A Novel

INTIMATE RELATIONS
WITH STRANGERS

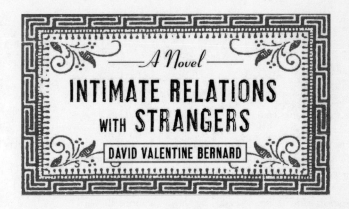

A Novel

INTIMATE RELATIONS
with STRANGERS

DAVID VALENTINE BERNARD

STREBOR BOOKS

NEW YORK LONDON TORONTO SYDNEY

Strebor Books
P.O. Box 6505
Largo, MD 20792
http://www.streborbooks.com

Intimate Relations with Strangers © 2007 by David Valentine Bernard

ISBN-13 978-1-4165-4036-6
ISBN-10   1-4165-4036-9
LCCN 2007923862

First Strebor Books trade paperback edition September 2007

10   9   8   7   6   5   4   3   2   1

Manufactured in the United States of America

For information regarding special discounts for bulk purchases,
please contact Simon & Schuster Special Sales at 1-800-456-6798
or business@simonandschuster.com

Dedication

For Antonia Francesca, Anastasia Corinthia, Amaya Sione,
Onyali Calista and future generations of Bernards,
who might one day find something useful in these words.

"Few are the people who know the meaning of what they are living through, who even have an inkling of what is happening to them. That's the big trouble with history…"

Richard Wright's *The Outsider*

Now that the killing was done, the soldier took a deep breath and allowed his mind to return to the woman. He remembered the way her eyes twinkled when she smiled, and the strangely erotic way beads of sweat would form on her long, slender neck. After a year of war, and months of captivity in this prison camp, the woman was the only thing left to him. She was like a drug, helping him to forget all the cruel things he had done, and all the cruel things that had been done to him.

He looked around one last time—as if to tie up any loose ends. The camp consisted of seven earthen structures—hovels—arranged in an arc. By turning his head from side to side, he could see the entire camp. Beyond the hovels, the Sahara Desert stretched to the horizon. The sun was a few minutes away from setting, so the sky was a rich orange hue. Glancing up, he noticed two vultures circling overhead. He nodded his head then, and looked at the dead bodies lying on the sand.

Like everything else, the story behind those bodies seemed impossible. The soldier wanted to lie down and dream about the woman, and forget everything that had happened, but his mind was dragging him back to the thing that had happened only ten minutes ago. There had been gunshots and screams, and the sounds of men rushing over the sun-baked earth. He had killed all five of the prison camp's guards. The men who had tortured and imprisoned him were now lying on the ground before him. He was still holding the gun. He looked at the thing in his hands as if the sight of it would make all this real, but it did not... After the killing was done, he had freed twenty of his fellow prisoners of war from their hovels. Once released, the men had scampered into the sand dunes beyond the prison camp. He had watched them from the camp, wishing them well as they crested the summit of the tallest dune; but he had known, even then, that it was only a matter of time before the Sahara claimed them.

Indeed, as he glanced up once more, he saw there were more vultures circling—and he could see others in the distance, in the direction his countrymen had fled. The thought of being devoured by vultures suddenly seemed right—natural. Now that the killing was done, he wanted to be a part of something real—even if it was only the food chain.

While these strange thoughts were going through his mind, there was a gust of wind within the prison camp. A miniature cyclone danced on the dusty earth for a moment before disappearing like a ghost. The gust of hot, arid air burned the soldier's eyes and left his nasal passages desiccated. The hovels had been sandblasted smooth by those desert winds. As he looked at the wall closest to him, it seemed to disintegrate in the wind, like a sand castle. He did not know if it was an optical illusion or not, but there was something beautiful about it, and he again felt a vague sense of peace at the thought that everything was coming to an end.

While he was nodding his head absentmindedly, something brushed against his leg. He sensed it even before it touched him. The usual tingling sensation came over him, and he looked down in time to see the same spectacularly white cat he had been seeing for months now. The cat arched its back as it brushed its flank against his leg. He had spent the passing months wondering if the cat was a figment of his imagination. It had always brought him good luck, and set him on the right path, but the rational side of him knew cats did not appear out of nowhere. In fact, while he was staring down at the creature, the glare from the setting sun reflected off its immaculately white fur, blinding him. Reflexively, he clamped his eyes shut; and even though his eyes were only closed for a few seconds, the cat was gone when he opened them.

After everything that had happened, he was not surprised. He was actually nodding his head again when his legs suddenly gave way beneath him.

The sound of his collapse echoed through the camp. Lying on the ground, he finally got a chance to look at his body. He gasped as he saw it; but on second thought, it made perfect sense. His body was bullet-riddled and bloody. Replaying the last few minutes in his mind, he realized he had been shot during the battle with the prison guards. Wanting to make his final moments comfortable, he dragged himself out of the glare of the setting sun, and leaned against the side of the hovel, where there was shade. Rather than being painful, the bullet holes were points of numbness. He had been shot at least once in each leg. A bullet was embedded in his left shoulder, and there were two in his abdomen. As the blood flowed, the points of numbness seemed to expand in diameter. Knowing these would be the last moments of his life, he closed his eyes and willed his mind to return to the woman.

—*Book One*—

THE BEGINNING
OF TIME

HOW THE LITTLE BOY
LEARNED TO DREAM

September 11th changed everything for America. That was a phrase the soldier remembered hearing when he was still only a little boy. Terrorists had attacked America, so America had gone out into the world to take revenge. The logic behind it seemed simple enough. Then again, everything seemed simple when you were only eight years old.

He grew up in the middle of Long Island, in a cul-de-sac where most of his neighbors were old couples. The few children were either too old or too young to be his friends and playmates. Yet, even though he usually played by himself, he was never lonely. Beyond his backyard, there was a small wood—a few hectares of trees, hemmed in by the highway and other people's backyards. This place was his. He claimed it the way lovers claimed their mates—with authority and the gratitude that so much pleasure could reside in one place. When he allowed his imagination to roam, the wood was easily transformed into anything he pleased. Muddy pits metamorphosed into lakes and oceans; boulders became mountain ranges and skyscrapers. Over the years of his childhood, the wood had been everything from distant planets to steaming jungles. Sometimes, when a cruel streak seized him, he would terrorize the many squirrels with his slingshot, pretending the bushy, darting creatures were monsters to be eradicated. Mercifully, his aim was never true, and the squirrels knew to run when they saw him coming.

In the beginning, his mother would smile and shake her head when she saw him acting out one of his elaborate fantasies. The running joke around the house used to be that if the world were to come to a sudden end, the little boy would go on playing as though nothing had happened. His mother used to say she was happy for his independence and resourcefulness, because they kept him out of her hair. As a fifty-year-old woman who worked full-time in New York City, she often had little time and energy left when she returned home. Many days, she left the house at six in the morning and returned after eight at night. Her husband, likewise, worked in the city, which meant the little boy was often left alone with his older sister, or whatever babysitter the cul-de-sac had to offer. The babysitters liked the little boy, because he would never bother them; and most of the time, when his sister claimed to be babysitting him, she would be locked in her bedroom with her boyfriend.

Before September 11th, the mother had never really considered the consequences of these things. However, the terrorist attacks had highlighted a quality in her son she had never allowed herself to see. On the morning of September 11th, she had emerged from the subway station at Wall Street just as the first plane hit. She had walked the three or four blocks to the World Trade Center complex, where her firm was located, and stared up at the scene in shock. In the immediate aftermath, people had thought it was an accident; many of the workers had stood around, thinking they would be allowed to go to work after the flames were put out. But then, the second plane had hit, and everyone had known it was no accident. The mother had been there to see people jumping out of eightieth-story windows, choosing death by sudden impact to death by flames and toxic fumes. The mother had been there when the first tower came crumbling down. At the horrific sight, she had run with a terror she had never thought possible, screaming as the cloud of rubble engulfed her. Because the subway stopped running, she had had to walk over the Brooklyn Bridge: herself and hundreds of thousands of other war refugees. They had walked in a silent procession, speechless and terrified. Once she was across the bridge, it had occurred to her the Long Island Railroad would probably not be running either, so she had hailed a cab. Some passersby, who had had the same idea, had asked if they could share the cab. Thus, four of them had set off for Long Island. They had tried to talk about what had happened, but one woman had started to sob uncontrollably, so they had driven in relative silence.

On the day that everything changed for America, her husband had been in the city as well. He was a doctor at a hospital in midtown Manhattan. A triage center had been set up at his hospital. They had made provisions for thousands of wounded people, but few had come; and as an urologist, the father's expertise had not been needed anyway. He had stood around in a state of simmering helplessness; on the hospital television, he had seen all the horrible scenes, but there had been nothing for him to do. Seeing the towers collapse, he had had terrible thoughts about his wife—who worked on the ninetieth floor. The wife had been one of those people who refused to get a cellular phone—who had thought it all a trendy fad. She had called the hospital from a pay phone; but in the chaos, the woman at the reception desk had forgotten to convey the message, and so the husband had spent the day thinking the worst. Around midday, when his fears had finally gotten the best of him, he had driven back to Long Island like a maniac. He had called home before leaving, but there had been no response, and the horrible thoughts had left him feeling hollowed out.

On the road, he had found himself looking at the other drivers. Their pained expressions had been those of people marooned in a wasteland. They had all rushed ahead desperately, secretly wondering if their homes and loved ones would still be there when they arrived at their destinations. He had passed people crying—people yelling into cellular phones; once, at a red light, he had seen a couple groping, her breasts exposed, their faces contorted with what was supposed to be passion, but which had struck the husband as the inner panic of those who thought the world was coming to an end. He had turned away, ashamed, as he recognized the same sense of panic within himself.

When he got home and saw the building was still standing, he had felt an almost insane sense of relief. The sight of his daughter sitting in front of the television had brought tears to his eyes. They had hugged one another, both of them crying as they tried to make sense of their fears.

As for the little boy's sister, she had known nothing about the attack until the little boy's elementary school called. She had been about to head to a class at the local college when the panicky woman from the elementary school called. The woman had been calling all the parents, so they could come and pick up their children. The sister had panicked as well, almost crashing her car twice as she sped to the school to pick up the little boy. She had cried on the drive home. Every few minutes, she had asked him if he was okay; but instead of waiting for an answer, she had only launched into another explanation of how terrified she was. In the beginning, the little boy had nodded his head when she asked him if he was okay; but by the end, he had only stared out of the windshield in silence as his sister worked herself into a nervous frenzy. As soon as the car stopped in front of their home, he had gone straight for the wood, and the sister had gone straight for the television.

The father had found her in front of the television when he came home; and half an hour later, when the mother came home, she had found them in the same position. On the screen, there had been the chilling scenes—which, by now, had been replayed hundreds of times. They had all hugged one another, and cried, trying to reassure one another things would be okay. As if on cue, the little boy's older brother had called from Albany, where he was working as a state senator's aide. The brother had cried as well, and kept repeating how unbelievable it was—as if the repetition would make it all believable.

The little boy had come in from the wood while the mother was crying on the phone with her first son. The sister had been sniffling on the couch, while the father held her around the shoulders and tried to keep back his own tears. At the sight of the crying adults, the little boy had stood frozen. Seeing the television was the source of everything, he had stared at the screen for a while, as if hoping to discover a secret. However, the scenes of planes crashing into towers, and skyscrapers crumbling, had reminded him of the time he found his brother's porn stash. It had been under a loose plank in his brother's closet—some old *Playboy* magazines and a videotape porno that looked like it had passed through many hands. He had put on the porno, initially intrigued by the extent of the human imagination; but instead of arousing him, those scenes of staged sexuality had only left him melancholy. All his life, he had been different. While others his age had been shocked and scandalized by the things they learned about the adult world, nothing had ever been able to surprise him. The fake shouts of ecstasy on the videotape had been a mockery of something he sensed within him. It was as if he had experienced something pure and good—something beyond all the mundane things people had come to call pleasure. He had sensed it within himself, in an untapped region of his psyche. He had searched his memories, trying to reenter the paradise he sensed within; but as always, nothing had come. Indeed, as he watched the videotape, the only concrete thing he had come away with was the realization none of it was real. He had wished then that he had never found the videotape—not because of his ruined innocence or anything that stupid, but because it had left him with a feeling of emptiness he could not understand. He had turned off the VCR, and fled into his wood, and spent the rest of the day trying to forget...

Likewise, when he entered the living room that day and saw the adults staring at the TV screen, the same queasy feeling had come over him. Somehow, the death and sorrow he saw on the screen had been a mockery of something he felt inside, so he had turned away from the television after about twenty seconds, and returned outside, to the wood.

The mother had watched all this while she held the phone to her ear. Her first thought had been that the little boy was too young to understand what was going on. She figured that maybe, in his naiveté, he had been unable to grasp what had happened. She had nodded her head, thinking that that had to be it. Accordingly, by the time he came in for his evening snack an hour later, she had had her speech ready. She had told him how bad men had attacked America, and how it was okay to be afraid. However, when she began to sob again, he had taken her hand and pressed it, so that she would look down at him. When they made eye contact, he had said:

"Don't be afraid, Mom, you're home now." He had smiled at her faintly—almost pityingly, she thought—before returning outside, to the wood. She had been too numb to speak. In the brutal aftermath of the words, she had been unable to make up her mind if what he had said was a good thing or a bad thing. She had walked back to the living room in a daze; and since then, an internal shudder had gone through her every time she considered the little boy. There had been something in his eyes when he said those words to her—either a precocious awareness of the world's inner dynamics, or a sociopathic coldness toward the weaknesses of his fellow human beings. The words had made her feel small and petty. They had been beyond her comprehension; and she had feared them, the way she feared all unknowable things.

In her darker moments, the mother traced everything to one cause: she had had the little boy too late in life (forty-two), by which time the zeal of motherhood had passed from her. With her first two children, she had been the self-sacrificing, hovering mother. Her first child—the little boy's older brother—had grown up craving her acknowledgement and approval in all things. Similarly, her daughter had been doted upon and spoiled—especially by the husband—and the girl had gloried in the attention, like a princess. However, the little boy had never needed her to explain a mystery of life to him; he had never needed to be calmed and reassured by the comforts that parents had to offer. Either he was some kind of emotional prodigy, or he was something horrible. It was either one or the other, and she trembled before both possibilities.

It was now nine months since September 11th. The little boy had spent those months trying to come to grips with the strange preoccupations of the adult world. Grownups had begun to grumble and whisper about unseen dangers; news reports had seemed like video games, with flashing graphics; everywhere, there had been images from faraway lands, of the spectacular bombings and assassinations that would ensure America's continued existence. Overnight, every house in the cul-de-sac had sprouted at least one American flag. Flags had been on cars and buses and trains and clothing; anthems and pledges of allegiance had become mandatory. All around him, the adults had seemed suddenly desperate to remember they were Americans—as if remembering were the key to maintaining the stability of the world. And yet, in their acts of remembrance, there had been something off-putting, so the little boy had left the adults to their games, and found solace within his own.

On the day of the incident, he was playing by a huge muddy pit in his wood. It had rained a great deal that week; and as he had developed a strange affinity for the feeling of warm mud between his toes, he had taken off his sneakers. Being filthy was one of the joys of childhood. Many an afternoon, his mother would have the hose ready when she called him in for the night. She would throw a bucket of suds on him, then hose him down like a dog. Of course, she could not always head him off, so several times a week, he would leave a trail of muddy footprints through the house; which meant that several times a week, his mother would go into a fit of madness and threaten to do him bodily harm.

Presently, it was late afternoon, and he was content because another day of imaginative play had gone well. In the muddy pit, the male frogs were fighting one another for supremacy. He knew it had something to do with sex—or at least the frog equivalent, which involved excreting a lot of slimy substances. He found the entire thing wondrously disgusting. Also, watching frogs fight was like watching a soap opera. By now, he had given names to all the players in the drama. He had decided which ones were villains and which were heroes. Sometimes, he sniggered when a frog he had come to hate lost out to a rival. Every once in a while, when a battle was not going the way he liked, he would poke the victor with a stick—so that he became the ultimate arbiter of frog justice: a kind of hovering frog deity.

That afternoon, as he crouched by the pit, the wind suddenly began to blow. On the trees, the leaves shook violently. The wind was so strong he almost lost his balance as he crouched there. His hand went down into the muck, but he managed to right himself. He stood up and looked around warily: the wind was warm, but as it blew against his skin, it made him shudder. Stranger still, the world seemed suddenly dark. The sun, which had been shining brightly only seconds ago, was gone now. When he looked up, the sky was a twilight gray, and seemed to be darkening by the second. He knew every tree and shrub in the wood, but everything seemed different now—as if something sinister had taken over. He became aware he was trembling; he wrapped his arms around his front, like someone freezing to death. And then, as the world passed a threshold of darkness, the wind suddenly stopped. More than that, everything stopped, as if God had put His index finger to His lips and shushed the world.

The little boy ran. He turned on his heels, almost slipping in the mud, and ran for his life. He ran toward his home. He had never been terrified before—not like this. He had experienced the insecurities and uncertainties of all human beings, but the terror he felt now was beyond all those things. As he ran, he feared not only for his life, but for what he had come to think of as his soul.

He darted around tree trunks and splashed through puddles. He could see the edge of his backyard now. His house rose up like an oasis. He ran faster—more desperately. He grunted and grimaced when he stubbed his toes on a root, but he did not scream, or stop, fearing the thing stalking him would be able to gauge his position.

He was running across the lawn now. He was almost there. In his haste, he practically ripped off the screen door. Within seconds, he was within the kitchen. Unfortunately, with all the mud and filth on the soles of his feet, he slid across the white tiles, before colliding with the table like a bowling ball. His mother had placed a pitcher of iced tea on the table a few minutes ago. It was toppled, along with the table. At the sound of the commotion, she returned from the living room, where she had been watching the news, and stared at the kitchen scene as if her head were on the verge exploding. She could not speak for about three or four seconds. At first, she did not even see the little boy (as he was still under the kitchen table). All she saw was the skid mark of mud from the door to the table. Eventually, she heard him gasping for air; and when she bent down and saw him, an insane gleam came into her eyes. In one brutal motion, she reached down, grabbed him by his collar, and wrenched him up. Soon, he was standing before her, his legs still wobbly.

"What the f…!" She almost cursed, but managed to catch herself. Her hands were still on his shoulders; she realized they had been inching toward his neck, to throttle him. She forced herself to let go of him. She took a deep breath and took a step back. He was staring up at her wide-eyed. She looked again at the muddy skid mark and her toppled pitcher. The iced tea was now dribbling across the floor. The rage was overcoming her again. That was when she glanced down and noticed his feet were bare. The little boy had a bad habit of leaving his shoes out in the wood; the mother had had to buy him a new pair of sneakers last week, because he had left the old pair in the wood overnight, and a raccoon, or some such creature, had ripped it to shreds to get to the salt. Seeing his bare feet, the mother's words got caught in her throat, as if they were choking her:

"Boy, where are your shoes?" She was trembling with rage; he opened his mouth, but the words would not come. She took a step toward him; he retreated a step. "Boy, tell me you didn't leave your shoes outside again!" She sprang at him, and grabbed him by the collar again—

"But Mama—!" He tried to explain about the suddenly darkening world and the thing stalking him in the wood, but the words again eluded him. This enraged the mother even more, so that her hands shook and her eyes bulged.

"Boy, get your shoes before I strangle you!"

The little boy ran again. He slipped against the tiles once more, but managed to regain his balance before he burst through the screen door. Even then, he left a huge, muddy palm print by the door, so that the mother screamed and seemed on the verge of chasing after him.

The little boy burst out of the house, but once he was on the lawn again, his pace slowed. The world was still dark and menacing and hushed. Before he knew it, he was crying. He was trapped: if he went into the wood, the thing would get him; if he went back into the kitchen without his shoes, his mother would beat him within an inch of his life. He was doomed. He stood on the periphery of the wood for about two or three minutes, sniffling and pondering his fate. Eventually, the mother spied him from the kitchen window and screamed out again. When he glanced back and saw her glaring at him from the kitchen window, he ran. He ran for his life, knowing his mother would come out and strangle him if he stood there any longer. Once in the wood, he did not allow himself to stop or to think. He ran like he had never run before. His plan was to grab the shoes and run back out before the thing in the wood got him. He did not allow his mind to think of anything else. All there was, was running.

At last, the muddy pit, and his sneakers, came into view. Yet, as he neared his prize, the old terror came over him again, and he slowed to a walk. He approached the shoes tentatively, as if they were the cheese in a mousetrap. He searched the surrounding trees and shrubs then, looking for the thing he could sense closing in on him. It occurred to him he could not hear the frogs croaking anymore. He frowned. When he reached the pit, he picked up his shoes, but he stood staring down at the pit. The frogs were gone. He bent lower, and stared. The pit seemed impossibly black. There was no reflection, so that he wondered if there was even water there anymore. In a strange sense, it was as if the infinite darkness took possession of him. He felt compelled to bend lower—to touch the darkness. He forgot about being stalked by a hidden monster; he forgot about his mother. For those few moments, all there was, was the darkness. He took both of his shoes in his left hand, and stretched out his right hand, to touch the darkness. His hand, he saw, was trembling. In fact, his entire body was trembling, but he still felt compelled to touch the darkness.

A bubble formed on the surface of the pit, as if something were churning below. He made out the bubble because it was a lighter hue than the surrounding darkness. The bubble formed, and then popped with an unexpected sound that reminded him of a belch. The air from the bubble was vile, and his face soured. He realized he was still stretching out his hand to touch the darkness, and pulled it back quickly, just as another bubble formed. Somehow, he was still crouched by the pit, mesmerized by the forming bubble. It grew bigger and bigger, until, to his amazement, it was about half a meter in diameter. A voice of prudence told him to step back. He stood up and retreated a few steps, but he was still mesmerized by the bubble. This time, the bubble did not so much pop as it imploded. It was sucked back into the darkness, and then ripples appeared on the surface.

His eyes followed the concentric circles, as if he were being hypnotized. Eventually, his eyes focused on something stirring in the center of the ripples. He leaned in closer, his eyes straining. He was still leaning in closer when the thing suddenly broke the surface of the darkness. It was not a bubble this time, but something with substance. He jumped when he realized he was looking at fingers. They were emerging from the darkness. And then, there came a full hand, and then the arm. He could not breathe. The surface of the pit bubbled. Vile-smelling froth formed on the surface. The little boy tried to step back. He may have moved, and taken a wobbly step, but it was not the frantic flight his body cried out for. The muddy pit was giving birth. He had never seen something being born before, but he saw it now. Within seconds, a nude body was expelled from the darkness, and then the afterbirth came out—chunks of clotted blood and unspeakable filth. The expelled body was coated with it.

As the little boy looked on in shock, the thing's head sprung up; it coughed, then vomited up some discolored fluid. The little boy went to run at last. He turned quickly on his heels, but almost decapitated himself when he ran headlong into a low-hanging branch. He did a near somersault, landing on his shoulder. The joint gave immediately, feeling like a knife slicing into shoulder. Either his clavicle snapped or he strained some neck tendons. His chin, which had taken the brunt of the blow with the branch, was split. For a moment, his visual cortex translated the onslaught of pain as flashes of light. Yet, even then, his first and only thought was to flee. With all the commotion, the creature's eyes darted in his direction. In the darkness, the eyes seemed like an abyss, drawing him in—

He screamed, and clamped his eyes shut, and screamed again, balling himself into the fetal position…

Either minutes passed or seconds passed—it all seemed the same to him now. His mother came running, followed by some of his elderly neighbors. Even then, he could not stop screaming. His mother grabbed him. The blood from his chin had spurted all over his face by then. The sight of his bloody face and lopsided shoulders must have been horrific to her, because she began to cry, even while she tried to calm him. Soon, however, some of the old neighbors noticed the creature—or whatever it was. It was still lying by the mouth of the pit. It was not moving anymore: it had not moved since he started screaming, as if the sound had stripped it of its strength. Some of the old neighbors went to the body and tried to rouse it. Someone yelled for an ambulance, and an old man shuffled back toward his home to make the call.

The little boy huddled into his mother's arms. It was the first time he had done that since he was a toddler. This terror was a new thing, opening him up to states of existence he had never thought possible. His mother was rocking him now; she kept repeating that everything would be okay. The old people were still congregating around the body by the pit. Maybe three or four minutes passed before one of the old women used a kerchief to wipe away some of the filth from the thing's face. That was when they discovered it was a girl. The filth had cloaked her and matted her hair to her head. However, once her face was cleared, they saw the girl was beautiful. The little boy got a glimpse of her through the old people's legs. Once he did, the previous terror died away entirely, and he felt only shock. In that instant, he was convinced he knew her. More than that, it was as if a connection existed between him and the girl that trumped even the one that existed between him and his family: between him and everything he had ever known. It was as if all those other things were irrelevant, and the girl was a conduit back to everything that mattered. She was lying there with her eyes closed, and the little boy was happy for it, because he had a sudden fear that the girl's eyes would be his undoing.

Some of the adults moved in closer to get a look at the girl, obscuring the little boy's view. The adults were talking wildly now, speculating about the filth—the chunks of clotted blood—and where the girl had come from. They wondered about the nudity, thinking maybe the girl had been abused and dumped here (since the highway was right next to the wood). The little boy listened to these things without fully understanding them. Now, they were conjecturing that a man must have dropped the girl there, then beat up the little boy when he came upon them. They asked the little boy if they were right, but by then he was too dazed to understand them. The pain now had him wrapped up and incapacitated, like a straightjacket.

More adults came. One of the old men took off his shirt to cover the girl. About two minutes later, the little boy's father came running up. Some old people had flagged him down as soon as he drove into the cul-de-sac. The father immediately began checking the little boy for wounds. He grew annoyed with the others, because they could not give him any definite answers on what had happened. The father tried to question his son directly, but the little boy had become bored with all the adults by then. The girl was the only thing on his mind—the only thing he could bring himself to consider. He wished everyone would move away, so he could stare at her again.

Then, within minutes, the police and ambulance were there. By now, the father had decided his son's injuries were not life-threatening, and had started checking the girl. The old man who had run back to summon the ambulance must have made it seem like a massacre, because six police officers and three ambulances arrived. They parked in the cul-de-sac and ran through the wood to get to the supposed crime scene. Most were middle-aged men with huge guts, so they were panting when they arrived. With the authorities there, all the adults seemed to be screaming now. The old people began telling the police and paramedics their various theories of what had happened. The little boy's father explained he was a doctor, and gave his assessments to the paramedics. For the little boy, everything passed in a blur. The girl was put on a gurney; some paramedics came and placed the little boy on another gurney. By now, the onslaught of pain had evolved into a dull ache. Of course, his body had gone into shock.

Next, there was the trip back to the cul-de-sac. It was impossible to wheel the gurney over the uneven, muddy earth, so the gurney had to be lifted. One of the paramedics lost his balance and tripped over a shrub. The little boy was almost sent flying, but the father, who had been jogging by his side, managed to grab the gurney. At present, half the adults were running back toward the cul-de-sac. The other half stayed with a contingent of police officers, who were cordoning off the crime scene. The girl and her paramedics reached the street first. She was put in the back of an ambulance; within seconds, she was off to the hospital. The little boy and his contingent reached the street as the girl's ambulance was taking off. The little boy was placed in the back of another ambulance. His mother got in with him, while the father yelled he would drive the car behind the ambulance. With all the sirens in the air, everyone had to yell to talk. The little boy was barely conscious by then.

The little boy had started to doze by the time they arrived at the hospital. In a strange way, the siren had lulled him to sleep. He had already begun to dream; and even then, his dreams had been of the girl. Both ambulances arrived at about the same time. Two medical teams were waiting outside the emergency room when they pulled in front of the hospital. One fastened itself onto the girl, and whisked her into the hospital. The other came for the little boy. The mother went with the little boy and the medical team. The father was about to follow, but some guards warned him to move his car if he did not want it to be towed.

They wheeled the little boy down the labyrinthine hospital corridors. His mind did not bother to digest what was going on. Soon, he was in the pediatric wing. There was a central ward with about a dozen rooms on either side. There were cartoon figures painted on the walls of the ward. Some wretched-looking kids were milling about in the central area, mostly with broken arms, and bald heads from chemotherapy, and that sort of thing. The girl had arrived ahead of him. She was taken into one room while the little boy was brought into the one next to it. Now, he was being undressed. A female doctor asked him some questions while he was stripped. Actually, they cut off his clothes. The doctor said his shoulder was dislocated. She used a stethoscope on him. It was cold against his skin, and he shuddered. The interminable minutes passed. He had a sudden desire to bite the doctor's hand when she wrenched his jaw open to look inside. He was poked and prodded and ordered about. They were going to give him an X-ray to see if there was any other damage. So, shortly after the perfunctory examination was complete, he was rushed to the radiology department. By now, he only wished they would leave him alone.

They had given him some pain drugs, which made him feel giddy. His shoulder was snapped back in place. They gave him a couple stitches for his chin... Through all this, his mother had either stood to the side, or held his hand. Her eyes were red from tears. The father joined them after he found parking. By that time, the little boy was back in the pediatric ward. It was true that doctors made the worst patients (and parents of patients) because the father was a nervous wreck.

The little boy allowed his mind to roam. While everything was going on, he had flashes of the girl emerging from the pit. It was strange that the sight no longer terrified him. Instead, there was a yearning within him now: a need to see the girl again, and be around her. Somehow, he had the sense everything would be revealed if he looked into her eyes.

While the pediatrician was putting him in a shoulder restraint, a middle-aged woman came in with a folder in one hand and a huge plastic cup of coffee in the other. It was more like a jug than a cup, and she smiled in a jittery way after she took a sloppy swig. In fact, she dribbled on her cotton blouse (which already had coffee stains on it). Everyone stopped what he or she was doing and looked up at her, as if to ask her what she wanted. She gave a preamble, the gist of which was that she was a police detective and had been assigned this case. The pediatrician said she was finished, giving tacit approval for the interrogation to begin. The doctor left the room then, saying she would return later to check on the little boy. The doctor opened the door just as the wretched-looking children in the ward were laughing at a joke or some other form of childish merriment. The sound was unexpected in the otherwise grim silence, and they all looked toward the doorway.

The detective asked the parents if she could ask the little boy some questions. Once she had their approval, she went over to the little boy's bed. She first placed her cup/jug on the nightstand to free her hand, then she proffered her hand to the little boy, for him to slap her five.

"How are you doing, homie?" she said, trying to be cool, but it was ridiculous coming from a middle-aged white woman. Her voice was so loud it startled him. As for her extended hand, his arm on that side was in the restraint, and he did not feel like stretching his other arm over just to touch her, so he only stared at her.

"I'm fine," he said simply. She pulled her hand back, and tried to mask the awkwardness of the situation by shuffling through her folder. Of course, the folder only had a handful of sheets of paper in it, most of which were blank for taking notes.

"I hear you're a brave little boy," she began again, hoping to work on his ego.

The little boy wanted to go to sleep. He looked at his parents, as if begging them to drive the woman away, but they had proud smiles on their faces.

When the little boy's gaze returned to the detective, she continued: "They told me how you saw that bad man hurting the girl, and cried out for help when he attacked you. You're a hero, you know that!" she said, nodding enthusiastically. "You scared him away!"

The little boy was still staring up at her in the same confused way, but then he remembered the old people speculating in the wood. The detective must have gone to the cul-de-sac and gotten their reports. He could not believe how wrong they were. At the same time, he knew he would never be able to explain the scene that had been flashing in his mind: the girl emerging from the muck. The detective still had a hopeful smile on her face, as if trying to coax him into believing their concocted story. When he looked, he realized his parents had the same expression on their faces. As he watched them, it occurred to him the adult world was probably not worthy of the truth.

The detective seemed to be waiting for a response, so he made a non-committal grunting sound to placate her. That was not what she had been hoping for, and her beaming smile faded away.

"Can you give me the details of how it happened?" she pressed him now.

The little boy saw no other course but to lie. He shook his head—or at least, he tried to. His neck was sore. She continued:

"Do you think you could identify the bad man if you saw him again?"

"No," he said this time.

"You don't have to be afraid," she said, taking his reticence for fear.

"We're here to protect you," she went on. "He'll never hurt you again—especially once we have him in custody."

"Okay," he said eventually, seeing she was waiting for an acknowledgment.

Mercifully, the detective seemed to conclude she was not going to get any more information from him tonight, so she turned to the mother:

"They said you were one of the first people on the scene. Did you see anyone running away?"

"No, I didn't even see the girl at first. I guess my attention was on my son. I ran toward the screams."

The detective sighed, then fetched her jug from the nightstand, taking another sloppy swig of her coffee. It seemed to rejuvenate her spirits, because she gave them another jittery smile once she was finished. After assuring the parents they should be proud of the little boy (and that the police would catch the bad man soon) she made her exit.

His parents were determined to stick around and "keep him company" once the detective left, but he wanted to sleep. When his parents began discussing how all this could have happened in their "wonderful little community," he closed his eyes and pretended to be asleep. They eventually took the hint, kissed him on the forehead, and left. Outside, in the ward, all sounds of childish merrymaking were gone. The children had probably been forced to go to bed.

He tried to sleep, but thoughts of the girl would not leave him. His mind kept going over the impossibility of what he had seen that afternoon…and the possibility of what the girl might be. In fact, when he thought of her, he wondered *what* she was, not *who* she was. He did not care what her name was, or where she had lived before this afternoon. Names, he knew, where what lazy people used to distract themselves from the true realities of life. Somehow, the girl was like the sun: her coming and going could affect the rhythms of life and death; regardless of what she was called, it did not change what she was, and the power she had over their fragile lives. In the few glimpses he had gotten of her, he had felt himself changing. In fact, it was impossible to go back to what he was. He was a different person from the kid who had entered the wood that afternoon.

He sat up in bed now, knowing he had to see her again. His parents had turned off the light. He now turned on the lamp on the nightstand. He felt a sense of excitement taking hold of him. He got out of bed, but his body still felt otherworldly from the anesthesia. His legs felt light: as if he would go bounding through the ceiling if he inadvertently took too strong a step. As such, his first steps were tentative. He hoped there were no guards outside to keep him from the girl. He only wanted to stare at her: he did not care if she was still unconscious. The sight of her would soothe him for the night. When he awoke in the morning, he would probably need another fix, and then another… Now that he had met the girl, he would only be able to exist from moment to moment—

The door burst open. He had been about to take another tentative step toward the exit, but he froze now, unable to believe his eyes. It was the girl! She was actually there, panting and wide-eyed. She was in a hospital gown now, just like him, and she was clean and beautiful. She took a step toward him, and he took a step. Her eyes were frantic. She scanned the rest of the room, as if searching for something; right before the door burst open again, she darted behind it. Now, an orderly was standing in the doorway. He, too, was panting and wide-eyed:

"Did a girl run in here?" the orderly yelled.

It took all the little boy's will to not look over at the girl. He shook his head—despite the pain. The orderly went to leave, but then turned back: "You need to be in bed," he said. There was a warning somewhere in there, and the little boy grunted to say he understood.

Within seconds, the door was closed, and the little boy and the girl stared at one another again. She seemed calmer now—grateful to him, perhaps. He wanted to talk to her, but he could not translate his thoughts into a cogent sentence. He could not even begin the flow of words, so he only stood there, staring. It was she who walked toward him. His insides quaked with every step she took. On her face, there was an inscrutable expression: a mixture of terror and relief.

Within moments, she was hugging him. Her bony little arms were clenched around his neck; he cringed from the pain, but he was so stunned he only stood there with his free arm dangling limply at his side. Within the ward, the guards could be heard running back and forth. The girl looked toward the door anxiously. Thinking quickly, the little boy took her to the attached bathroom. He turned on the light and closed the door, so that soon they were standing face-to-face in the cramped quarters. She was quivering, still with a terrified expression on her face. He held her upper arm, and spoke for the first time, saying:

"The guards won't hurt you."

However, seeming to come to her senses, she blurted out, "We have to get out of here." In the cramped quarters, her voice had a disturbing resonance.

He frowned. "What are you afraid of?"

She thought about it for a moment, but realized she had no idea. She detached from him—he had still been holding her arm—and scratched her head, as if it would trigger her memory.

"Are you okay?" he asked again.

She looked up at him momentarily, but then went back to scratching her head. "...I don't know," she whispered at last.

He ventured: "I saw you when you came out of the mud." By her expression, he saw she had no idea what he was talking about. He lowered his voice then, saying, "What's the last thing you remember?"

"...Running," she whispered. She looked past him for the first time and caught her reflection in the mirror. She frowned, and stepped closer, brushing past him. "How did we get so young?"

"What?"

"We're kids," she said in bewilderment.

He chuckled, as if to ask what else they were supposed to be.

She talked to him via the mirror; her face remained grave: "We shouldn't be so young. This is all wrong."

His smile faded. He touched her shoulder, so that she turned and faced him again. "How old do you think you are?"

The same confused expression was on her face. "I don't know," she said at last. She was about to go back to scratching her head, but he grabbed her hand. "This is all wrong," she said in bewilderment. "You and I are *grown*. …Married."

"Married?" he almost screamed. The word echoed in the bathroom. And then, "I'm only eight."

"You're not eight," she said as if annoyed with him. "…Don't you recognize me?"

His mind returned to the strange feeling he had had the moment he saw her face; he remembered the feeling he had always had, that there was something else beyond all this—something that made this life seem like a pale imitation of living.

The expression on his face made her feel vindicated. "You know me," she said decisively. "We were together. All of this"—she looked about warily— "…it's not real."

"What is it then?" he started cautiously.

She thought about it, but when her mind could not offer anything definitive, she only began to cry again. She took a step toward him, and he hugged her, wrapping his free arm around her. He did not know if he believed her or not. He did not even know if he understood what she had said. He only knew he did not like to see her cry. She returned his hug, then she kissed him—not in the quaint, adorable way of little children, but with wild abandon. He felt her tongue in his mouth. She pulled him to her, so that he winced again from the pain. They were both in the hospital gowns, naked under the thin fabric; as the kiss continued, his free hand, following its own volition, caressed her back. Her gown was unfastened in the rear, and he felt her skin—the warm, smooth flesh at the bottom of her back. His hands moved lower, brushing against her small, boyish buttock—

Sensations were being stirred within him—a feeling of bliss that left him feeling dazed and drunk. He had to pull away from her before he lost himself completely. He was panting when they detached. His eyes were wide.

"…We were making love," she blurted out when they detached.

"What?"

"That's the last thing I remember. We were grown and married, and we were making love before you went to work…and then I was running down the street…and then I was here." The description seemed vague even to her, and she began to cry again.

He still could not stand to see her cry. Somehow, her desperation became his desperation—as if they were one entity. He held her again: it seemed right. And the closeness of her body left him feeling complete—content. All his life, he had been hollow: she filled him up, and satisfied him. At that moment, he knew he loved her—that he had always loved her. He did not try to make sense of it. They were kissing now. As before, it was not the kiss of two children, but something else entirely. He pulled her to him, despite his dislocated shoulder. Indeed, with thoughts of love within him, he felt no pain. The kiss seemed to go on for minutes. He closed his eyes and allowed himself to be pulled into it. He felt almost giddy—carefree and light. …He was drifting now. At first, he thought the love had made him high, but when he opened his eyes, he gasped. The hospital bathroom was gone; as he looked around, he saw they were drifting through a dimension of light. There was no up and down: all there was, was the light. His first thought was that it was a dream—that he had fallen asleep after his parents left, and this was all a fantasy. Either way, he knew he did not want to lose the girl. He held her tighter, suddenly terrified of losing her within the infinite possibilities of this place. Then, as he stared over her shoulder, into the light, he realized there were scenes taking place all around him. He saw one from a village in the primordial heart of Africa—something that seemed from the beginning of time. Inexplicably, years passed as he stared into the scene. Children turned into adults; adults became old or died. The same was true for the hundreds of other scenes. As he looked from one to another, hundreds of years of history played themselves out before his eyes. He saw tribal wars, and slave ships. He was there to see America take its formative steps. He saw all the contradictions and hypocrisies of history: declarations of independence being made at the same time that slavery became entrenched; he saw the expansion of wealth and hope at the same time that others were damned to nightmarish servitude. There were revolutions in industrialism—hulking factories that brought wealth and pollution and social disruptions. He saw the systematic butchery of the Civil War, and the barbaric westward surge of Americans who believed God had given this land to the white man. In fact, he was there for all the wars—all the excuses men of power made for their greed and bigotry. He saw the despair wrought by the course of human history; he saw all its advancements and dead ends and regressions.

That was when he realized he was impossibly old. It was a rational conclusion to be drawn, because the hundreds of scenes in the dimension of light all had a person who looked exactly like him. For hundreds of years, he had been struggling and suffering. He did not know how it was possible, but he knew it was so. The girl had been in all those scenes as well, sharing in his suffering and bewilderment and joy—

He suddenly realized he was not holding her anymore! He panicked and looked around, but the girl was gone. In fact, as he drifted through the light, he felt as though he, too, were fading away. Ties that had bound him to the world were loosened; new ties came into being, washing away all that had been there before. For a moment, he was certain he did not exist. For a moment, he forgot about the cul-de-sac and his parents and his wood. It was as if all the remnants of his old life were being cleared away, so that a new host could take over his body—

A sickening sensation came over him—as if he were in an elevator whose cables had snapped. He was falling. His stomach felt like it was moving up his throat. He wanted to scream, but he was afraid his guts would come out of his mouth. As he began to flail his arms and legs, he realized he was no longer in the shoulder restraint. His dislocated shoulder not only seemed healed, but as if it had never been injured. He instinctively touched his chin, seeing there was no wound there either.

That was when the sensation of falling stopped, and he found himself standing on solid ground. At the speed he had been traveling, he had expected his body to splatter, but there was only a feeling of disorientation as the world started to form around him. Within seconds, he realized he was back in the wood, standing next to the muddy pit. Somehow, it was again Friday evening—he knew it instantly. He looked down at the pit, but there was nothing supernatural about it anymore. The frogs were croaking and fighting in the muck as usual. He looked around, at all the familiar sights, but he knew this was all wrong. He suddenly remembered his parents and the cul-de-sac; a lifetime's worth of memories came flooding back. The hundreds of years of history he had seen while drifting through the light were effaced from his memory. A remnant of that vast history did stay with him, like the aftertaste of bitter medicine; otherwise, it all left him. He remembered the girl. He scanned the wood for any sign of her, but she was gone. Without her, nothing seemed right. It was like waking up to find his heart or lungs had been taken out. The sensation was disturbing—brutal. When his body could no longer take the strain, the world went black and he fell to the ground....

An unknown period of time passed. His mother, who was about to call him in for the night, saw him from the kitchen window, stumbling out of the wood with blood smeared over his clothes, face and hands. She screamed and ran out to meet him. ...His skin was cold and clammy; his eyes were blank and unresponsive. For those first few moments, he merely stared into space with a kind of slack-jawed dementia. His father was home by then, and ran out to help. Seeing no wounds, they bathed him and put him to bed. But even as the little boy began to regain consciousness, his first realization was that they had forgotten about the girl. In fact, it was as if that entire afternoon had been edited out of existence. All trace of the girl was gone from their eyes; and when he tried to talk to his father about the muddy pit and a trip to the hospital, the man only shook his head and looked at his wife with concern, convinced his son was still delirious.

Over the next few days, his parents tried to pretend nothing had happened. They told themselves the little boy had not been covered in blood. They convinced one another it had been one of his childish games. In time, the little boy fell in line with their world of make-believe; but when he was alone, he would find himself thinking that none of this was real, and that it was only a matter of time before he again held the girl in his arms.

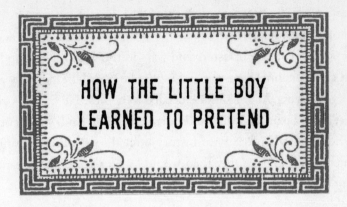

HOW THE LITTLE BOY
LEARNED TO PRETEND

Months passed. Summer gave way to fall, and the little boy returned to school. He tried to embrace his old routine, but he could not pretend he was the same person he had been a few months ago. He knew the world was not what people thought it to be. In fact, he had always known. Merely from observing the world as a child, he had sensed secrets and hidden possibilities behind what the adult world called reality.

For the first time in his life, he felt isolated. He had never needed to talk to anyone before, but for once he yearned for a confidant. He knew if he went to his parents or teachers and told them what had happened, the words would never be able to reach them. It was not empathy or intelligence his parents and teachers and peers lacked, but a spiritual awareness. He and the girl were beyond time and all the mundane things that made human lives seem rational. People who saw things others could not, were either geniuses or madmen, and he accepted both possibilities.

The only thing he knew for sure was that from his earliest memories, he had been waiting for something. The girl's visit (real or imagined) had satisfied something in him. His mind kept going back to how he had screamed when the girl emerged from the muddy pit. It was as if he had been saving his emotional energy all his life, so he would be able to release that scream. Now that the scream was out of him, everything seemed clearer. He knew love now, but he also knew terror. The terror confronted him at all times, so that he grew wary of going out into the world. He rarely played in the wood anymore, fearful that something else would emerge from the pit. Instead of going outside, he plopped himself down on the couch and watched news reports on all the disasters and wars in the world. He found a Middle Eastern cable channel that was so graphic he usually felt queasy after a few minutes of viewing. Yet, he felt he needed to be sick. He had to force himself to digest all the pain and filth and horror he could find, so he could reconstruct the hundreds of years of history he had seen while drifting through the dimension of light. Only then would he be able to understand the true meaning of the girl's visit.

Typically, once the little boy's school bus dropped him off in front of his house, he would enter through the kitchen, grab a snack from the fridge, then go to the couch to watch the news shows. About two weeks into the new school term, he returned home around half past three, as he usually did. He was standing in front of the fridge, staring in to see what was there, when he heard strange creaking noises coming from the basement. The door to the basement was right next to the fridge, and he snuck down to investigate the noise. At first, he thought rats or raccoons had gotten into the house again. However, when he got to the floor of the basement he saw his sister and her boyfriend having sex. There was the initial shock of course, but then he laughed at the ridiculous sight of his sister lying on the couch with her legs thrown over her boyfriend's shoulders. At his laughter, his sister screamed in embarrassment and tried to clothe herself; her boyfriend, annoyed that their session had been interrupted, stood there with his flagging, condom-wrapped erection, his arms akimbo as he grumbled and shook his head.

For weeks afterward, the little boy found himself having to suppress a laugh every time he saw his sister. She only scowled at him—until about three weeks later, when she took her revenge. That day, the little boy returned from school to find the sister's boyfriend waiting in the house. The boyfriend grabbed him as soon as he stepped in the door, and punched him in the face and stomach. His sister was there as well, with a smug look on her face as she cheered on her boyfriend. Threats were made. Once released from the boyfriend's grip, the little boy ran to his room in tears. He cried more from the injustice than from the pain. Yet, when he searched his mind, he knew his sister had always been like that. He would never have told their parents about his sister's act: the only threat she had had to endure was his laughter. Yet, she had never been someone who could stand to have something over her. They had perhaps never been friends, but after what she had done, the intimacy of siblings was destroyed forever.

Halloween came and went. For the first time, the little boy did not bother to get a costume and go trick-or-treating. With only a handful of kids in the cul-de-sac, he usually had a near monopoly of the old people's candy. When he did not visit their homes, the old people came to ask if he was okay. The mother made a joke about her little boy getting too big for trick-or-treating, but the entire thing disturbed her, and she talked to her husband about it when he came from work. She often had reports for him nowadays. The little boy's sudden need to watch that Arabian news channel troubled her. She found herself thinking maybe the little boy was being indoctrinated in terrorism—receiving some kind of subliminal message from the channel. At one point, she even thought about contacting the FBI about it, but the husband talked her out of it. In fact, in most of their discussions about the little boy, the husband took it as his duty to convince her that the little boy was a normal eight-year-old (even though he was just as disturbed by their son as she was). For this reason, their conversations about the little boy usually left them both feeling uneasy and/or dishonest.

As Thanksgiving approached, the parents allowed themselves to believe the family get-together would "bring the little boy back to them." That was the phrase the mother kept using—as if gatherings of distant relatives had miraculous powers over strange little boys. The mother was planning an elaborate feast. Relatives they had not seen in over a decade had been invited—about fifteen in all. The mother lost herself in the work, experiencing the numb, peace-like feeling people had when there was too much work and a tight deadline. In addition to the distant relatives, their first son would visit from Albany, and their family would be complete. With all that, the mother was convinced everything would take care of itself, like one of those made-for-television movies.

It was now the day before Thanksgiving. The kitchen was overflowing with ingredients for the feast. The old refrigerator they had stored in the basement had to be re-commissioned. The little boy only had a half-day of school, and returned about one in the afternoon to find his mother in the kitchen, working herself into a frenzy. There were sauces and various side dishes to be prepared. On the mother's face, there were daubs of flour; her eyes were wild; and as she was a messy cook, her clothes were stained with all the dishes she had prepared thus far. With so much work to be done, the mother had commandeered the sister's services. Under regular circumstances, the sister was useless in the kitchen, but that was even more the case now, as she had broken up with her boyfriend two days ago. She was chopping garlic half-heartedly, and sighing dramatically every few seconds. The little boy noticed she was dressed in her mourning clothes: pink shorts, a pink T-shirt, and pink, fuzzy slippers—all of which had the same trendy logo prominently displayed, like some kind of evil incantation.

The little boy had poked his head into the kitchen to see what was going on. His curiosity was quickly satisfied. In fact, he was about to close the door and go watch some TV when his mother suddenly shrieked. The little boy and the sister stared at her. There was a horrified look on the mother's face:

"I forgot to get the cranberries!"

"I guess I can go get them, Mom," the sister said with another sigh, as if going to the store would be a great act of courage and self-sacrifice on her part.

"No—you stay here and watch the pots," she said suspiciously, knowing she would not see her daughter for hours if she were allowed to leave. That was when she looked up and noticed the little boy. "You can come with me, son," she said brightly, as though the entire thing were pure genius. Of course, the little boy did not want to go, but the mother was soon grabbing her handbag and gesturing for him to come. The little boy and his sister ignored one another conspicuously. Soon, the mother and the little boy were walking out of the back door, toward the garage. She practically jogged, and he matched her pace.

During the drive to the strip mall, there was a (mostly) one-way conversation. It was more like a series of soliloquies on the mother's part, about how great the Thanksgiving dinner was going to be, and how it would be wonderful to see her first son again. The little boy did not exactly ignore her, but he listened to her the way he now watched the news shows: with an awareness that most of it was a repetition of things he already knew (or of things designed solely to elicit a desired response from him). Since the incident with the muddy pit, she had spent most of her time with him trying to "fix" him. He had become bored with the entire thing, but was always respectful toward his mother, and patient with the madness of the adult world.

It was about a fifteen-minute trip to the strip mall. Every other household must have had last-minute shopping to do, because the mall was packed. The mother had to drive around the parking lot twice before she found a free parking space. She was about to exit the car when the little boy pointed out she still had flour on her face. She spent a few minutes wiping it off, and fixing her hair, then they headed across the lot, to the supermarket.

Besides the supermarket and the usual spattering of fast food joints, the strip mall also had some office space. The local congressman had his office here, and it was next to the supermarket. As the mother and the little boy approached, they realized a dozen or so people were marching in front of the congressman's office. They were holding signs and chanting, and trying to get passersby to take their literature. Most of the protesters seemed to be of middle age or older. The entire thing seemed pathetic—especially in the face of all the antagonism and indifference they received from passersby. As the little boy drew closer, he realized they were chanting, "Stop the war! Bring the troops home now!" An old black man seemed to be at the vanguard—or at least, his voice was the loudest. He was standing on the curb, trying to hand out fliers.

After the mother had gauged the situation, she took the little boy's hand and pulled him along, as if the protesters were perverts exposing themselves in public. Something about watching them was shameful—almost prurient yet the little boy could not tear himself away. Their voices droned. Their protest seemed more like an act of penitence—like something prisoners might be forced to do—rather than something anyone would do willingly.

The mother and son were almost to the curb when the old man noticed them approaching. He was taking a flier from his stack, in order to hand it to the mother, when his eyes came to rest on the little boy. The moment they did, the old man gasped and moved toward them. Soon, he was standing in front of them, staring down at the little boy.

"It's incredible!" he whispered. He stretched out his trembling hand to touch the little boy; the mother wrenched her son back. Even then, the old man stood staring at the little boy, repeating how incredible it was. At last, the mother lost patience:

"Excuse me!" she screeched, so that the old man jumped and seemed to come to his senses.

"I'm sorry, ma'am. It's just that your grandson—"

"He's my son!" she screamed now, insulted by the assumption she was too old to be the little boy's mother.

"I didn't mean anything by it," the old man tried to apologize. He seemed flustered now. He had a messenger bag slung over his shoulder. It was full of the fliers he had been giving out. Assuming he was trying to give her a flier, the mother started to walk around him, but he once again stepped into her path. "I'm an artist," he explained, taking a sketchpad from the bag.

"I'm happy for you," she said sarcastically, preparing to leave again—

"No, wait!" he pleaded. He quickly flipped open the sketchpad, shoving it before the mother and son. "Look!" he said, breathing hard.

The mother looked and stood frozen: "What is this?" she said at last, her voice unsure and apprehensive. In the sketchpad, there were dozens of por-trait drawings (the old artist flipped through some pages) and all the drawings were of the little boy.

"What's going on here?" the mother said now. An unnamed terror grew in her eyes as she watched the pictures. "Why have you drawn my son?" she said, finally looking up at the old artist.

"That's what I'm trying to tell you, ma'am—I thought I was drawing a random figure: an idea I had in my head. I've been working on a series of paintings for months now. These drawings are studies I've been doing."

The mother still did not understand. "But why did you draw my son?"

"I don't know," he said, frustrated that she was not catching on, "—it's just a face that's been in my head. I can't explain it."

She stared at his head suspiciously, as if trying to detect something under-handed. ...And the drawings were perfect. She looked down at the sketch-pad once more. There was no chance of the drawings being coincidental facsimiles of the little boy. That was her son on those pages. The old artist had captured the little boy so perfectly that the mother had a sudden impulse to rip the pages to shreds, in order to free her son's soul—

"You're shaking," the old artist observed, staring at the mother closely. "I didn't mean to startle you...it's only that this thing is...is incredible." (Some-how, he could not get beyond that word). It was then that a gentlemanly impulse overcame him, and he proposed, "Can I get you something to drink?"

The mother looked around warily—as if searching for an escape route. At that moment, the protesters' chants reached a droning highpoint. She looked at the protesters sharply, then back to the old artist with new suspicion, remembering he had been with them—

"Please, ma'am," he implored her again. "Let's sit down and talk—"

"Talk about what?" she said combatively.

He looked at her helplessly: "About your son."

"I don't see what there is to talk about...just because my son resembles something you scribbled!" And then she ran, pulling the little boy behind her. She had not intended to run, but the need seized her. She ran all the way into the supermarket without turning back. However, the little boy looked over his shoulder as his mother wrenched him along; and in the old man's eyes, there was the disillusionment of a man watching his dreams playing themselves out in the light of day.

The mother seemed suddenly scatterbrained. She had put half a dozen superfluous items into the shopping cart before the little boy reminded her she had come there for cranberries. She seemed anxious about returning outside, and being at the mercy of the old artist. However, when she was on the checkout line, she looked out of the window and saw the police carrying away the protesters. She was relieved the old artist would be gone, but the dread continued. In fact, she did not talk at all on the trip back home. She merely stared out of the windscreen, periodically nibbling the fleshy lower part of her thumb (as was her habit when she was on-edge).

When the little boy and the mother got back home, the first thing they noticed was the flashy new car parked in the driveway. It was parked next to the now beat-up Saab the father had gotten the sister when she turned sixteen. Since there was no space, the mother had to park on the street. She got out of the car with an annoyed expression on her face; but just then, there was a hail of laughter from the house. It was as though there was a full studio audience in the house; and when the mother realized her first son must have arrived from Albany, she began to run to the house. The frown she had been wearing turned to a grin. She forgot about all the groceries she had to unload, and practically banged the door down in her haste to enter the house. Soon, her shrill, excited laugh could be heard above the cheering as she saw her son.

The little boy was still outside, by the car. He looked over at the flashy car, noting the expensive rims and tinted windows, then he walked toward the house. The mother had left the door open. There were over a dozen people in the house. Most were the old neighbors, who had come to greet the cul-de-sac's favorite son. In the living room, the brother and mother were still hugging and laughing. Soon, the sister joined the scrum, so that the old people started to cheer and clap and talk excitedly amongst themselves. The brother was tall and handsome. He laughed easily, and his eyes were bright and inviting. The little boy stood on the periphery, watching it all. For the first time, perhaps ever, he wished he belonged. Rather, he wished there were a side of him that wanted to rush into the familial hug. However, as he watched the scene, the only thing he could think was that none of it was real. He remembered the old artist at the mall. He was not even close to grasping what that could have been about, but he knew it was part of the thing he had sensed since the girl emerged from the pit.

He was mulling over these thoughts when the brother looked up from the familial hug and noticed the little boy. The man let out his loud, inviting laugh, and beckoned for the little boy to join them. The little boy went to them. Soon, he was in the midst of them, pressed between their bodies. His mind was blank.

Someone made a joke. One of the old men brought up one of the brother's childhood antics, and the adults laughed. The little boy tried to hear—tried to bring the words of the joke into him so he could be one of them—but he was somehow immune to their joy.

Some more of the neighbors arrived. The front door was still ajar, so they simply walked in. The brother was moving toward them now, shaking the old men's hands and kissing the old women on the cheek. As the brother touched them, it was as if he were a priest blessing his flock. Some of them, in their strange, euphoric way, seemed to genuflect when he greeted them. The little boy could only stare: none of it was real—

He had to leave. He could not explain it, but he had to leave. He retreated to the door; when he was outside, he realized he was panting. Something told him to run, and he ran. He wanted to exhaust himself. Within seconds, he was in the wood. Most of the trees had shed their leaves by now; and as he ran, the dead leaves at his feet were kicked and crushed. He liked the sound it made. Somehow, the sound drowned out a voice of panic within him. But when he looked around to get his bearings, he saw he had run to the pit. He slowed, then stopped at the encrusted rim of the pit. The frogs were long gone; instead of muck, it was filled with the dead leaves. The little boy stared down at the pit, feeling suddenly melancholy. He wished the girl would reappear and take him away from all this. He did not want to go back into the house—into that place where nothing was real. He wanted the girl to return to him, so she could show him more of the forbidden knowledge. That was how he had begun to think of the hundreds of years of history he had experienced. Maybe, when she touched him again, the scenes would finally make sense to him. Anything seemed possible at that moment.

…A voice or impulse told him to see what was beneath the dead leaves in the pit. He picked up a long stick and began digging—pushing the leaves aside so he could see what was there. The wind gusted. It was not violent, but strong enough for more leaves to be blown into the pit. He stopped digging and looked around warily. The sun was going down. In the growing darkness, the foliage-free trees seemed like the hands of monsters. The boughs were like the long, creepy fingers—

All at once, the wind died. The wind-blown leaves came to rest with a kind of grim finality—as if the wind would never ever blow again. The little boy dropped the stick. Looking down, he saw his hands were trembling. And then, in the dead center of the pit, the leaves began to move—as if something were burrowing within the pit. The little boy remembered his wish for the girl to reappear. The prospect of seeing her again was the only reason he did not run. Nevertheless, as the leaves churned slowly, his muscles were quivering—preparing for a dash, if it came to that.

He bent closer, to get a better look; as he stood there in shock, some fingers appeared from beneath the dying leaves in the pit. This time, instead of muck, the fingers—and the emerging hand—were covered in dust. The little boy could not move. With effort, he forced himself to take a breath—to suck air into his lungs. Now, an entire left arm was coming out of the pit. The little boy stared, but barely saw. His mind was frantic. By the time it occurred to him the arm was a boy's, the dust-covered head came out of the pit. It was a black boy's head: the hair was short, coarse and curly. Within seconds, the rest of the dust-covered body was expelled, as if the kid's grave had regurgitated him. The little boy took a step back—

The kid's body convulsed, then there was a long, rasping inhalation as the body took its first breath. The little boy was still standing there when the head jerked up and the eyes opened. The eyes were bloodshot—so red that barely no white showed in them at all. As the little boy stared at the bloodshot eyes, he realized something: the kid with the bloodshot eyes had been in some of the scenes in the dimension of light.

The kid began to stretch out his hand. At the sight of those dusty fingers, the little boy retreated another step. The little boy was about to run; but just then, the kid with the bloodshot eyes let out a low moan. The little boy stopped, uncertain. He thought maybe the kid was hurt. He took a tentative step closer to the kid, and then another. He opened his mouth to ask the kid if he was okay; he was just leaning in closer to get a better look, when the kid lurched at him. Whether the kid was only desperate to touch him or wanted to rip him to shreds, the little boy did not wait to find out. He turned and fled; just like when the girl appeared, he almost ran headlong into the low bough again. He remembered to duck. There was a shrub to hurdle, and he did it in one athletic stride. Unfortunately, there was another shrub right next to the first, so the little boy only managed to take one step before he tripped over the second shrub. With the adrenaline flowing through him, he was on his feet within seconds. He glanced over his shoulder, in case the kid was chasing…but there was no one there. It was so unexpected that he stopped, staring at the pit. The voice of panic was still telling him to run; but he knew, somehow, that it was safe now. The kid with the bloodshot eyes was gone; the pit was undisturbed. Either the world had reset itself again, or he was losing his mind. It was either one or the other, and he nodded his head in grim acceptance.

He remembered his brother at that moment. In a flash, he recalled how he had fled into the wood, hoping to block out the feeling that he did not belong. In the face of everything, he was glad the kid with the bloodshot eyes was gone. Maybe the kid's touch would have been like the girl's touch, severing his ties to the world. He did not want to be pulled away from the world anymore. At least for a little while, he wanted to pretend he was like the others. He wanted to be with them, laughing and hugging: a normal eight-year-old. These were his thoughts as he began walking back toward the house.

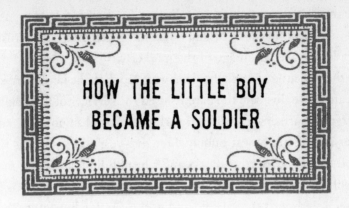

HOW THE LITTLE BOY
BECAME A SOLDIER

The little boy went home and tried to pretend. The Thanksgiving dinner went well. He made a concerted effort to laugh when jokes were made. He picked up his brother's habit of putting people at ease, and found, to his amazement, that he was good at it. By the end of the Thanksgiving weekend, the mother was celebrating the success of her plan, convinced her machinations had finally "brought their little boy back to them."

When the little boy returned to school, he fell in line with the pursuits and pastimes of his classmates. He picked up sports—football and basketball—and discovered he was untouchable. When it was time to play games, he was always the first to be picked. In the classroom, he had always been a relatively good student, but when he began to pretend, and to apply himself, he quickly rose to the top of his class. Like all lies, it became self-perpetuating, so that after a while, he was no longer conscious of trying to pretend.

Even then, in his private moments, when he allowed himself to be honest, his mind always returned to the girl. When he conjured her, he did not see her as a child anymore, but as a woman, with a full, supple body. In his fantasies, he, too, would be grown, and he would be making love to her. The images were so vivid that he often wondered if they were more than fantasies. Like always, the only thing he knew for sure was that the girl (real or imagined) was the key to everything.

Since the first war was going so well, America now decided to start up a new one. It was like a business: product demand was high, so they rushed out a new model to take advantage of the market.

Now that the little boy and the sister were feuding, she never agreed to baby-sit him anymore. Instead, the parents used the services of the neighborhood babysitter: a fourteen-year-old girl with pigtails and a bubbly personality. In fact, her entire family was bubbly. Her five-year-old sister was the neigh-borhood darling, with rosy cheeks and a head full of curls. Her mother had supposedly come from a long line of "stay at home moms," and was practically never seen without her embroidered apron. As for her father, he was the "cool dad" of the cul-de-sac, and was never seen without his trademark smile. The bubbly babysitter was earnest about her job, and always came equipped with a million activities to keep the little boy occupied: board games and other wholesome standbys that made the little boy want to bang his head against the wall in boredom. Yet, she was so nice that he felt guilty about telling her how childish and idiotic he found the entire thing.

The babysitter's father was a reservist in the Army; and as America prepared for a new war, he was called up. The entire cul-de-sac threw a party to send him off. He was literally the life of the party, telling jokes and speaking with an almost religious certainty about how he was going overseas to protect America. The little boy did not know if he believed it or not, but he wanted to believe. Like everyone else, he wanted to see certainties where there were only doubts and questions; he wanted to see unassailable truths were there were only shadings of the truth. He did notice, however, that the babysitter seemed more bubbly than usual. Her natural ebullience seemed to go into overdrive—as if she were on some kind of emotional caffeine. She laughed louder than he had ever heard her laugh before, as if she were desperate to match her father. At every moment, she was at his side, holding his arm, as if she were desperate to be a little girl again....

About a month after her father was deployed, the bubbly babysitter had a total personality change. All at once, she began going about the motions of rebelling against the adult world. Instead of pigtails and the "proper" dresses she had always worn, she reported for babysitting duty in dark Goth make-up and painful-looking piercings in her tongue and eyebrow. On top of all that, she had on a strange crinoline mini-skirt with neon orange thigh-high stockings. The little boy's mother was wary, but she was in a bind, since she had to finish a special project at work.

Instead of their usual board games, the babysitter left the little boy to his own devices; to all questions, she either shrugged or delivered her trademark, "Whatever" with bored indifference. After the little boy's mother was gone, and they were alone, she went behind their house to smoke a cigarette. He could tell she was still in the experimental phase of her habit, because he heard her coughing.

When she came back inside, he was watching TV in the living room. He was on the couch; she plopped herself down on the adjacent loveseat, which was perpendicular to the couch. She sat with her leg thrown over the arm of the loveseat, so that he could see her crotch. She had on a neon green thong, but it barely covered her thatch of pubic hair. He was not so much shocked as confused. He looked at her face for a clue: she was staring ahead blankly; his eyes returned to her crotch—the bulge of her pubic mound. He stared; her legs remained spread; her gaze remained distant. …The sight of her crotch aroused him instinctively; as he stared, he thought about the girl from the pit—all the fantasies that had graced his dreams and daydreams since the events of that magical summer a year ago. However, as he watched the babysitter's eyes again, he saw they were the eyes of a scared little girl.

The realization short-circuited his lust, and he sobered. Maybe it was only then that he saw her clearly. "…You miss your father, don't you?" he said at last.

She looked over at him, surprised—disarmed by the simplicity of his question. A helpless expression came to her face, breaking the mask of teenage apathy. Her leg came down; she crossed her legs and looked down at the floor, her eyes softer—more human. The little boy felt sorry for her. Now that her father was off fighting in America's latest war, she was locked in a battle with her fears and uncertainties. He did not know if she would win, but at least she seemed human again—and real.

They spent the rest of the evening talking. Sometimes, it was serious—

like the terrible dreams she had had about her father; but most of the time, it was about nothing in particular: the humanizing trivialities of life.

Time progressed, and he matured into a handsome, athletic young man. With his ability to put people at ease, he acquired many friends—but as he was always pretending, he never had close friends. The same went for his eventual girlfriends. Invariably, they initiated contact and pursued him; at best, he tolerated them. Even when he hugged and kissed them, he did so without any true passion—since he saved his love for the girl of the pit, who was literally the girl of his dreams. His girlfriends became hollow surrogates for the girl. After a while, he always felt sorry for them, and a little guilty—which was why he never had girlfriends for long.

Despite these complicated dynamics, he still became the most popular person in his high school. On the sports field, no one could touch him; in the classroom, he grasped the lessons so easily that the entire thing often bored him. Like his fantasies of the girl, he often swore he had experienced it all before—had learned all the lessons and played all the games in a previous life, and was stuck in a repeating loop that only he could sense. Luckily, such thoughts were never with him for long.

By the time the young man entered his senior year of high school, the wars of September 11th were stretching into their tenth year. To assuage the public, the politicians and generals pretended there was no war. They outsourced the killing to militias and warlords—whom they called freedom fighters. Every once in a while there would be a massacre, or reports of an American bomb that had missed its mark—but as Americans were always willing to abide horrific casualties when the people being killed are not (white) Americans, these things were easily relegated to the back of the national consciousness.

Up until late April of his senior year, the young man's life seemed outwardly perfect. By any objective measure, he was a great success. He had been accepted to Harvard. He had applied more out of curiosity than because of a desire to attend. They had offered him a scholarship. The final agreement was still on his desk, along with the other acceptance letters and scholarship offers. He was to be the valedictorian of his high school—no one else was even close to him. On top of that, he had led his school to championships in football and basketball. Major college sports powerhouses had offered him athletic scholarships; famous coaches had visited his home, trying to coax him to their programs. The letters were all on his desk, the last ones unopened. Every day, his mother asked him if he had decided which school he was going to attend. His teachers and coaches did the same thing. He told them he was merely weighing the options. It was not until the end of April when he realized he was terrified of the future.

The passage of time had unnerved him since the day the girl's touch brought him to the dimension of light. He feared time the way people feared snakes and spiders, and all the other stealth predators. The future was an ambush; with each passing day, he felt trapped and cornered. He could not explain any of this logically, but the certainty was within him. ...Then, one morning in April, he woke up feeling doomed. The day was bright and beautiful, yet he felt like a condemned man. He tried to reason it out, but it made no sense. He tried going about his life as usual, but the anxiousness continued. After a few weeks, he realized he spent his days waiting for something bad to happen. By May, it took all his willpower to keep up his pretenses.

He bought himself some time by deciding to go to Harvard. Everyone cheered; but deep down, he knew the time for pretenses was coming to an end.

In the final weeks of school, he retreated into himself. He kept his friends at bay; he stopped stringing on the girls jockeying to be his lovers. At home, the mother began to worry about him again. Fortunately for him, that entire year, the mother was distracted by his brother's U.S. Senate campaign. It had all happened quickly. The young man did not know the details. He only knew everyone loved his brother, and that his brother's smiling face was often on TV now, accompanied by glowing endorsements and a Pollyannaish cornucopia of campaign promises. Even the sister was doing her part to keep the mother distracted. She now lived in Los Angeles, where she was a talent agent. The mother usually called her up a few times a week to get the latest celebrity gossip. With all that, the young man could fade into the background and await his fate without too much nagging.

It was now two weeks until graduation. The seniors were all suffering from "senioritis," so the final weeks were replete with field trips and movies and a host of other activities that required little concentration. It was a beautiful Friday, and the day's field trip was to midtown Manhattan. The young man was the last one to disembark from the school bus. The rest of his classmates—about eighty in all—were already walking up the stairs to The Museum of American Art. He had pretended to be asleep on the bus, so that no one would bother him. Even when he was outside, he trailed behind them, wary of the various cliques. For a moment, he considered walking away from them all. He wanted to wander the city by himself. For the first time in years, he craved the solitude he had had as a little boy playing alone in his wood.

His history teacher—a short, elderly woman who reminded him of a bulldog—saw him lagging behind, and yelled at him at the top of her voice. Her voice was so shrill even people on the other side of the street turned to see what was going on. The young man moved toward her, embarrassed. Yet, even when he was in the museum's grand marble atrium, he lagged behind the others. Ahead, he saw his prom date. She was a cheerleader, and was surrounded by a clique of popular girls. Since the prom, she had been snubbing him; as he had not tried to seduce her, she had been spreading the rumor he was gay. The young man could not be bothered. His eyes moved to some loud football players and their hangers-on. They were laughing at someone's punch line. The comedian spied the young man and waved at him, intending for him to join them, but the young man pretended not to see. He bent down and spent a couple minutes untying and tying his shoelaces. When he looked up, the last of his classmates was filing past the ticket counter. The young man ran up to join them, so he would not have to pay, but as soon as he was clear, he turned the corner and walked away on his own.

The museum was packed—mostly with tourists and other kids on field trips. He spent about fifteen minutes wandering through the various exhibits before a combination of anxiety and boredom got to him. He felt hungry and restless. He was thinking he would leave the building and find a pizzeria when he came upon the main exhibit. It was jammed with patrons. People were streaming into the gallery. There was a huge placard in front of the door, giving a biography of the artist. Apparently the exhibition was a retrospective for a famous painter who had recently died. The young man had skimmed through half the biography before his eyes came to rest on the artist's picture. When they did, and he realized he had met the artist before, he shuddered. It was the same artist from the strip mall all those years ago…

He found himself walking, but as if in a trance. There was a chalky film on his tongue; his mind seemed suddenly short-circuited and useless. His classmates were all in the gallery. They seemed stunned. He did not realize why until he looked at some of the paintings hanging on the wall. There were dozens of historical scenes, all of which had the same figure at different stages of his life. The young man moved toward the picture closest to him. He brushed past some of his classmates; and when he did, they looked at him as if they had seen a ghost. In fact, all his classmates were looking at him that way now, because he was the person in all those paintings. Like the scenes he had seen in the dimension of light, the pictures portrayed him over hundreds of years of history. The young man glanced to his left, where his prom date and her retinue were staring at him, unsure of whether to be scared or amazed—

The young man fled. He did not run, but instead turned away from them and exited the room. A few people began to whisper. He did not turn back. Frantic thoughts flew through his mind, but he made no effort to decipher them. He only knew he had to get out of the building—put some distance between himself and the paintings. He felt sick. If his stomach had not been empty, he was sure he would vomit. He moved quicker: the front entrance was in view now. The atrium was still packed: he bumped into a few people; each time he did so, he put up his hand as a sign of apology, but he did not stop or look back or say anything.

At last, he was outside. He took a deep breath, but the city air was not of the type that could refresh. In fact, it burned his lungs. He slunk down the stairs, grabbing the handrail to maintain the pretense of balance. He did not stop once he reached the bottom. He kept walking. Soon, he was walking across the street. Luckily for him, traffic had stopped for the red light. He walked on in a daze. He stared ahead, barely seeing. Maybe five blocks passed this way. Eventually, he stopped and looked around, feeling a sudden sense of despair. He wanted to cry—but for a reason he could not articulate. He wanted to run—to continue fleeing—but he knew it was pointless. He had spent the last nine years running: the time had come to stop and face the thing he had come to think of as fate. On the next block, he saw a subway station. Nodding his head, he walked toward it.

He took the downtown train to Penn Station, then he took the Long Island Railroad. His mind sputtered along for most of the trip, as if fearful of where its thoughts might lead. As the cul-de-sac was only accessible via the highway, he had to return to school to pick up his dilapidated Saab. It was the same one his father had bought for his sister about twelve years ago. When his sister left for California, she had left the car behind—not so much as a gift to her brother, but as forgotten trash. To start the car, he had to connect two wires under the hood. He did so now, and headed home in the same dazed state.

Once he entered the cul-de-sac, he parked in front of his house and headed straight for the wood. Within minutes, he was standing over the pit. It was muddy again—considering all the rain they had had lately. The frogs were croaking; everything was as it was all those years ago, when the girl emerged from the pit. He did not know what exactly he was to do to make the thing happen, but he knew the moment of truth had come. In fact, soon, the wind began to blow, and the sky began to darken. When he looked at the surface of the pit, he saw there was no mud there anymore. Instead, there was the black void he remembered from the last time. He braced himself. His skin crawled, but he kept telling himself to stand his ground—

Fingers broke the surface of the void; the young man took a deep breath, and waited. Soon, an arm appeared, and then a torso. The young man only stared. Before he could make sense of it, a man's body was expelled from the pit. As the man's back was to him, he could not see the face. However, the same chunks of filth were spilling out over the rim now. The young man took a step back to keep from dirtying his shoes and pants. The man's body was gaunt—as if starved—and covered in filth. The young man held his breath—both to keep from smelling the stench, and to listen for any sign that the man was breathing. The man's back was still to him; the young man was about to walk around the pit, to see the face, when the body gasped and began to cough. This brought the young man to his senses, and he bent down to help. His hand touched the man's skin—the slick coating of filth. The man seemed to be hyperventilating now. At the young man's touch, the man turned to him. His eyes were wild—panicked—as if he had just seen hell. It took a few seconds for the young man to recognize the bloodshot eyes. It was the same person from the last time—only older. However, the smell of rancid blood and filth was now turning his stomach; he had to fight the urge to flee—even if it was just to take a breath of fresh air. He remembered the man with the bloodshot eyes had been in the scenes in the dimension of light—

The man was stretching out his hand now. The wild look of panic was still in his eyes. The young man was debating whether he should take the man's hand when the man was suddenly wrenched back. When the young man looked, he saw the man's legs had been pulled back into the pit. A hoarse cry escaped from the man's lips. His body was wrenched back again, as if the devil were pulling him back to hell. Now, his torso was the only thing left sticking out of the filth. He was crying now—disconsolate. His eyes were frantic—pleading for the young man to help him. The young man had only stood there, stunned, but as the pleas reached a desperate pitch, the young man went to the rim of the pit and grabbed the man's hands. With the filth that covered him, it was impossible to get a grip. At most, they touched for two or three seconds before the man with the bloodshot eyes was pulled all the way into the darkness; but in those seconds, the young man saw it all. He saw a scene in a desert somewhere—there were sand dunes and hovels all around him—and the man with the bloodshot eyes was screaming. There were two turbaned men there with guns, and the man with the bloodshot eyes was their prisoner. One of the turbaned men rose a gun to the man's head then, and pulled the trigger, so that a single, thunderous gunshot sounded. …After that, there were more scenes of the man being gunned down and stabbed and thrown from buildings and run over by cars. It was as if the man had spent eternity dying—suffering in his own private hell.

The young man shuddered, feeling the weight of the man's pain and suffering. He stumbled back a few steps, then collapsed to the ground. He was losing consciousness quickly. He felt doomed—as if he were running out of time to figure out what all this was supposed to mean—

Move! he told himself. He had to remain conscious. He could not waste any more time. Unfortunately, he only managed to crawl a few meters before he passed out.

Anywhere from a couple minutes to a couple hours passed. He awoke with a shudder. He was still in the wood, lying prone in the mud. He raised his head off the ground and looked at his clothes. He was still covered in blood and filth, but it was dry now—caked-on and stiff. He sat up with effort. He remembered the man with the bloodshot eyes—the entire sequence of events. Once again, he saw all the man's death scenes. He glanced back at the pit, but it was again a normal pit; the frogs were again croaking. He looked away and scanned the rest of the wood, as if he had misplaced something.

He remembered what had happened in the museum today—all those paintings of him throughout history. Everything was swirling in his head now; but out of all the chaos, one thing became clear to him: the man with the bloodshot eyes, the girl and himself were all joined by something monstrous. What that thing was, he still could not begin to guess, but he could feel it gathering about him.

With effort, he got to his feet. By the placement of the sun in the sky, he guessed it was perhaps about six or seven o'clock. His parents would be home now—if they were not already. He took a few steps toward his house before it occurred to him he could not let his parents see him like this. The caked-on filth still covered him: at the sight of him, his parents would only panic and ask questions he could not answer. He remembered his car: he had some workout clothes in the back seat. He began walking toward the cul-de-sac. When he got to the street, he looked and saw his parents' cars were not there yet. He sighed: that was one less thing to worry about.

He went inside the house, but he walked like an old man. In the bathroom, he took off his clothes and showered under a hot, stinging blast of water. The day's events flashed in his mind again, and he began to weep. Now that he was home, he allowed himself to be sick—and to let out everything he had kept bottled up inside. A wave of nausea incapacitated him; he tried to vomit, but only ended up dry heaving stomach juices. His throat burned and he felt wretched, so he turned off the shower and stumbled back to his bedroom. Once there, he crawled into bed and slept a horrible, dreamless sleep that was more like being dead.

His mother awakened him about two hours later. He gasped as she shook him. His throat still ached from the stomach juices. The mother was staring down at him with an anxious look on her face. She saw he was sick. She began:

"The school called me—said you had disappeared." When he only stared up at her confusedly, she continued, "Are you okay?"

"I'm fine," he whispered with his sore throat, "—just a stomach ache."

She was still unsure. "Is that all it is?"

He wanted her to go away—not because he had any animus toward her, but because he knew he had no answers to the questions in her eyes. "Maybe some soup would help?" he suggested at last. She stared at him a few seconds, then nodded and left the room. He closed his eyes, hoping to get some rest, but his mind only flashed with the day's events. He grimaced.

About fifteen minutes later, his mother returned with a tray of chicken noodle soup. The smell of it turned his stomach, but as his mother looked at him hopefully, he knew there was nothing to do but eat. His mother began to spoon-feed him. The entire thing annoyed him, but the only thing to do was endure it. Unfortunately, the smell of the soup was making him queasier by the second. He was halfway through the bowl when his stomach rebelled. He barely had time to lean over the side of the bed and vomit into the waste bin. Once he was through heaving, he groaned again, lay down in bed and closed his eyes. His mother was distraught, but he felt too weak to acknowledge her. She took away the bin, and he went back to sleep.

Some time later, his mother and father awakened him from the same dreamless sleep. It was night outside. The young man's head throbbed. His parents had turned on the light, and his eyes burned. When his eyes adjusted to the light, he saw his parents' faces were tense and unsure. His father felt his forehead. Apparently, the young man had a fever. The father made conjectures about food poisoning, and asked the young man what he had eaten. The young man wished they would go away.

Now, the father was saying he had to get some fluids in him. The mother asked him if he thought he could eat something again, and he nodded his head. The father suggested soup without spices. The young man drowned them out; but in a strange way, his sickness bridged the distance that had built up between them. After months of respectful distance, his parents finally felt useful and needed. His mother took a strange sort of joy in tending to him, and bringing him soup. He let them have their joy, even while a sick feeling in the pit of his stomach reminded him there was a puzzle to solve, and that he was running out of time.

Eventually, he managed to get to sleep; but when he awoke from the same horrible, dreamless sleep on Saturday morning, the sense of panic only intensified. The dreamless sleep was an ominous sign—as if his body were preparing for death. He was sick all day Saturday as well. …And then, it was Sunday morning. He awoke feeling haggard and beleaguered, and terrified of going back to sleep again. The dreamless sleep was worse than any nightmare or vision he could have had. He stayed up late on Sunday night, reading and watching TV—and anything else he could think of to keep him awake—but on Monday morning, it was the same thing: awaking to the realization death was out there, waiting for him.

He decided to go to school—not because he felt better, but because school would be something to distract him. His legs were wobbly beneath him as he walked downstairs. His parents asked him not to go, but the young man knew it was all out of his hands. He felt enslaved by the flow of time. In the car, nothing seemed right. As he drove to school, the world outside the window seemed off; noises and scents all seemed warped, as if the universe were coming undone. On top of that, he could not get over the feeling he was doomed.

He stared blankly ahead as he drove. He noticed the car ahead of him was going too fast. The light at the intersection was turning from yellow to red. The young man stepped on the brakes, but the car ahead of him sped up, trying to beat the light. It was horrible. There were people in the crosswalk—dozens of people…mostly kids on their way to school. The car ahead of him ploughed into them. People were screaming…trying to run. A few of them banged into the windscreen, shattering it. When the driver finally managed to stop the car, he got out and looked at what he had done. It was a middle-aged man in a cotton sweat suit. He had probably just come from the gym, or the local park, because his clothes were soaked with sweat.

Like many of the other drivers, the young man got out of his car—since the road was now clogged. The scene was sickening: blood and guts…mangled kids. People started screaming at the man in the sweat suit; a parent came up and punched him in the face; another started to choke him. Fortunately, others intervened to break up the fight. The young man returned to his car. He shut his door and locked it. There were sirens in the distance. Looking around him, he realized if he made a U-turn, he could escape the scene. He had just put his car in reverse when he sensed something in his peripheral vision. Among the crowd that had gathered to watch the sickening scene, there was a man's form; but instead of flesh and blood, the man was a blurred shadow. The young man tried to look closer—and corroborate this impossible thing—but that was when another crazed parent lunged at the man in the sweat suit. The parent had a baseball bat in hand, and it took about six bystanders to keep him from murder. The young man's eyes had instinctively moved to the people struggling with the parent; when he looked back to the place where the blurred shadow had stood, there was nothing there. His skin crawled.

Something told him to escape while he still could. He put the car in gear, and executed the U-turn. Yet, even as he drove away, he had the sense none of it was real. He felt that if he were to turn around, he would see all the actors going about their business; all the mangled kids would be getting up and wiping away the fake blood. He did not look back. He forced himself not to look; but he knew, deep inside, that it was only a matter of time now before everything came to an end.

Twenty minutes later, he entered his first class—his history class. He kept seeing those mangled kids. He remembered the entity on the periphery of the mob: the blur in the form of a man. His mind tried to go to it, but he shuddered at the possibilities.

It was toward the end of his history class that there was a scream in an adjacent classroom. That other class had been watching the news for a social studies project. When several students from that class began to scream, the young man's history teacher went to investigate the commotion. She warned her students to stay in their seats. However, as the seconds passed, and more students in the neighboring class cried out, everyone in the history class streamed over to the other class. Even before the young man saw the thing for himself, he had known. He was actually the last one to leave the history class. He walked as if in a trance. When he got to the class, some of the students were already crying and hugging. He looked over at the TV screen, but only allowed himself to nod his head when he saw the smoldering remains of the White House.

A few minutes later, there was the announcement that the president and half the cabinet had been blown to bits by terrorists. For the first few hours, there was total chaos and disarray; people were crying in the open—not so much because they loved the president, but because reality, as they had known it, had come to an end. His classmates and teachers fled home, hoping to find stability and reassurance with their families. There was no formal school closing: people just left. On the streets, everyone seemed jittery. Mothers clutched their little children; friends and lovers gripped one another with a desperation he had never seen before.

He got home about midday. His parents were not home, and he was happy for it. He turned on the living room TV, seeing the culprit had already been identified. A regime in Saharan Africa had supposedly been the staging ground for the terrorists. There were already photos of the terrorists—passport photos with impassive faces that seemed monstrous, considering what the men had done. No one could figure out how they had gotten a bomb into the most restricted area in America—especially such a massive bomb. The young man watched all the speculation for about an hour before he dozed off.

The phone awakened him: it was his sister calling from Hollywood. She was crying and distraught. He wished he could feel compassion for her, but her sobs only annoyed him. Her cries seemed fake, like everything about her. He had never forgiven her for what she had done—mostly because she had never sought his forgiveness. He tried not to be rude and petty, but he found he could only give her one-word answers: no, to if their parents were home; yes, to he had seen the news. It went on and on like that for about twenty minutes. She went in circles, asking him the same questions. As was her habit, she did not wait for his answer, but instead used her question as a prelude for long, disjointed explanations of her fears and theories. Mercifully, his parents entered the house while he was on the phone with her. After a mandatory hug—given the circumstances—he handed over the phone and retreated to his bedroom.

He lay in bed thinking. He knew the president's murder was only an inconsequential ripple in time: another illusion in a series of illusions. The challenge now was to struggle against the illusions—to see things as they were, regardless of where he ended up. He had to figure out what to do next. Instinctively, he turned on the television in his bedroom, and it was all there for him. The stations were now showing file footage from the African country. Apparently, there had been a civil war there for decades now. On the screen, there were images of refugees and war-ravaged villages; but against the backdrop of human suffering and desperation, there were the sand dunes he had seen when he touched the man with the bloodshot eyes. There was the same cloudless blue sky, deceptively beautiful against the scorching sun. It was all there for him, calling him. All he had to do was look beyond the illusions.

He walked back downstairs. His parents were still on the phone. They each had a receiver and were having a three-way conversation with their daughter. The young man got something to eat—some leftovers. When he walked back into the living room, the TV was still on, and the same images were there: the sand dunes, the deceptively beautiful sky. He knew then he had no choice but to go to that place. He did not know if he believed in destiny and fate, but the flow of history was pulling him to that place, so he nodded his head imperceptibly.

And then, the brother was on the TV. The young man had been about to head back upstairs when the broadcast came on. The parents screamed for the sister to turn on the channel, then they sat down to watch the show. …The brother had always had a knack for being in the right place at the right time. He had been visiting Congress when the attack happened. The news crew had literally been walking the halls when they came upon him.

The brother's facial expression was a combination of pain and resolve. He began slowly, recapping everything that had happened that day; but soon, he was highlighting the reasons for vengeance and fortitude. He made everything so simple. He identified the brutal, terrorist-sympathizing despot who had conspired to do this to America. The African country's hundreds of years of written history and geography and culture were subsumed in one evil man. America's wrath would be the right hand of God—those were the words the brother used. Yet, they were words Americans understood and liked. In the halls of Congress, bystanders began to clap; across America, people clenched their fists and nodded their heads, allowing themselves to believe the inevitable war was to be God's will. The young man only stared, genuinely awed by the force of it, even while he knew it was all fake.

As the brother had stated it, the resulting war was inevitable—like the impulse to scream once someone had stepped on one's foot. The war was a transcendental event: Americans surrendered to it the way converts surrendered to a new religion. In the aftermath of the White House bombing, it was not so much a new president that Americans cried out for, as a priest able to interpret the will of God. The laws enacted by the new government were like edicts from God. The new government's policies were like the ones mandated by ancient high priests, where everyone was either a believer or a nonbeliever—and where the nonbeliever was a sinner to be eradicated, either through conversion or death.

The young man shocked everyone by joining the Army; but by then, all he could think about were sand dunes and deceptively beautiful skies.

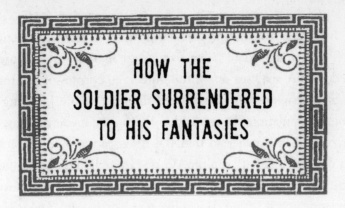

HOW THE SOLDIER SURRENDERED TO HIS FANTASIES

A week after he graduated from high school, the young man was sent to Georgia for basic training. By the second week of basic training, American military might had already routed the African army. The few African tanks were left charred on the roadsides. Long columns of African soldiers surrendered every day. Indeed, most of them simply took off their uniforms and walked away, so that African resistance seemed to evaporate the moment the Americans appeared on the horizon. At basic training, the main concern among the recruits was that they would miss out on their chance for glory. They had dreamed of going to war and coming back to ticker tape parades; but after three weeks of war, the American flag was flying in the capital. The only thing that marred the aesthetic perfection of the victory was that the "brutal, terrorist-sympathizing despot" remained unaccounted for. Now that the war seemed to be all but over, capturing the despot was the only thing that kept people's attention.

On all the news shows, there were daily (and sometimes hourly) reports of the despot being cornered in a desert enclave or holed up in a shantytown somewhere. Without fantasies of battlefield glory to keep them going, the new recruits hoped they would be sent over in time to be able to capture him. They held their breaths every time there was a despot sighting, and sighed in relief every time the sighting proved false. In fact, speculating on the despot's whereabouts became a national pastime. People discussed it at the office water cooler and while they were waiting for their commuter trains. Unfortunately, about a month after the invasion, it was revealed the despot had been killed in the opening hours of the war (along with his junta). The Pentagon had taken so long to announce it because they had had to do DNA analyses on all the butchered corpses of the regime. The terrorists had supposedly assassinated the men before blending back into the general population. That was the story in the media anyway. They said the terrorists had done it so that the Americans would never be able to prove a definite link between the White House bombing and the despot.

Whatever the case, by then, Americans were ready for the war to be over. They became bored with it. It was like a movie that did not satisfy: they left the theaters grumbling and wondering where it had gone wrong. With no more despot sightings to distract them, people were forced to digest the daily trickle of death: five Marines killed by a roadside bomb in an unpronounceable desert province; another six gunned down in an ambush.

Every day, it was something else; some days, the numbers were larger and the deaths more gruesome. The perfect little war Americans had envisioned was turning into a nightmare. When the politicians and generals could not put people at ease, the media conglomerates brought out historians and academics, who explained all the things people had not wanted to hear before the war began. They explained how Americans had inserted themselves into what was already a bloody civil war. They revealed how hundreds of thousands of people had been killed, raped or maimed—even before the Americans rolled into the desert. When the Americans first appeared on the horizon, the factions opposed to the despot had cheered and provided logistical assistance. Unfortunately, as the Americans had come to the desert to take revenge against terrorists, they assumed any man they saw with a gun was a terrorist. It was only a matter of time before they bombed the factions with whom they were supposedly allied. In the chaos of the initial invasion, one desert village looked the same as another; one turbaned man with a gun was indistinguishable from another. Naturally, after a few weeks of mistaken bombings and massacres, all alliances were called off. By the time the Americans rolled into the capital as conquerors, all the African factions came to realize they hated the Americans more than they hated one another.

Crude alliances were made; ancient blood feuds were forestalled as the people of the Sahara dedicated themselves to the task of killing Americans. If there had ever been any actual terrorists in the country, they stoked these resentments. The resentments became a new religion—a new pagan god, to which they could pray and sacrifice their lives. After the first few weeks, it was no longer a war between armies, but a war between believers. On one side, there were the wretched men of the Sahara, who openly professed their willingness to blow themselves up for their beliefs; and on the other side, were the Americans, who declared their resolve to be more brutal and uncompromising than these madmen.

Back at basic training, the new recruits followed these developments with a certain amount of alarm. Where Army censors and patriotic American journalists left gaps in stories, the new recruits filled in all the gaps with their imaginations. And then, odd rumors began to circulate about the war—like the despot was not really dead. Even after the Pentagon announced his death, there were still daily sightings of him. A nomadic desert caravan claimed to have seen him. Supposedly, he had appeared in the desert—like a mirage—and sat down to have tea with them. The nomads were shown on the news, shivering and clutching their heads. At first, the news broadcasts mocked such sightings; television comedians did entire acts on them. Yet, the sightings continued. Even after the military declared the entire thing to be a well-orchestrated hoax, the despot kept appearing. The man would show up at people's shacks at mealtime, as if his tastes had gone from the caviar and champagne he had enjoyed with his junta, to the gruel the locals made out of the American-issued relief aide. In time, commando units were sent to all the sightings (just in case). The military pointed out the despot was appearing in several places at once—which was impossible. They again made declarations that the entire thing was a hoax, but the multiple sightings only corroborated the belief some of the Africans had always had: the despot was a ghost, haunting the desert. After a while, even the American troops on the ground began to report sightings of him. He always disappeared out of back doors before he could be captured. Several units insisted he had faded into dark corners of shacks and disappeared.

The soldier already believed in ghosts and other impossible things, so these strange developments did not concern him. Indeed, while the other new recruits began to have their doubts about joining the Army, the soldier could think of nothing but sand dunes and deceptively beautiful skies.

He still did not dream anymore; when he closed his eyes for the night, he would be taken away to the nowhere place. He always awoke with a sense of panic; his first thought was always that he was running out of time. For this reason, he usually felt sick in the morning. Yet, as he excelled in everything the Army put before him, he was sent to commando school after basic training. The training was like the games he had played in the wood as a child. Even among the Army's best, the soldier excelled. No one could keep up with him; and for once in his life, he was rewarded for losing himself in games.

Right before the soldier was deployed to war, his brother made a visit to the base. It was all part of his brother's campaign for the U.S. Senate. Having a sibling in the Army was judged to be beneficial by the brother's campaign manager, so a photo shoot was set up. His brother's campaign manager had called the soldier to set up the event (not his brother, himself). His brother stormed into the Army base like a force of nature—along with the media. Before the soldier knew it, they were upon him; his brother's arm was around him, and the soldier nodded to whatever his brother said, while onlookers cheered and photographers took pictures. A few minutes later, just as abruptly, his brother was gone, and all the reporters and onlookers departed as well, like planets being wrenched along by the gravitational force of the sun.

A few days after that, the soldier and his unit were loaded onto a transport plane and flown to the Sahara. It was the middle of the afternoon when they arrived. The soldier had a window seat; and as he stared down at the war zone, he felt his insides go numb. Even from the air, the city seemed like a nightmare place. Maybe "city" was the wrong word. City denoted order, whereas what the soldier saw from the window was a cancerous growth of human desperation. After an hour of seeing nothing outside the window but sand dunes and the deceptively beautiful skies of the desert, the city emerged from the nothingness. The plane flew high, in order to outwit the shoulder-fired missiles that had brought down two transport planes already; but with the eerily clear skies, the soldier could see it all. He got out his binoculars and stared out of the window at the countless kilometers of shantytowns—maybe two million crumbling little structures, populated by five million or more desperate little people.

Most of the people in the city were refugees—from war and famine and the dissolution of civilization. With the civil war, and the American invasion, most people had been without set homes for over a decade now. The de facto refugee camps encompassed most of the city. There were few genuine streets—only corridors through the shantytowns. These corridors were always unreliable, because they might tomorrow be covered over with trash and shacks—like wounds that sealed themselves with ugly scabs. In the center of the city, there were high-rise buildings—not skyscrapers, but buildings that perhaps reached seven or eight stories at most. Yet, even on the streets with high rises, there were shacks within alleyways and on the sidewalks, as if the shacks were a kind of mange, spreading over the skin of the city. In the distance, the oil derricks stood out like giant mosquitoes, drawing sustenance from the diseased host. An American base was in that direction, forming a protective ring around the derricks, so that the parasites could keep on feeding...

The soldier's eyes gravitated back toward the city. Below, a fire seemed to be raging. Before he was deployed, a general had given them a briefing on what they should expect: a PowerPoint presentation with pictures of refugees and armed insurgents—who, in many instances, were the same people. The general had warned them that when the shantytown fires started, there was nothing to do but let them burn—as water was scarce, and the closely packed shanties made for good kindling. Now, as the soldier looked out of the window, he knew no slide show could do justice to what was below him. It was as if they were descending into hell—if not *the* hell, then a man-made equivalent.

Staring down at it all, he had a sudden awareness of the failure of human beings—the *filthiness* of human beings, in fact. He wanted to flee from it, but the plane was making its final descent, and he was a soldier. He had never been the patriotic type, but he knew his duty; and in the back of his mind, there was the hope that this place would solve all the mysteries of his life.

Either way, after the plane landed, his fate was sealed. When the commando unit exited the transport plane, the Sahara's heat ambushed them. The heat rose off the asphalt runway like a ruthless spirit. The airport was about ten kilometers from the city. The soldier could make out the city's ugly outline on the horizon. The airport, itself, was a hideous, searing patch of cement and asphalt in the desert. The sun was hateful. There was something about the glare that was alive and menacing. The unit moved quickly toward the hangar—where there was shade and the illusion of cooler temperatures. However, in the gaping entrance of the hangar, there were about a dozen flag-draped coffins. The coffins were to be loaded onto the transport plane: new recruits in, corpses out. And there were about thirty wounded soldiers there as well—lying on gurneys as they waited to be evacuated out of the war zone. There were men with missing arms and legs…missing faces in some instances.

The sergeant of the soldier's unit pointed to the coffins and wounded men in the same threatening way he pointed out everything to the new recruits. "That's where you end up if you fuck up!" he yelled. However, there was a hopeful proposition beyond the threat: the consequences of war could be outwitted; if you did everything correctly, you would stay alive. To the sergeant, there were no random occurrences or mistakes in war. Everything was precise and manageable. For the new recruits, there was hope in the sergeant's proposition—even while the sight of the coffins and butchered men curdled their blood.

When they reached the hangar, a grinning colonel greeted them with the speech he used with all new recruits. The word "victory" was inserted into practically every sentence. The first time the grinning colonel gave the speech six months ago, the African war had just started, and the new recruits had cheered. This time, when he finished the speech, there was silence: an uneasy awareness on all sides that a lie had been told. In the grinning colonel's eyes, there was an emerging sense of anguish, which he tried to hide even from himself. There was something shameful about looking at it, so the sergeant tried to salvage the situation by making his unit salute the man; and then, once the man had dismissed them, the new recruits were put on a truck and driven to their base.

When he was in the back of the truck, driving toward the base, the soldier's nose began to bleed from the hot, arid air. Some of the men in his unit said it was "a sign." …Maybe there was something about the Sahara that bred superstition. Like all the invisible perils of desert, the heat seemed alive and menacing. After a while, the men noticed themselves whispering when they talked about it—as if it were a demon, hovering over their shoulders.

The next morning, there was another sign for the men to worry about: a sandstorm came out of nowhere, causing all operations to be grounded. The veterans viewed the storm with grim acceptance, but the new recruits looked around wide-eyed as the barracks moved beneath them. The sound of sand scouring the outer walls and windows was like the roar of a predator. The sand found its way into every crevice. Even when the skies were calm, the sand usually got into everything—into one's clothes and hair… onto the floors of the best-tended rooms. But when the sandstorms came, the sand would seem like something Biblical—a plague to hide from: a vessel of Divine vengeance, from which only prayers and a personal covenant with God could provide deliverance.

The next day, the soldier's unit had their first mission. They left the heavily fortified base at dusk, and entered the city. At least sixty percent of the shacks had blown down in the storm, and the wretched people of the desert were trying to reconfigure heaping piles of rubble and trash into homes. Because of the storm damage, and all the rubble lying on roadways, it was impossible to navigate the maze of streets. The soldier's unit had to navigate by GPS.

There were dead bodies along the streets—dozens of them. There were corpses whose flesh had been scoured off, and people who had been crushed or impaled by the flying debris of their homes. Nobody bothered to count the corpses. The vultures feasted in the open in this place. Some of the locals welcomed the beasts, and tossed corpses onto a pile for them to devour, as there was no time to dig graves nowadays.

The soldier's unit reached their destination about eight at night. The supposed terrorist's house was composed of brick, so it was actually standing. Following their training, they knocked down the man's door and rushed in to find him sleeping. The man seemed about sixty or seventy at least. The women and children of the house began to scream and cry and plead his innocence while the Americans wrestled him to the ground. In time, the presumed terrorist was handcuffed and hooded. …Then, there was the search through the house, uncovering a machine gun and a few hand grenades. The presumed terrorist tried explaining he only kept these things for his own protection. Growing desperate, he said whatever words of English he knew—trying to bypass the interpreter and talk directly to the Americans. Unfortunately for him, the Americans were not there to hear him, only to capture him. They led him away, to be held at another base deep in the desert, until he could prove his innocence. In this way, their first night of war came to an end, with frightened women and children crying in the aftermath, and men morosely following the roles dictated by power and might.

The men of the soldier's unit were proud of themselves after their first mission. They had faced death and come away unscathed. They were reassured by how easily it had gone. However, the soldier knew, even then, that there would be horrors to come. While the other men celebrated back at the barracks, giving one another high fives, the soldier lay in his cot with his eyes closed, wishing he could dream and forget.

The days began to pass like that. When the Americans drove through the shantytowns, there would be the most deathly silence. The people would disappear. In parts of the city where hundreds of thousands of people were packed in like sardines, there would be no one outside, no one talking…no sounds at all, except for the droning engines of the Army vehicles. When the soldier did see people, he would notice their eyes. There would always be something unwholesome there—a kind of spiritual infection, as if they had seen too much death and been blighted by God. The soldier realized the people had the same look in their eyes that the wretched stray dogs had. Everyone shooed the dogs away as soon as they came near, and kicked them and threw things at them, so that the dogs learned to be kicked and shooed without any protest. Like the dogs, the people accepted their fate, and came to realize that living was only a laborious form of dying. In their eyes, deep down, there was a yearning for death—a sense that death was a blessing, which might save them from undue suffering.

A week or two after the soldier's first mission, he killed his first person. It all passed in a blur of adrenaline and terror. His unit and he were at a check-point, supposedly looking for an escaped terrorist. They were stopping cars and asking questions of those inside—an undertaking that was ridiculous at best, since they did not have an interpreter with them. Few of the people they stopped spoke English, and no one in his unit spoke the local language. The soldier and his sergeant approached the car. While the soldier went to the passenger side window, his sergeant went to the driver. The sergeant ordered the driver to roll down his window, but the driver had no idea what he was saying. After about fifteen seconds of this, the sergeant began to scream and bang on the window; but the driver, incensed for whatever reason, only screamed back at him in his own language. In the meantime, the soldier kept his gun on the passenger—as he had been trained to do. The passenger was a youth—most likely the driver's son. The driver must have reached for something, because the sergeant suddenly screamed, "Gun!" When the sergeant began firing at the driver, the soldier instinctively pulled back on his trigger as well, watching in sickly fascination as the youth's head exploded. The other members of the unit joined in the firing—compelled by some kind of collective terror. As for the soldier, he found he could not release his finger from the trigger. He only stopped firing when there were no more bullets. The bullet-riddled vehicle literally smoked afterwards... and the two dead men inside sat slouched over. No gun was found...not even a rusty penknife was discovered in the subsequent search of the vehicle. The area was cordoned off; curious people in the neighborhood were told to disperse at gunpoint—in case a riot broke out. Neither the sergeant nor anyone in the unit talked about it afterward, but they all knew they were murderers.

In time, there were more deaths, so those first murders became relegated to the murky dreams that possessed them when they slept: montages filled with murder and regret and all the things their commanding officers told them to banish from their consciences. Of course, as the soldier did not dream anymore, the images were simply whisked away to the nowhere place within him. The only drawback was that while he was awake, he still had to see and experience the many horrors around him. To shield his mind, and soothe his conscience, he began to play a rhetorical game with himself. Every time he pointed his gun at someone, he said, "I'm only pulling the trigger: the gun does the rest." He would repeat this in his mind, sometimes mumbling it aloud, so that it drowned out all his thoughts. He told himself what happened after he pulled the trigger had nothing to do with him. After a while, he really began to believe it.

Some of the other new recruits found solace in the sermons of the Army chaplain. The chaplain was a harried little man with an evangelical fervor. He kept talking about bringing God to the heathens, but he was too terrified to go beyond the walls of the Army compound. He talked to the men about faith and righteousness—and the Divine correctness of the war; but at night, the men would hear him crying out in his battles with his personal demons—those spawned by his nightmares and those spawned by the horrors of the waking world. After a few months, he transferred out of the war zone, and returned to America, where he could sermonize about heathens and God's will from the safety of rural Tennessee.

About two months after entering the war zone, the unit had its first casualties. It happened while they were out on another nighttime raid. They were getting ready to break down the door of the house and storm in, when there was a sudden hail of gunfire from across the street. Three soldiers were injured; one soldier got hit in the back of his neck and died instantly. The sergeant later said it was a one in a million shot, finding a crevice between the victim's helmet and flack jacket. It was a bad omen. The dead soldier's best friend was particularly distraught. Supposedly, they had forgotten to follow their pre-battle ritual, and had left themselves open to evil. Like the soldier, who told himself he was merely pulling back on the trigger, the other men all had their pre-battle rituals by then. Some said little chants; some did dances; some caressed amulets and pictures of loved ones. No one laughed at even the stupidest rituals. When you believed in nonsense, yourself, it was hypocritical to lampoon the foolishness of others. If anything, the men were suspicious of those who did not seem to have superstitions. When a bomb exploded in a group of soldiers and only one man got hurt, you either believed in the randomness of death, or you believed something you had done had shielded you. Maybe it was the way you had tied your boots that morning, or which side of the bed you had gotten out on, or what you had eaten for breakfast. The possibilities were limitless, and some of the men set their minds to exploring every one of those possibilities.

Even while the soldier excelled in the Army, he had never been "one of the guys." He was cordial enough with the men, but he did not really have any friends. The other men did not trust him, somehow, because he was too good a soldier. He was too self-contained. Outwardly, he showed no frailties, needs or fears. Once, during a raid, some insurgents had them pinned down. The soldier rushed into the building by himself, and single-handedly killed four insurgents. He then walked out of the building as though nothing had happened, and waved to the rest of the unit to come. He was the first of them to get a medal. He routinely saved their lives and took the actions that guaranteed them victory in battle. The men praised him openly; but in their honest moments, they knew they were afraid of him. He terrified them for a reason they could not quite place. It was always as though he were beyond this place: as though he did not have fears in battle because he knew, some-how, that he could not die. His superiors liked him, however, because he made them look good.

Back at the base, the TV room was usually packed. News stories from home (all censored, of course) were of particular interest to the men. News reports were literally a link back to America—to the people for whom they were risking their lives. Besides reports on the war, which were always sanguine—and, as such, resented to some extent by the men—the big story in the news was a celebrity sex scandal. A famous actor had raped his Mexican maid and gone on the run to avoid going to jail. There were sightings of him everywhere—like there were sightings of the deposed despot. There would be reports detailing how the actor had had plastic surgery or been smuggled out of the country. A few days later, there would be contradictory reports, but they would be given in a way that did not invalidate the previous reports. It was as if previous facts did not matter anymore. The important thing was the next sordid detail: it did not matter if that detail did not fit in with what had passed before or what was to come. The only thing that mattered was that it was new.

The men of the soldier's unit would come back from their missions, still trembling and on-edge, and go to the TV room to discover the actor had been spotted in Iceland by two tourists bathing at a hot spring, or that he had purchased the services of three prostitutes in Thailand. Every day it was something else. After a few months, it was the fleeing actor, and not the war, that became the main news story. Some of the soldiers were captivated by the story—just as the entire nation back home seemed to be. However, others— the true believers, who still believed they were in the desert to defend democracy and the American way of life—thought those back home were ungrateful.

To the soldier, it made no difference at all.

As the war progressed, the men searched for ways to hold onto their humanity. The most popular was to hand out candy to the local urchins. Typically, children were the only locals who were brave (or stupid) enough to approach the Americans. It was not unheard of for a misinterpreted gesture to get someone killed by an anxious American soldier—which was why the adults usually ran for cover when they saw the Americans approaching.

One day, the unit was driving through a shantytown when little children ran out for candy. They were all in rags for the most part—urchins of a peculiar sort, who sometimes had families, but who roamed free most of the time, because their families could do nothing for them. A simple act like handing candy bars to the local urchins went a long way to keeping men sane. Some of the new recruits had their families send them massive quantities of penny candies for this purpose. They needed the act more than the urchins. The only thing the urchins got was empty calories and rotten teeth: the soldiers got a cheap form of self-respect.

One of the men of the unit was well known to the children, because he carried a side bag full of candy. The children called him "Candyman" (after he told them to call him that). On that day, when the children ran up for candy, Candyman got out of the vehicle and waved at them like a visiting dignitary. One or two other soldiers got out of the vehicle as well to hand out candy, but most of the men stayed within the vehicle, since they did not have candy to distribute. All at once, there was something in the air like gunfire. Candyman reacted instinctively; and the next thing they knew, he gunned down a little urchin girl. Somehow, the smile she had been wearing at the prospect of candy was still on her face. Candyman was disconsolate. About four days after the incident, he was in the bathroom by himself when he screamed out. When the others ran to investigate, he told them he had seen the smiling urchin girl standing by the stall, putting out her hand for candy. Candyman pointed to the spot, his hand trembling as he stared into the empty space. After that, he had a total mental breakdown, and had to be sent back to America.

To some extent or another, they all saw ghosts—whether it was merely in their dreams, or in full-fledged apparitions putting out their hands for candy. As one roamed the barren landscape of the Sahara, it was at times impossible to differentiate ghosts from the living. Many of the living were ghosts who did not know they were dead; many of the ghosts were people who did not know they were alive. Among the people the soldier passed on his daily patrols and missions, he saw the faces of people he swore he had seen dead—and the faces of people he, himself, had killed. He told no one. After a few months, he realized he did not even flinch anymore when the ghosts of his past confronted him.

As in all wars, there was a budding realization amongst the soldiers that the generals and politicians all lived in another reality. Sometimes, there would be broadcasts, and the soldiers would gather around the television to hear their president describing impossible things: they were winning the war;

morale was high. Some of the soldiers were desperate to believe. Indeed, some knew it was their duty to believe their superiors' lies. Some, on the other hand, grew bitter and cynical.

In time, the men on the ground began to experience a kind of self-destructive satisfaction from outwitting their superiors. It was self-destructive because these officers had the soldiers' lives in their hands. Nevertheless, outwitting them became a pastime. Once, they replaced a training tape with a porno, so that when the general was in the middle of his briefing, shouting, "We must penetrate deep into the enemy's core!" a porn starlet appeared on screen, her legs spread wide as she inserted a dildo into herself. The soldiers in the briefing laughed out—some of them even fell out of their seats. The general was so embarrassed that he left the briefing screaming, "You cocksuckers!" to all the laughing men. He commissioned a full investigation, and would have court-martialed the culprit if the prankster had not bribed the investigator with the best porno from his DVD collection. Everyone had needs in the desert.

Indeed, war had a way of making people yearn for all kinds of sordid things. Once soldiers found themselves in foreign lands, surrounded by death (and the threat of death), they either learned how to fantasize, or they became victims of the surrounding nightmare. After a few months in the war zone, the men talked about sex constantly, obsessed not so much with the act, as the normalcy that the act entailed. One of the men claimed to have a mistress in one of the desert villages, but everyone knew he was lying—since an American alone in the villages would be lynched and strung up as a warning to others. That had happened once, when two soldiers wandered away from their stalled vehicle. They were found a few kilometers away, their body parts ritualistically strung up on a line, like laundry.

There were no rendezvous in the desert. The soldiers all stuck to their camp, and told stories, and masturbated to whatever fantasies their corrupted minds could muster.

About seven or eight months into their tour, the saga of the fleeing actor and his maid came to an end when the grinning couple appeared at a news conference. They were hugging and kissing as they announced they had just gotten married in Las Vegas. It was the perfect Hollywood ending to the story, and the press loved it.

A few days after the marriage announcement, when there was a void in the nightly news reports, the president visited the men at the base. They were having dinner in the mess hall when the president suddenly popped out of a side door. The soldiers were excited while he was there talking about victory and God's will and the American way of life. They did not mind that they were kept at bay by the Secret Service, or that only officers were allowed to go up and take pictures. They were all excited during the moment, but the moment was short; and within minutes, the president was whisked out of the same side door, with his Secret Service bodyguards and handlers and camera crews surrounding him like a school of remora. After the man was gone, there was a great confounded silence in the mess hall, as if to ask themselves what had just happened. Eventually, the men filed out in the same confounded way, and returned to their barracks, or reported for missions, and went about their lives as if nothing had happened. The soldier remembered his brother then, and thought about how politicians were always disappearing into the nothingness, leaving people to wonder what the hell had happened.

As the war progressed in this way, time began to seem unhinged and unpredictable. Sometimes, it whizzed past in a blur of adrenaline and terror. Sometimes, it crawled at an excruciatingly slow pace, so that time, itself, seemed like a prison. By now, the soldier had been in the desert for about nine months. For the troops, everything had become routine by now, even their madness. The soldier was still able to insulate himself from the surrounding reality by his battle chant. However, around the nine-month mark, his body reacted to the reality of the world around him, even while his mind was still numb. One morning, he found himself sobbing uncontrollably. It startled him in the mess hall, where he was eating the Army-issue slop. First, a tear rolled down his cheek, confusing him; and then, his body convulsed. He ran to the latrine, bewildered by the tears that would not stop. And then, hiding in the stall, he began to remember all he had seen and done in the war zone. It was only through an extreme act of will that he was able to stifle the sobs, and shove them back into the innermost depths of his consciousness. However, from then on, the war ceased to be a game to him. It was not exactly real to him either—since war was never real—but he saw it as it was.

His ability to blind himself had been the only thing sustaining him through the war. Without his blindness, the soldier began to experience all the little pieces of horror he had been blocking out. For the first few days after his perceptual breakthrough, he was deluged by so many horrors that he thought the tidal wave would sweep him away. He tried reciting his battle chant, but the trick refused to work. He returned from his first two missions sweaty and distraught, knowing he would not last long.

It was after his third mission that a strange new sense began to take over him. The third mission had gone badly. They had rushed into a house and gunned down about six people: a man, his wife, daughters and sons... The first of the soldiers to enter the shanty had seen a gun leaning against the wall, and started firing. The family was wiped out. The wife was pregnant. After the shooting, her belly oozed blood and amniotic fluid. The men all stood around staring at it, feeling sick. They were so engrossed in the scene that they did not notice the youngest son, a twelve-year-old, was not yet dead. He grabbed the gun lying against the wall, and shot four of the men in the soldier's unit. Two were killed; the other two were merely hit in the legs. However, the soldier was standing right in the middle of them. In fact, he was standing in front of the two men who were killed, so it was as if the bullets had magically swerved around him. It was the sergeant who came to his senses first, and gunned down the son; but from then on, the soldier could not get over the feeling that he could not die. It was more than good luck or chance. He had the feeling that his inability to die would reveal the world to be an elaborate hoax. The purpose of the hoax was uncertain, but as he thought about it, he came to the conclusion that the first step in uncovering the deception was to try to get himself killed. Once his inability to die was established, the world would be revealed as a stage show. Beyond the curtains—somewhere backstage—someone was controlling all this, pulling the strings of a million marionettes, so that the deception could keep on going.

He knew the thought was paranoid and sick, but he had to acknowledge how he felt. His suspicions about the world would confront him at unexpected times. He would be on a mission, being shot at, and a voice would tell him to jump up from behind cover and charge the men shooting at him. He did it once, and was not surprised when the bullets missed him. The entire thing passed in a miraculous blur, and then he was nodding his head as the terrified rebels fell before his gun. He got another medal for that, but he only nodded his head, waiting for the purpose of the hoax to be revealed.

It was around this time that the soldier began to miss his parents. The emotion hit him suddenly, like a blow. All at once, he found himself calling them, and *needing* to call them. The only way men ever survived war zones intact (both physically and mentally) was if they managed to hold onto something in the real world—be it their home or loved ones. The soldier did not know if love had ever been applicable between his parents and him; nevertheless, during his free moments, when he was feeling self-indulgent, he would allow himself to daydream about his parents and the cul-de-sac. In time, he was calling them a few times a week. His parents were surprised by this new onslaught of attention, but they were grateful that their son seemed to be warming to them at last. While they talked over the phone, he would pretend he was still a child, listening to them from the safety of the kitchen table.

This was how the soldier surrendered to his fantasies.

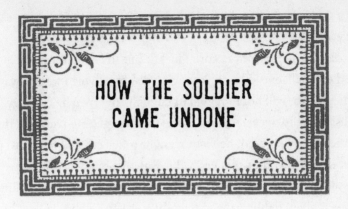

HOW THE SOLDIER
CAME UNDONE

During his time in the war zone, the soldier had gotten into the habit of walking around the base before his unit went out on night time raids. He would walk inside the base's perimeter walls, willing his mind to be still. As his sergeant was always telling them, a soldier's job was to forget everything but his orders. For a soldier, there were no yesterdays and no tomorrows, and even the present was only a nightmare dreamed up by someone else. ...That was what his sergeant would say; so, when the soldier went on his pre-mission walks, he would allow himself a few moments of indulgent fantasy before he willed his mind to be clear. Most times, he would think about his parents: how much he missed them and their home on Long Island. Invariably, his thoughts drifted to the girl of the pit. He would see her grown now, her body perfect and supple under his gentle touch. This would always be the final step before he cleared his mind and walked back to the barracks.

Typically, these walks would only take five to ten minutes, and he would come back looking resolute and ready for war. However, on the night when everything began to unravel, he was gone for half an hour. His sergeant came looking for him, concerned, because their mission was supposed to begin in five minutes. The sergeant exited the barracks and spied the soldier through the darkness. When the sergeant called to the solder, the young man came stumbling up, looking dazed. At first, the sergeant was going to ask him what was wrong, but he prided himself on being a strict disciplinarian, so he screamed:

"Get a move on, soldier! Quit walking as if you need to change your god-damn tampon!"

The soldier tried to move more quickly, but the disillusioned expression on his face did not change. The sergeant glared at him (which was his way of telling the soldier he was still not moving fast enough) and then he re-entered the barracks. Inside the barracks, the rest of the unit was getting ready for the mission. When the soldier entered, he went straight to his cot and began to put on his gear. Several of the other soldiers had frowned at him when he entered, noting the strange expression on his face. However, the sergeant was yelling at them again, telling them to hurry up, so the others got up and headed out of the room. The soldier was the last one left, and the sergeant yelled at him again, saying:

"Move your ass, goddamn it!"

The soldier bundled the rest of his gear in his arms, and ran out of the door. The other men were getting into an armored personnel carrier when he got outside. As soon as he got in, the door was closed. In addition to the sergeant and the other soldiers, there was an interpreter and a lieutenant. The interpreter was a scrawny old man who claimed to have been an English teacher before the war, but whose sentences were so convoluted that the soldiers did not bother to ask for translations half the time. They kept him along as a kind of mascot, and made crude jokes about him to his face, which he never understood, but which he would nonetheless smile at, in his demented, toothless way. The lieutenant was a young man straight out of West Point, who always kept a certain professional distance from the others, as if military decorum demanded it.

The personnel carrier headed off, through the night. There was still a dazed, disillusioned expression on the soldier's face. He began to put on the last of his gear. He needed to clear his head and figure things out. Yet, when the soldier looked up, he became aware everyone was staring at him. They stared at him because his agitated state was an aberration. He had always been calm; in everything, he had always been fearless—a perfect model of what a soldier was supposed to be. Seeing their eyes now, the soldier felt self-conscious. He tried to smile to reassure them, but all he could manage was a nervous grimace. He realized he was trembling slightly. He inhaled deeply, hoping to calm himself, but it was no use.

This was usually the time when they made wisecracks about one another, in order to put the unit at ease before the start of a mission. When men faced death on a daily basis, they were always on the look out for bad omens, and the soldier's strange behavior was the worst of omens. Suddenly exasperated, the sergeant snorted in disgust and addressed the soldier again, saying, "What the *hell* is your problem?"

The soldier opened his mouth, but he had no idea where to begin, so he shut it, shaking his head in the same disillusioned way. He was staring at the floor.

"Soldier!" the sergeant yelled, annoyed. The soldier looked up at him helplessly. The sergeant continued: "Whatever it is, get it off your goddamn chest now, before we start the mission." And then, sarcastically: "What happened? Did your girlfriend tell you her new man has a bigger dick than yours?"

The rest of the unit laughed. The soldier tried to laugh, but his lips somehow refused to comply. He looked up at them apologetically, as if embarrassed by his lips' shortcomings. This reaction made the laughter cease.

"What is it, son?" the sergeant asked again, his tone strangely compassionate. And then, falling into his old superstitions, "Whatever it is, you'd better tell us. You can't have us going into battle worrying about you. Tell it now, so we can all move on."

The soldier looked at them helplessly. Under regular circumstances, he would have kept it to himself, but the thing that had happened tonight was so extraordinary that he felt compelled to talk. He took a deep breath. "I...I don't know where to begin."

"Start from the beginning," the sergeant coaxed him.

The soldier nodded. He looked at the unit apologetically again, and took a deep breath. "...I went out for my walk—you know, like I always do." Everyone else in the unit nodded, remembering his routine. The soldier went on: "...I was walking along the wall, like always. My thoughts were just drifting, you know...Anyway, I looked up, and there was a man there. He seemed to pop out of nowhere. I looked up, and he was there."

"What do you mean?" the sergeant asked. "He wasn't one of us?" he said, meaning if the man was with the Military.

"No," the soldier said, shaking his head gravely. "He was in a business suit. His shoes...I remember his shoes were shiny: *polished*. That's how I knew he didn't belong there. You know how the desert dust gets on everything. It was like he had just popped…" The soldier shook his head. When he looked up again, everyone in the unit was frowning at him. He felt embarrassed and foolish. "I'm sorry—"

"Finish your goddamn story, soldier," the sergeant chastised him. "Tell it now and get it out of your goddamn head." Of course, the sergeant's favorite word was "goddamn." He used it as a crude exclamation point in practically every sentence—especially when he was angry or anxious.

The soldier stared at him, then nodded when he saw no choice but to continue. "…Well," the soldier began, "he was standing there when I looked up…the man with the shiny shoes. …And then he began to speak."

"What did he say?" one of the other men asked when the soldier faltered.

"He said he knew me—that we were friends. I tried to look at his face, to see if I could place it, but the strange thing was that no matter how hard I looked, it was as if he had no face—as if his entire face was a shadow. I think I spent about half a minute trying to see his face. …I don't think I heard what he was saying at first—I was staring at his face…trying to see it…"

The sergeant spoke up again, losing patience: "You're saying you met an intruder within the perimeter wall, and he didn't have a face?"

"…I know how crazy it sounds." When the soldier looked around the unit, he realized even the lieutenant, who usually read mission orders during these rides and pretended to be too engrossed to hear their banter, was staring at him. The soldier felt even more self-conscious. However, knowing it was too late now to keep quiet, he went on, "…I started to listen to what the man was saying. …He told me about this mission—about everything that's going to happen."

Everyone stared at him, but then the sergeant laughed out, saying: "A ghost appeared to tell you the future? Why the hell can't you fantasize about women like the rest of us?"

The other men laughed, but it was a mirthless kind of laughter—as if they were desperate to believe it was a joke. The soldier tried to laugh as well, willing to admit that it did sound silly. Unfortunately, he had a sudden flashback of what the man with the shiny shoes had said to him, and he shuddered.

The laughter died down.

The sergeant sobered, and spoke up again: "You're serious about all this? Some ghost man popped out of nowhere and told you what's going to happen on our mission?"

"Yes, sir."

"Then tell us then," he said sarcastically, trying to joke again, but nobody laughed this time.

The soldier nodded anxiously. "…The man said we'd go to the complex and find it deserted. There won't be a damn thing there…but then I'll see a white cat."

"A *cat*?" the sergeant interrupted him again.

"Yeah, he said I'll see a white cat; and that if we all follow it, we'll stay alive."

"*What*?"

"He said we'd die if we didn't follow the cat."

"Die how?"

"I don't know. He just said we'd die—all of us—if we stayed in the building. Our only chance to live is to follow the cat."

"Goddamn!" the sergeant exploded. "What kind of fucked-up story is that to tell before a mission!"

The other men in the unit agreed, and began to grumble amongst themselves.

"I'm sorry," the soldier apologized. "…I told you it was weird. I didn't want to talk about it."

"Well, keep out of our way on this mission, goddamnit!" the sergeant screamed again.

"I'm sorry, sir," the soldier repeated. He stared down at the ground, because he could sense the other men glaring at him. He willed his mind to wander. He conjured images of his family. He thought about how he had called his parents today, hoping to pacify a strange, nameless feeling that had been building within him lately. Unfortunately, when the soldier called his parents, something strange had happened. A woman whose voice he had never heard before had answered the phone; when the soldier asked her who she was, she had said she was his mother. He had asked her questions—trying to test her—but she had ignored him, and talked excitedly about her house redecorating plans. It had driven him over the edge, and he had found himself screaming and cursing. Still, even then, the strange woman on the other end of the line had only moved on to how beautiful her flowerbed looked. He had slammed down the phone and redialed his parents' number, but there had been no answer, and he had walked away, looking dazed and wretched.

The soldier shook his head. Even that memory seemed farfetched. Was he coming undone? Maybe. ...Maybe he needed to come undone. He thought about that for a moment, allowing his mind to accept the possibility that madness might have its benefits....

Outside the vehicle, it was deathly quiet in the sprawling shantytowns—except for the intermittent sounds of gunfire and sirens. Within the armored personnel carrier, the men were still brooding over the bad omen of the soldier's story. There was still none of the cheerful banter that usually prepared them for battle. However, the men prepared nonetheless. Some of them stared into space, conjuring their intimate fantasies; some closed their eyes and said prayers—either to gods or men or chance, itself. Across the aisle, a corporal was leafing through a miniature edition of the New Testament, the pages of which had become grimy from sweat and the Army-issue grease they used on their guns. The corporal's lips were moving as he mumbled Bible passages. The soldier had the sense it was indecent to watch the man, so he looked away. He scanned the rest of the unit then, suddenly desperate for something to reassure him. There was nothing, so he preoccupied himself by fastening his flack jacket. His mind returned to the man with the shiny shoes, and he grimaced. ...He had not told his unit how the man had disappeared. One moment, the soldier had been looking at him, trying to digest what he was saying; and then, the next moment, the soldier had found himself looking into the darkness of the African night. The soldier had not told the other men how he had cried out—how he had tried to run, but been frozen by some kind of mortal terror....

The personnel carrier was driving on a paved road now—the soldier could tell from the sound the tires made as they gripped the asphalt. The unit was nearing the target for the night. The soldier felt suddenly sick. He hoped he was wrong about everything—that the man with the shiny shoes had only been a figment of his imagination. Hopefully, this mission would progress the way dozens of their other missions had progressed, and he could go back to the barracks and sleep. He was exhausted, as if all the nights of dreamless sleep had reached some cataclysmic threshold. He felt tonight would be a crossroads in his life. Either everything would come to an end tonight, or he would find himself on a new path, struggling against new horrors....

The door of the personnel carrier opened. This was a relatively opulent neighborhood: there were asphalt streets and brick walls here. However, the night seemed repulsive—like something dead and rotting. With no sewage system in the sprawling shantytowns, the stench of excrement was always in the air. A wave of intense heat ambushed the unit as they exited. Some of them coughed on the hot, dry air—and the pestilential stench it carried. A stray dog had been sleeping in front of the presumed terrorist's home. It fled as they emerged from the vehicle. It ran down to the next compound, then crouched behind a pile of garbage, watching them timidly—but not barking. The unit moved quickly. They had done this so many times they hardly had to think. The sergeant glared at the soldier, as to tell him to stay out of their way. In turn, the soldier bowed his head and slouched to the rear. Two other soldiers kicked at the front gate, and it collapsed onto the dusty ground. The unit ran up to the door of the house. The door was quickly kicked down as well. They entered, screaming out "Clear!" as they progressed through the empty rooms...but then, at last, after about thirty seconds of searching and screaming, they realized there was no one in the house. Following the lieutenant's orders, a quarter of the unit fanned out to the backyard, looking for bunkers—but there was nothing. Eventually, they all congregated in the living room. The soldier, who had stayed back, came walking up with the same dazed expression on his face. The others looked at him, remembering his story. The lieutenant grew annoyed with them; refusing to give in to superstition, he made a call to headquarters, talking in an overly loud voice about how they had been given bad intelligence.

Yet, while the lieutenant talked over the radio in his stage voice, the rest of the unit grew increasingly anxious. All of them stared at the soldier. Their rational minds told them men with shiny shoes did not pop out of thin air and foretell the future, but they looked at the soldier as if he had all the answers. Even the sergeant stared at him, his eyes unsure. As the soldier stood there, waiting for the thing to happen, his skin felt hypersensitive. His mind seemed in shock; and then, as he glanced out of the living room window, he saw it. Initially, there was a white blur, and then he saw it clearly: the white cat, sitting in the middle of the yard, staring at him. When the others saw the expression on his face, they followed his eyes. A few of them gasped. Even the lieutenant stopped in mid-sentence and stared out of the window. Some of the men took a tentative step closer to the window, to get a better look. All of their hearts were beating savagely in their chests.

The soldier found himself walking. His legs took over, and he moved toward the door. Soon, he was in the backyard. He was walking like someone in a trance. The other men followed him. Only the lieutenant and the interpreter stayed behind. The lieutenant was probably still trying to resist his superstitions, and the interpreter probably had no idea what was going on.

Once the soldier was outside, he suddenly emerged from his trance. He shook his head to clear his thoughts, but then jumped when he saw the rest of his unit was standing behind him. Their eyes were wide and desperate. Through the window, the soldier could see the lieutenant arguing with whoever was on the other end of the radio; the interpreter was still standing by his side, looking out of the window uncertainly. The sergeant gestured to the cat then, as if to remind the soldier. The cat was still waiting there patiently. The soldier turned around and faced it, amazed that it was actually there. He took another step toward the cat, and the men behind him took another step as well. The cat was purring, and the sound was like nothing the soldier had ever heard before. Somehow, the purring soothed him—filled him with a sense of peace. On top of that, a tingling sensation was taking hold of his body. He felt lighter—freer. Nothing else existed while the cat purred. He was transported away from war and death, and all the things that had been eating away at his soul.

Understandably, when the cat began to walk away—through the broken gate of the backyard, and into an alleyway—the soldier followed. The other men followed in his wake, but he was hardly aware of them. He was still overcome by the fuzzy sense of peace the cat's purring had instilled in him. For the first time in months, he was more than a mindless killing machine. He felt as though all his wartime sins had been absolved. All the murders he had committed in the name of America and his panicky fears were washed away. He smiled. In his delirium, he probably laughed out loud in the night. He heard nothing but the purring—saw nothing but the cat…

The cat walked about fifty meters away from the building. Yet, as the soldier followed it, that journey seemed beyond all definitions of distance and time. What was in reality only a walk of eighty seconds, seemed more like fifteen minutes. Each step was a step away from all he had known—and all that had been killing him. By the time the cat stopped and stared back at him, he was so dazed he approached it haltingly. It had stopped beneath a streetlamp; and for the first time, the soldier saw the color of its eyes. They were the most startling shade of blue he had ever seen: an almost phosphorescent aquamarine. He stumbled up to the cat; as he crouched down, and stretched out his trembling hand, he was already smiling—already giving praise and surrendering the last of his will…but just as his fingers were about to touch the cat, there was an explosion behind him, and he was knocked to the ground by the blast. For a moment, he lay semi-conscious on the ground. Some of the other soldiers had fallen on top of him. The first thing the soldier did when he opened his eyes was to look for the cat. It was gone; but then, as there was a secondary blast, he looked around, realizing the explosions had come from the house his unit had raided. Huge plumes of red flames rose into the air. He could feel the heat from where he was on the ground. Looking around, he saw the other members of his unit. They were getting up groggily—

"Did the lieutenant make it out?" someone asked.

"No," someone else answered, "—he was still in there."

They all stared at the scene, and then back at the soldier. One realization shone in all their eyes: the soldier had saved them from certain death. They were now willing to follow him anywhere. Their sudden neediness was startling and repulsive. Even the sergeant was looking at him beseechingly. The soldier wanted to escape from them, but his attention went to the huge

plumes of flames dancing about the building. There was something mesmerizingly beautiful about the blaze. He took a few shambling steps toward
the building before another explosion made them all turn their faces away
and shield their eyes. If the lieutenant and the interpreter were still in there,
then they were both dead. There was no question about it. In a strange way,
the soldier was too numb to be panicked, but he was acutely aware of their
position: of their isolation here in the middle of nowhere. He began running, and the others followed him. He cut through a neighboring yard, then
ran through another alleyway—so he could get to the front of the building,
where they had left the personnel carrier. However, as soon as he reached
the mouth of the alleyway, he saw the vehicle was also engulfed in flames.
The entire thing had been an ambush! No doubt insurgents where hiding
in the shadows at that moment. He looked over his shoulder then: the sergeant was the closest one to him. The man again nodded, as if to say he was
ready to follow the soldier's will. The others nodded as well. The soldier
gestured with his hand, then they all turned and fled back into the darkness.
The soldier had no idea what was to be done now, but as he was about to
give in to the hopelessness, he saw the cat waiting at the end of the alley.
The cat had saved them all—protected them in this world of insecurity and
death. Understandably, by the time the cat began to lead them away, the
men went without hesitation.

The soldier stumbled along behind the cat, and the rest of the unit followed
him. The cat's pace was calm and steady; yet, the men were so on-edge they
felt as though they were running. Most of them were panting and out of
breath. Some gagged on the ever-present stench from the shantytowns. In
their haste, they paid little attention to their surroundings. They were
being drawn deeper into the sprawling slums of the city—into places where
even the most battle-hardened troops of the Army refused to go without
tank cover and air support. The only thing keeping them from being discovered was the fact that most people barricaded themselves within their
homes after dark. This was the case not because they respected the American-

imposed curfew, but because they respected their lives. The sounds of crumbling civilization were in the air—gunfire and screams and sirens. The sounds came from every direction. The fleeing men would have felt surrounded and trapped, but the cat was there, showing them the way to salvation.

They were still in the paved section of the city, where an occasional streetlamp provided light; but in most places, the darkness was pitch, and only the preternatural glow of the cat's fur allowed them to follow it through the darkness. The soldier's mind remained blank, but after about five or ten minutes of following the cat, it was as if a switch in his mind were suddenly turned on. New memories confronted him: a chaotic montage. He saw the girl from the pit running down a city street. She was grown now—just as he pictured her in his fantasies. All at once, he remembered the story the girl had told him, about how the two of them were married, and the last thing she remembered was running down the street—

"Soldier!"

The sergeant grabbed him before he fell; another member of the unit stepped forward to support him. At that moment, something exploded a few kilometers away. Yet, the blasts were so powerful that the men felt the reverberations in their chests. They staggered back. When they looked in the direction of the blasts, they realized it had come from the American base. They listened closely, discerning the sick wail of the base siren. As their apprehensions grew, they turned to the soldier. He was still swaying and unresponsive; and at the sight of him, they remembered the cat. They looked ahead to see the creature disappearing into the darkness—where there were the remains of a bombed out building. The men moved quickly, desperate to keep the cat within sight; they pulled the soldier along behind them as an afterthought. It was the cat, not the soldier, that mattered to them now. Unfortunately, once they got inside the bombed out husk of the building, they realized the cat was gone. The two-story building had no windows, no door and no roof. People had scavenged the bricks, wood and metal to make their shanties. As a consequence, the inside of the building was eerily clear of rubble. There was nowhere for the cat to hide: it simply was not there.

Without the cat, the men began to panic; the soldier was still in a daze, trying to absorb the chaotic memories. The sergeant shook him by the shoulder to revive him. Several of them began to talk at once, asking what had happened to the cat, and what was going to happen to them. All the questions were addressed to the soldier, as if he had the answers. The questions went on and on, until the soldier came to his senses and screamed, "Shut up and let me think!" He was panting. He remembered something: "...The man with the shiny shoes—"

"What about him?" the sergeant asked anxiously.

"He said I'd remember the girl."

"What girl?"

"After he told me about the mission, he told me I'd remember the girl."

"*What* girl?" someone else asked.

The soldier ignored him, amazed by his own memories.

Somehow, seeing the insane gleam in the soldier's eyes brought the sergeant back to his senses, and it occurred to him he was supposed to be in charge. He remembered they had radios, and that they could call headquarters to request pick-up. "Specialist," he ordered the communications officer, "contact headquarters and tell them our situation." Giving orders again felt good. However, the specialist was staring at him uneasily:

"I tried before, sir, but there was no response."

"Then try again, goddamnit!"

The specialist talked into his equipment, but all they heard was static. And then, after about three seconds, a screaming, disembodied voice came out of the speakers:

"...Base bombed! We're under attack! Send reinforcements...!" In the background, they could hear men screaming. The siren was piercing. They could hear machine guns and bombs going off...and then there was silence—more static.

None of the men could breathe for two or three seconds. Eventually, one of them whispered: "That explosion we heard...they blew up the base!"

The sergeant typically screamed when he was anxious. Now, he yelled: "They're just under attack, that's all! I'm sure the base is still there!"

"But they got cut off," another man said, staring ahead in shock. "They're *gone*."

"We don't know anything yet!" the sergeant screamed, but the doubts were clear in his voice. He grabbed the handset from the communications officer now, as if the man were not up to the task. He gave his codename and asked for acknowledgement, but there was no response.

"What the hell's going on?" another man whispered.

"Maybe the radio's broken," the sergeant suggested.

"It's working fine, sir," the specialist said, "—there just isn't any response from the base." To prove his point, he turned some dials on his equipment and picked up a radio broadcast: some strange, tinny music that sounded eerie in the night.

"Turn that off!" the sergeant screamed, frustrated.

When the specialist complied, they made out the whine of aircraft engines overhead. They looked up in time to see about fifteen American attack helicopters flying toward the base. The helicopters had come from the direction of the airport, which meant the airport was probably still secure; but since such a large convoy was an ominous sign, their innards shook.

There was silence for about five or six seconds, as the men thought about how they were going to get out of this. At last, one ventured: "Sarge, do you think the lieutenant…" The man did not finish the sentence.

The sergeant shook his head, looking lost for once.

Someone else spoke up: "He should have followed the cat, like the rest of us."

The corporal, who had before been leafing through the grease-stained pages of the New Testament, spoke now, saying: "I'm not so sure that cat was God's doing."

"What do you mean?"

"God don't operate like that," the corporal said.

"We were saved, weren't we?"

"God don't operate that way—that's all I'm saying."

"What the fuck are you talking about!" a couple of the soldiers screamed at once.

Gesturing to the soldier, the corporal went on, "What if that was a demon he spoke to when he went out there by himself." He was talking quickly now, sounding defensive. "A demon tempted us, and we fell for it."

One of the other men scoffed: "I see your ass followed behind the cat, the same as us."

"I gave in to fear and temptation," the corporal conceded.

The men were about to get into a full-blown argument, but the sergeant stopped them. "Shut up—*all* of you, goddamnit! We've got to remain calm."

However, no sooner had he said these words than one of the men gasped and pointed. He had been by the window, looking out for pursuers. The men all turned to get a glimpse of a small animal on the street. It darted into the darkness before they could confirm anything.

"What was it?" the sergeant demanded.

"The cat!"

Now that they could not count on being rescued by men, they turned again to superstition and the impossible. They all rushed out of the building now, chasing after a cat they realized too late was not *the* cat. It was only a regular alley cat. The soldier came up behind them, still dazed. By then, they were out in the open, in the middle of the street. Common sense told them to run back to the bombed out building, where there was at least cover. However, before they could act, the first bullet rang out from the darkness, and the corporal stumbled back, his face blown off. After that first shot, bullets seemed to come from every direction. The men tried to duck for cover, but some of the shots were coming from the direction of the bombed out building. They were cut off from retreat—trapped. There was nowhere to go. Another member of the unit dropped. By now order had left the men. Some of them remembered what the corporal had said before he died—about the cat being the devil's work. As such, as they ran, they feared not only for their lives, but their souls.

The soldier ran, but not with the fear of the others. His old suspicion came back: the sense that he could not die, and that all of this was a cosmic hoax. While the others screamed and panicked, the soldier only ran ahead, staring blankly into the distance.

After a few minutes of this, he turned around and saw there was no one behind him. There were no other members of his unit and no pursuers. There were gunshots—because there were always gunshots at night—but they seemed distant. The soldier was alone—the last one left. The realization was chilling.

Keep moving! That was the thought that sustained him. Now was not the time to stop and think—or to mourn—or to ask himself what was happening. Thoughts about cosmic hoaxes left his mind for the moment, and he became a regular man again. He looked around, trying to get his bearings. He was entering what seemed to be the market district of the city. There was a huge square ahead of him. During the day, it would be filled with thousands of vendors and shoppers. However, at this time of night, it was deserted, except for the refuse blowing eerily on the breeze: some plastic bags and empty cans gliding across the hard-packed earth. To the left, there was a four-story, war-ravaged office building, which overlooked the market like some kind of defeated sentinel. On the outer wall of the building, there was a vicious pasquinade of the deposed despot. The soldier looked at it curiously for a moment; but just then, he heard footsteps behind him—and men screaming in the angry, guttural language of this region. The soldier ducked into a recess in the façade of the office building. The recess was not itself a doorway, but only a place where the bricks and mortar had collapsed. Inside, there was shattered glass and litter on the ground; whatever furniture there was, was rusting and misshapen—from the fire that had gutted this building. A charcoal smell lingered about the place, along with a more astringent odor of burnt plastic and excrement. Looking up, he saw a gaping hole in the ceiling, from which a light emanated. The soldier meandered over to the light, curious to see what it was. When he got close enough, he saw the upper floors had all collapsed. The hole went all the way to the roof, so that the soldier could see the moon.

The footsteps—and voices—of his pursuers blared in the air; the soldier fled deeper into the darkness, stumbled over some refuse, and then fell heavily to the ground. His pursuers seemed to scream louder at the sound of his collapse—as if they had heard him. Foreign languages had a tendency to sound mindless and repulsive. To the soldier, that language suddenly seemed evil—as if its words were dark incantations. The sound of it made his skin crawl, so he leapt up and ran for cover. In the gutted building, the incantations echoed like bomb blasts. His pursuers were running faster now. There seemed to be dozens of them. The soldier was running blind; he had to stretch out his hand in order to navigate through the darkness; but even then, he banged his limbs against jagged metal and collapsed concrete—

At last, he ducked behind a mound of rusting metal. He stared into the darkness now, and aimed his gun toward the hole in the wall—since it was the most likely place for his enemies to enter. The moment of reckoning seemed to take forever; but at last, he saw their silhouettes appear against the hole. He made a conscious effort to quiet his heavy breathing. His finger was trembling on the trigger, and he grew worried he would fire the gun inadvertently, losing whatever tactical advantage he had. His enemies, knowing they had cornered him, were whispering amongst themselves now. They were wearing the baggy clothes of the region; their turbans made their heads seem grotesquely large, as if they were demons—

One of the men yelled a command; at the severe pitch of the man's voice, the soldier removed his index finger from the trigger, flexed it in nervous preparation, and then replaced it on the trigger. Now that the cat had disappeared, he felt as though he had been abandoned in hell. He tried to conjure his old sense—that he could not die—but he felt weak and unsure.

His pursuers were entering the building. They were sticking close to the wall, wary of venturing into all the rubble—where the soldier hid. There were at least six of them. The soldier prepared himself to kill, and to die— *if he could die*—

One of his pursuers began to venture into the rubble. The other militants seemed to be directing this one with their whispers and gesticulations. From his place of hiding, the soldier got ready. The approaching militant was moving cautiously—but he was coming straight for the soldier! The soldier had a clear shot; he was just about to pull back on the trigger when the militant stepped beneath the hole in the ceiling, and the moon's rays highlighted his face. It was only a boy—maybe fifteen at the most…and the boy had the most angelic face the soldier had ever seen. It was not angelic because it seemed perfect or innocent, but because it seemed so human. Angels came to men knowing all the pain and sorrow of the world; and in the boy's eyes, there was a startling awareness of all the brutal things human beings did to one another—

And then, the soldier became convinced the boy had seen him, because the boy's eyes widened, and the barrel of his gun began to move in the soldier's direction. The soldier had had his machine gun trained on the boy all that time; he was about to pull back on the trigger when there was a sudden, inexplicable hail of gunfire. Beneath the aperture, the boy screamed out in agony and collapsed to the ground. The militants along the walls began yelling and firing their guns wildly. By now, the soldier had ducked down. The boy was crying on the ground—the same series of garbled words, over and over again. At first, the soldier thought the boy's comrades had shot him in the back; but after a moment of confusion, he noticed some of the gunfire was coming from outside (through the windows and holes in the collapsing wall).

In a moment of relief, he became convinced the men firing outside had to be his countrymen! Now that the cat was lost to him, he once again had faith in men. He imagined tanks and armored personnel carriers full of dozens of troops. Unfortunately, in time, he came to realize the men outside were screaming the same guttural language as the militants inside. This was nothing but another sectarian/ethnic turf battle. Maybe now that the American base was gone, the militants were celebrating by killing one another. Anything was possible in this insane war....

The soldier did not want to be in the real world anymore. He wanted to return to his fantasies, in which the girl of his childhood dreams was his to hold and caress. In fact, as the bullets whizzed over his head, he wanted to turn his back on reality entirely. He wanted the cat to reappear—either from a dimensional rift or his own corrupted imagination. He did not care at this point: he only wanted an escape hatch from reality—

One of the militants outside the building must have been hit, because an anguished cry echoed throughout the gutted building. The soldier unconsciously clamped his hands over his ears to shield himself. He had heard that cry too many times over the months; all the death cries he had ever heard were accumulating within him, like a poison. He felt as though he were nearing the critical dose—that if he did not get away from the insane wars of men he would succumb to the poison. His hands were trembling over his ears now. More death cries joined in a sick chorus; the soldier gnashed his teeth, bracing himself against the full weight of death and madness.

The boy who had pursued him into the rubble was not screaming anymore. The soldier imagined him either lying dead or breathing his last painful breaths as he prayed to his God. All enemies were brothers in death and suffering; and as the soldier prepared to die, all the sounds of the outside world—firing guns and yelling voices—seemed to resound in the air. The soldier clamped his eyes shut and held his gun close...but when he opened his eyes, there was silence. In the distance, there were gunshots and sirens; but in the building, and the immediate vicinity, there was silence. In his mind, he had closed his eyes only milliseconds ago; but when he opened them, and looked out on the still world, he knew a much longer period of time had passed—minutes or hours. What had happened? Had he passed out...? It was still nighttime outside. If anything, the night seemed darker. He poked his head out from behind the rusting refuse, and looked about warily. He was about to tell himself he had imagined the entire thing—that militants had not pursued him into the rubble; that a sectarian battle had not broken out—but he saw the boy's corpse sprawled on the ground; and near the wall, the soldier saw the boy's fallen comrades. They had all been wiped out in the gunfight...

The soldier sighed—not because he was relieved, but because he knew he had come undone somewhere along the line. He did not know when exactly it had happened, but he knew he was lost, and that it was too late to return to the world of normal men.

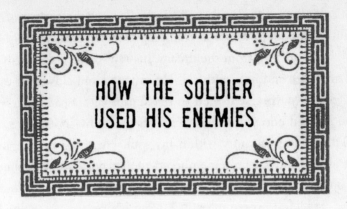

HOW THE SOLDIER USED HIS ENEMIES

Somehow, the soldier slept. Exhaustion overcame him suddenly, and he was pulled into a nightmare. It was the first dream he had had in about a year. He was walking down crumbling city streets; when he looked up, there was a blood red night sky. He noticed someone walking on the next block; and when he looked more closely, he saw it was the girl from the pit. She was older now, and infinitely more beautiful. He could not believe his eyes. There, at last, was everything he had ever wanted. His spirits soared; but when he went to take off running after her, he realized his legs were frozen; when he tried to call to her, he discovered he was mute. The woman was everything he had ever wanted, and everything he would ever want; but with each passing second, she drew farther and farther away from him. The universe was mocking him: showing him a glimpse of paradise, so that he would spend eternity chasing after something that would never be his. His spirit broke at last; his body slumped—

And then, at the last moment, before the woman disappeared entirely, the soldier noticed something in his peripheral vision—a blur in the form of a man, standing on the curb, observing him. He jumped back, too terrified to scream or breathe. It was the same blurred man from the day that car plowed into those kids in the intersection. Back then, he had thought the entire scene had been staged; now, as his dream self watched the blurred man fade back into the nothingness, he remembered the man with the shiny shoes—

The dream ended. He was panting as he awoke. His face was contorted and his eyes were wild. Dawn had just broken; in the early morning light, the ugly, rusting metal of his surroundings seemed otherworldly. Yet, as his mind was still reeling from the dream, his senses were short-circuited. He could barely see and hear and feel. He groaned and closed his eyes. …His mind eventually worked around to the source of his panic: the realization that the blurred entity and the man with the shiny shoes were one in the same. He felt the certainty within his soul. He could not begin to guess what it all meant, but he remembered the corporal's rant, about the man with the shiny shoes being a demon, tempting them to their doom—

A loud, creaking noise pulled him from his reverie. Actually, his senses suddenly began to work again. The creaking noise seemed impossibly loud. Nine months' worth of battle memories flashed in his mind, and he grabbed his gun. He scanned his surroundings, but could not figure out where the noise was coming from. His gun was trembling in his hands now. Recollections of the cat and the gunfight came back to him in a flash; he remembered the bombing at the American base—the fact that the base was probably not even there anymore. He grunted—like someone who had received an unexpected blow—

The corpses of the militants—the boy and his comrades—were still there. They corroborated everything: he stared at them uneasily for a moment, but the creaking noise was still in the air, grating against his nerves. Looking to his left—through a hole in the crumbling wall—the soldier saw two men shuffle past. In the early morning light, there was something unreal about them—as if they were ghosts. As he could not see their legs from his position beyond the window, they seemed to be drifting past. He crept closer to the window, crouching low, so he would stay in the shadows. The market was slowly filling up. Looking down the street, he saw an old man was approaching with a donkey-drawn cart. When the soldier realized the creaking was coming from the cart's wheels, he sighed.

The cart was heaped high with produce of some kind. The donkey walked with its head bowed, straining. At its side, the frail-looking old man shuffled with a stick in hand, hitting the donkey every few seconds, with strokes that seemed more habitual than wrathful.

There was something surreal about watching the people in the market going about their lives. For one thing, they went about their lives silently—almost dispassionately—as if they were all under a spell. No one was talking; people did not acknowledge one another or make eye contact. Considering everything that had happened last night, the soldier wondered if they knew what had happened to the American base. Either they did not know, or they did not care. Maybe they had seen too much war to allow themselves to believe it made a difference. Maybe, like the soldier, they had stopped thinking of the war as something controlled by men, and instead viewed it as a demonic punishment: a self-perpetuating hell.

It was then the soldier knew he was through with war. There was no way he could go on any more nighttime raids or patrols. He could not face any of it again. The war was like everything else in his life: a staged event designed to trap him. The only thing that had ever seemed real was the woman, so he said to hell with everything else: the war, the Army, his family and so-called friends. The woman was the key to his salvation. He had to find her again; and if she was only a figment of his imagination—a product of his lifelong madness—then he was willing to give up the last pretenses of his sanity, in order to embrace that madness.

Presently, he peeped out of the window again—to get his bearings and plan how he was going to get out of there. As dawn struggled with the darkness, there was the illusion of mist in the air. When he looked closer, he realized the mist was actually dust particles; and when he examined the sky, it occurred to him a sandstorm was on the way. He had gotten a sense of the desert by now. There was a charge in the air—something brutal that left him with an instinctive sense of panic.

The idea of the storm gave him the impetus to act—to get away from this place. If he was through with the war, the first thing he had to do was get rid of his Army fatigues, and find some clothes that would allow him to blend into the local population.

That was when he remembered the dead militants from last night. He realized he could cloak himself in one of their billowy outfits, use one of their turbans to conceal his face, and sneak out of the market. Where he would go after that, he had no idea. He only knew the woman was out there, somewhere, and that he was willing to overturn heaven and earth in order to find her. Suddenly enlivened by his new plan, he rushed over to the corpses. Rigor mortis had set in, and they were all frozen in the poses they had had when they breathed their last breaths. In the heat, the corpses were already bloated; and in death, their bowels had released and soiled their clothes. The soldier wrestled with the arms and legs of the first militant he came upon, before giving up and deciding on one who had died in a relatively straight position. He had to wave away the flies. No doubt maggots were already growing within their body cavities. ...He found his mind returning to the first time he had seen a dead body. It had been during basic training. Most of the new recruits had entered the Army with all the false expectations of youth. The patriotism that had driven them to enlist had been influenced by the melodrama of Hollywood war movies; recruitment commercials had made the Army seem like a game, so many of the young men had come expecting the brutal fun of little boys' games. The rude awakening had come quickly; and by the second or third week, the disillusionment had been dulled by routine, so that the young men of the Army had settled into their fate, and become what the Army called "good soldiers." Just as the soldier had been the golden boy of his squadron, there had been another golden boy in the squadron that trained side-by-side with them. The drill sergeants of both squadrons would place bets on their respective golden boys. Like the soldier, the other golden boy had excelled at everything with an almost supernatural effortlessness. In the fourth week of basic training, the golden boy's gun had exploded in his face during firing practice, taking off part of his skull. He had lain there in shock, going into convulsions as the frothy blood of the brain bubbled down what was left of his face. Both sergeants had rushed over, but the new recruits had only stood on the periphery, seeing death for themselves—free of boyhood delusions and Army propaganda...

The soldier was still undressing the corpse, moving with the languidness of someone whose mind was elsewhere. The corpse had been shot in the head, which meant its clothes were relatively blood-free...but there was still the feces and urine that the body had released. After he had disrobed the corpse, he found himself looking at the man's shrunken genitalia. He did not know what his thoughts were, but he knew he was disturbed by whatever revelation hovered on the outskirts of his consciousness. He lost himself in the work to be done. He had to clean away some of the feces in his newly acquired clothes, so he ripped the top of another militant's clothing, and cleaned up the mess the best he could. He worked distractedly, holding his breath and not really looking directly at what he was doing. When his new garb was ready, he began to undress himself. It felt good to take off his flack jacket. His skin could breathe again after all these hours. He would not be able to wear the flack jacket with the militant's clothes, as it would be too conspicuous. His helmet was also out of the question—as were his Army-issue, camouflaged boots. He took off his shirt and boots, then decided he would cut his pants at the knees, wearing them as a barrier between the militant's soiled clothes and his skin. He was still moving slowly; more than once, he had to steady himself, as to keep the vomit down. Besides the feces, and the sickly odor of blood, the militant's clothes had a pungent stench. The clothes seemed stiff—as if caked with layers of a tragic, ultimately hopeless, life. He looked at all the militants now. They were young men—in their mid twenties at the most—but what had any of them really fought for? It all seemed so pointless now. Maybe the militants had had religion and nationalism to guide them in their empty moments, but the soldier knew he had had nothing.

Now that he was clothed, he instinctively checked the pants pockets of his new garb, and found some neatly folded papers. He opened them cautiously, and saw they were covered in handwritten text. The writing had so many flourishes that the soldier concluded it had to have been made by the hand of a woman. In fact, as the soldier allowed his imagination to roam, he concluded the pages were a cherished love letter. Maybe even militants needed love (and thoughts of love) to keep them going. In that light, he was glad someone else had killed these men. He did not want to be responsible for any more broken hearts and mothers' tears. He did not want to create any more widows and orphans—or add to the self-perpetuating cycle of violence.

He was through with this war. He knew that to survive, he would probably have to kill again, but he was through with all the pretenses that made war seem rational and justified. If he was to be mad, then he wanted to own that madness, so that if he ever got out of this alive, he would be able to cast that madness off—like an ugly, restrictive raincoat, after the storm had passed.

After giving it some thought, he decided the best way to carry his gun was to conceal it in cloth. He cut off another militant's clothes, then wrapped the cloth around his gun. He would not be able to fire the gun in an emergency, but it would be too conspicuous to carry in the open. In reality, there were guns everywhere—just as there were militants everywhere. At night, all these things came out into the open; but during the day, the forces of self-destruction hid themselves away, like cockroaches biding their time until they could come out and devour the crumbs of civilization.

The soldier wondered if he should keep his dog tags or not. If militants discovered them on him, he would be killed on the spot. Then again, if he attracted the attention of militants to the point where they wanted to search him, then he was as good as dead anyway. He would keep his tags—if only so that his body could be identified.

He took off his boots now, and put on the militant's sandals. The sandals were two sizes too big for him, but he could not be bothered. After this, he took the turban of another militant (since the donor of his clothes had been shot in the head). When that was done, he stumbled off a little way and sat down amongst the rubble. He was out of breath, since he had been breathing shallowly to mitigate the various odors. The turban had a dank odor, and felt clammy against his skin. His scalp crawled, as though the previous wearer of the turban had had lice. The soldier tried not to think about it.

Checking his supply stocks, he saw he had two energy bars left. Unfortunately, his stomach was too unsettled to keep down food. Instead, he drank the last of his water. Despite everything, he felt hopeful for once. Now that he was through with war, he felt as though he had been given a second chance to live.

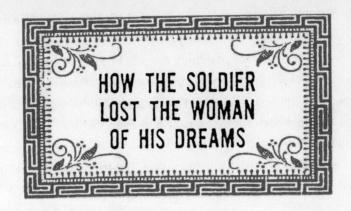

HOW THE SOLDIER LOST THE WOMAN OF HIS DREAMS

The soldier was about to take a step toward the opening in the wall when there was a sudden, plangent sound. It was as if the air were weeping. The soldier's first thought was that the sandstorm had arrived…but it did not sound like the other sandstorms he had experienced. After the initial outburst, there was a wail, which grew in intensity, until the soldier became convinced his gutted hiding place would come crashing down on his head. Looking out into the marketplace, the soldier expected to see the market goers screaming and running from the first stinging assaults of the sand—or whatever was approaching on the wind; but when he looked, everyone was frozen in place. They were staring down the street, to the soldier's right. They all seemed shocked. The soldier was buffeted between the impulse to flee for his life, and a yearning to know what was going on. He ran to the window then, still carrying his bandaged machine gun in his hand. At first, he tried to be circumspect, and stay in the shadows, so that those outside would not see him, but there was no way he could see far enough down the street without going outside. As the wailing grew more thunderous, his curiosity worked on him like a kind of madness. Something occurred to him: the noise in the air was chanting—dozens of voices screaming in unison. There was life and power within the chanting; he felt himself being drawn to it. At first, he stood at the window. Then, as he surrendered to the thing outside, he leaned out of the window, in order to see down the street. If others could view him or not, he could not care by now. There was magic and life in the chanting, and that was all that mattered....

The first time he saw the marching throng, he felt his heart quicken. It was like nothing he had experienced during his time in the war zone. There was no adrenaline-induced preparation to kill and be killed—none of the deadly instincts that had been eating away at him from the inside, like cancer. The wind was forcing him to squint now. The sight of the marching throng should have filled him with consternation, but there was a sense of hope in him that he could not understand.

The throng was perhaps twenty-five meters away. Their many tramping feet threw dust into the air, so that they almost seemed to be gliding down the street. Against the reddening sky, the entire thing seemed like an image from a dream. ...And then he realized the throng was composed exclusively of women. There were about one hundred of them—from old women in the formless gowns that were seen everywhere, to young, western-looking women in slacks.

He missed women. There was a universal dynamic in his longing—something that went beyond sex, but which his corrupted mind could probably only conceptualize as a sexual yearning. As he stared at the women, he suddenly felt homesick and lonely. Now that he thought about it, even the local men had looked homesick and lonely during his time in the war zone. For the local people, the reality of rape mobs, bandits and snipers had destroyed what was left of the social fabric. When Westerners saw the lengths the locals were willing to go to keep women out of the public eye, they complained of inequality and sexism. Yet, as the soldier had come to see it, women were not hidden away because they were valued less, but because they were valued more. In a society that had come apart at the seams, young/"respectable" women were like jewelry: if carelessly exposed in public, they might be stolen. One could argue about the dehumanizing aspects of being valued, and being protected, but freedom and equality were always myths; in a war zone, they were self-indulgent fantasies.

The soldier took a deep, cleansing breath. The chanting women were a kind of lyrical counter-spell to all the things that had been killing them.

The soldier suddenly wanted to chant with the women, so that their beautiful words could fill the emptiness of this place. The moribund silence of earlier that morning was gone at last. The people of the marketplace remained silent and still, but the women compensated for all their inadequacies. The women were circulating life through the stagnant air. Their clenched fists were the implements of a much-needed revolution—not against a regime, or any of the meaningless things men fought against, but a spiritual vacuum....

Before the soldier knew what he was doing, he crawled out of the window and stood outside, staring at the women. The women were coming straight toward him, and all he could think was that he wanted to be in their midst. A side of him almost wanted to be trampled by them. ...And he again saw the variety of the women. Some were in long gowns and veils; some walked in business suits; a few were even bareheaded, with jeans and T-shirts. He felt new life entering him. He trembled and stepped forward—like a worshiper following God's will...but the women were still coming—rumbling up to him with a power he knew he was not yet ready to withstand—so he stumbled back into the wall and let the first waves of protesters pass him by. He could have reached out his hand and touched them, but he kept his hands at his side. They passed him like a warm wave. His head swam with the odor of them—the very reality of them. And their words were more thunderous now. He felt the world shaking beneath his feet—as if all their stupid institutions were being demolished.

He must have seemed insane as he stood there with a simpering smile on his face, but no one seemed to be looking in his direction. As the first waves of protesters went by, he stared into their faces, hoping perhaps to latch onto their strength. ...Then, as soon as he saw the woman, he felt his stomach tighten. He knew her instantly; and when he realized why he knew her, and from where, he felt his mind go light. It was the girl from the wood—older now, and stunning, just as he had seen her in his fantasies.

All he could do was stare. The woman's eyes were bright and searching. While the other protesters screamed their chants, she was silent and self-contained. Her eyes seemed to be the gateway to everything he had ever wanted. She saw him staring at her, and stared back at him—at first only with passing curiosity, and then with awareness. He did not know if that awareness was merely her seeing through his disguise, or the realization that they had shared an improbable past together. Either way, she stared at him, cataloguing and dissecting everything that he was. Against the onslaught of her eyes, the soldier had the momentary urge to cover his face with the turban—to flee. Yet, on second thought, it seemed pointless to hide from her. In fact, he did not want to hide. Even if he and the woman were strangers, he wanted to see her and be seen by her. Even as a stranger, there was life in her eyes—and that attracted him, like food to a starving man. She wore one of the loose-fitting dresses of the region; and around her neck, there was a white scarf. Maybe she had used the scarf to cover her head previously, but it was off now, and her long, curly hair was free, dancing on the steadily increasing wind. In the five or six seconds it took her to walk past him, she seemed to see everything he was. Her eyes narrowed with understanding…and then she was gone, lost in the crowd…

The soldier panicked at this; as he lost sight of the woman, the strange spell passed from his system—or at least its influence was reduced to the point where he had the presence of mind to hide his face with the turban. His skin tone and features were passable for this region; but he sensed, instinctively, that his movements—his very manner of walking and being— were a sure giveaway that he was an American. He had to cover as much of himself as possible, so people would not have the urge to look at him too closely. He checked to make sure he still had the gun: he was so dazed he could not be certain. He looked down at the wrapped thing in his hand; then, still unsure, he squeezed it to verify the weapon was actually underneath those swathes of cloth.

The protest passed him. It had probably taken about twenty seconds for the entire throng to pass, but he felt the change within him. The woman was the key to everything—he knew it. Whether it was the same girl from his improbable past or not, he could not care by now. He only knew he needed to be around her. He needed to see her and be seen by her. He needed to feel the spell taking hold of him again, the way a drug addict felt the need for his next fix only moments after coming down from the high.

He set off after the protest. Had the woman recognized him, or merely been gawking at the strangeness of him? He pushed these thoughts from his mind. Now was not the time for reason. This was a world of extremes, so the only way to survive was to live beyond the bounds of everyday possibilities. In a flash, he relived the last few hours, seeing ghosts with shiny shoes, magical cats…and then there was the catastrophic attack against the American base. Reason was dead; logic was irrelevant. All that there was, was faith in the impossible.

The women continued down the street, past the market—toward what he believed to be the center of the city. He jogged a little way, to catch up to the protest, then he followed about fifteen meters behind them, hoping only to catch a glimpse of the woman. It was perhaps thirty seconds before he made out the woman again. Those seconds were like torture. His previous yearning for her was now a full-blown religion: a new way of contemplating the universe. …The white scarf was still around her neck; her long hair was still dancing. As if sensing him, she turned and looked back at him for a few seconds. He was unable to discern her expression from that distance, and this frustrated him. He felt cut off from her—and from all hope. She was like the cat to him now, leading him to the next phase of his destiny.

Typically, a demonstration like this would have attracted the authorities. Troops should have come; helicopters should have been scanning it from the sky; roadblocks should have been set up by now, in order to steer and defuse it…but there was nothing, and this again confirmed the extent of the attack against the American base. Yet, the woman was there, guiding him toward the next phase of his destiny. Now that he had found her, he knew that returning to America—and his parents—was no longer important to him. He had his old sense that there was another reality beyond this one. He could not begin to guess what it was, but he knew the woman was the key to everything…

He scanned the landscape now, as to get his bearings. Strangely enough, the streets seemed to be getting narrower as they moved toward the center of the city. On this block, a series of five-story apartment buildings fenced them in. With the approaching sandstorm, the sky was getting darker now—

as if the day had passed in a few minutes, and the gloaming were setting in. People were coming to their windows now—hundreds of people—looking down sleepy-eyed at the passing protest; from the shacks that lined the alleyways, people were coming out as well. The soldier felt suddenly conspicuous. The turban was already about his face, but he touched it to make sure.

That was when he noticed some militants standing on the roof of an upcoming building—about six of them. He saw the men and made out the guns slung over their shoulders. Directly across the street from the building, there were more men on the roof. They had guns as well…and something in their hands that he could not make out from the distance. And then, one of the men stepped to the edge of the roof—a man with a white turban and cloak. The man's long, black beard waved fitfully in the wind. Something about him seemed unmistakably ominous—as if he were a figure ripped from the pages of the Bible or Koran: a vessel of God's inescapable vengeance. The soldier felt his heart quicken: he knew an ambush when he saw one—

"Look out!" he screamed for the first time. With all the chanting, his voice was lost. Those first words were actually hoarse; he cleared his throat and tried to scream again, but by then the men on the roof had begun to fling the things in their hands—bricks. The first brick landed with a thud on the head of an old woman. She staggered back, too stunned to scream. However, those around her screamed when they saw her bloody face. And more bricks were falling now—a hailstorm of bricks. The women began to run, clutching their bleeding heads. Some of them turned and ran back toward the soldier. They were actually running in all directions now. The defiant chants were gone now; the women's screams reminded the soldier of dogs being beaten by their master. There was something disheartening about it, and he stood indecisively for a moment. Yet, when he remembered the woman, he began to run. He almost collided with a dazed matron, who stumbled toward him with her broken jaw hanging loose.

After searching the fleeing protesters desperately, he saw the woman. She was crouching on the ground, trying to help a prone figure. The militants were still flinging bricks. Suddenly charged into action, the soldier got out his gun. He grabbed hold of one end of the cloth that covered it, and flung the rest into the air, causing the gun to unravel and twirl in the air like a top. He barely managed to grab it before it fell to the ground. Then, he was firing at the rooftops and running toward the woman. As the other protesters had fled—or been carried away unconscious—the woman was out in the open by now. She was still bent over one of her fellow protesters—another matron whose head was bleeding. As the soldier approached, he and the woman stared at one another. In his haste, the turban had again unwrapped, revealing his face. He looked at her helplessly, and then he rescanned the rooftops for any sign of the militants. By some miracle, the men on the rooftops seemed to have been scared off by his gunfire. He looked back at the woman again. She was still crouching over her friend, but she stared up at him in the same enigmatic way as before. Maybe it was to shield himself from those eyes that he moved so quickly. First, he slung the gun over his shoulder by its strap, and then he bent down and took the unconscious protester in his arms. The protester was short and plump; and while he was not exactly straining as he held her, he had to get used to the weight. He and the woman stood up together. At first, there was a standoff. Her enigmatic eyes came up against his boundless yearnings; but then, seeming to come to the conclusion he was harmless, she nodded and began to lead him away. They jogged for a little while, until they got to the next corner, then they began to walk.

With his new burden, the soldier was out of breath. The woman was looking at him critically: "Why are you here?" she asked him suddenly. Her English was so precise it seemed British.

"You speak English," he said in surprise.

"Yes, I speak excellent English, but you make a horrible African," she said, looking over his clothes. There was something teasing in her voice, and he had to stare at her for a moment before he realized it. He had to remember what a joke was. When he did, he smiled—maybe more in relief than anything else—and said:

"Can you give me any tips?"

They stared at one another, both perhaps amazed by their odd conversation.

But at that moment, there was an inarticulate yell behind them—maybe blocks away—and they both turned toward the noise. There was nothing to be seen, however, and they looked at one another uncertainly. That look of softness and vulnerability was in her eyes for an instant, before she looked ahead and picked up her pace.

"Come this way," she said to him then. The soldier nodded eagerly: now that the woman had made him smile, he knew he would follow her anywhere.

The wind was picking up. Luckily for them, the gathering storm kept people—and potential attackers—off the streets. As the wind was at their backs, their eyes were spared the stinging blast, but he could feel specks of sand on the back of his neck as he walked. The sensation was unsettling. Also, it was growing darker by the moment, and the wind had an ululating quality, which was eerie on the empty streets.

They had walked in silence for about three blocks now: past shoddy-looking apartment complexes, which, in the gusting wind, seemed as sturdy as cardboard boxes. In the soldier's arms, the unconscious protester was still bleeding from her head. It was not heavy bleeding, but it was dampening the soldier's already soiled clothes. The blood chilled him for a reason that had nothing to do with temperature; and as they walked along like that—in silence, fleeing from the impending dangers of men and nature—he was overcome by the need to hear the woman's voice again. He searched his mind for something to say, and then he blurted out:

"There have got to be easier ways to get your morning exercise." He had hoped to make her smile, but the wind was so loud he had to repeat himself. By then, the humor seemed strained.

The woman glanced over at him, as if she had forgotten he was there. There was a hopeful smile on his face; she nodded equivocally, and returned to looking straight ahead. After a few seconds, she said, "There are lots of easy things in the world, Mr. American."

He felt stupid and uneasy. And the idea that the woman walking next to him could be the girl of the pit—or even that that girl could have existed at all—suddenly seemed silly to him. Logic told him to resist such thoughts. There was a sickness within him: that was the most logical explanation. Maybe he was so desperate for some morsel of human affection that he was seeing what he wanted to see—reconstructing the ghosts of his past fantasies. He nodded his head now. Still, as he glanced over at the woman, he could not deny his emptiness. He needed to talk to someone. Somehow, he felt as though he would be able to talk himself out of his madness. He looked over at her hopefully again, saying:

"Do you know what happened to the American base?"

She looked at him and frowned: "You really don't know?"

"No, I was on a mission when it happened."

"It was bombed last night. A couple thousand soldiers are dead at least. The survivors fled back to the airport. Your president appeared on TV a few hours ago, saying America was going to hit the so-called terrorists hard. Ten thousand more troops are being sent over."

"Shit," the soldier whispered. "...It's out of control."

"It's been out of control for a long time now."

The soldier sighed: "It'll never end."

"It will end if we stop it," she corrected him.

He looked over at her uneasily: "That's what your protest was about?"

This time, she did not even look up at him; he wondered if she had heard him, but he was wary about asking her again. It required a certain amount of courage to interact with her. Just when he was telling himself he should keep quiet and forget about the entire thing, she began:

"When I was little, maybe about five years old, the civil war broke out." Her voice startled him. It was clear and forceful. And the strange thing was that as she talked, the wind seemed to die down. She said the words calmly— in a natural voice, without shouting or raising her voice in any way—and yet they were somehow louder than the wind. It was almost as though her words did not have to travel through the air: as though he were hearing them within himself. "...Everything went crazy," she went on. "When the government troops attacked our village, everyone picked up and ran. It was the only thing to do. Hundreds of us joined hundreds and then thousands of refugees from other villages. It was women and children, mostly. My father had been working in the oil industry, but after the troops chased us out of the village, we never saw him again. Even to this day, nobody has any idea what happened to him. There were rumors: that everyone working in such-and-such was killed on such-and-such date...buried somewhere in the desert....

"My mother followed the refugees to a camp near the border. There were maybe half a million people there—maybe more. I had never seen a city before: never been around more than the few hundred people in my village. The refugee camp was like hell. The air carried death—all kinds of plagues from bad sanitation. The water became contaminated. You'd smell people as they died...and there were so many deaths that there was nothing to do but stack the bodies up outside the camp. Sometimes, entire families would die, and people would just leave them there. A mother would die, and her toddlers would starve. Sometimes, you'd see little kids wandering about: motherless, homeless, begging for food...Everyone became a beggar in the camp. International donors sent aide. They shipped in food and water, tents... everything...but it was the government that decided who got the stuff. ...There were these ration cards in the camp. Depending on which tribe you belonged to, or which tribe they thought you belonged to, they'd give you a different color ration card. ...We'd sometimes have to wait on line for five hours in order to get food. Sometimes, when you were finished with the breakfast line, you went straight for the lunch or dinner line. Or you'd wait on there for hours, only to hear they had run out of food. Everyone knew it was all a game. There was always food; and if you had a little money—or were willing to have sex with the food distributors—you got food. Everyone knew what was going on, but people accepted it, because they had to eat...

"One day, my mother and I were on line from sunrise. It was past noon and we hadn't eaten yet. The food distributors were sitting in front of the tent with the food. There was a tarpaulin blocking the food from view, but when the wind blew, you'd see the food stacked high back there. Anyway, the food distributors were lounging at a table in front, joking amongst themselves. Their laughter traveled down the long line of hungry, desperate people, mocking us. When my mother couldn't stand it anymore, she screamed, 'Enough!' and rushed up to confront them. Everyone looked at her in shock; the men stopped laughing and looked at her as she came up. 'You sit there laughing while children starve!' she screamed. 'What kind of animals are you!' Everyone was still in shock: the words lingered in the air, like something their minds couldn't decipher. I was still on line with the others. That's when one of the food distributors came from behind the desk. As if only then digesting what my mother had said, he reared his arm back and hit her. I must have closed my eyes to avoid seeing the blow, because the next thing I knew, my mother was lying on the ground. The man returned behind the desk, and the others continued their conversation, as though nothing had happened. They left my mother lying there, unconscious. On the line, nobody moved—nobody said a word…not even me."

"You were only a kid," the soldier said.

The woman ignored his attempt to make her feel better. Maybe she was even annoyed by it as she continued, "…We stood there, like cows on a slaughter line. After about five or ten minutes, my mother regained consciousness. She got up like a wounded animal, stumbling on unsteady legs. The food distributor guys looked at her and laughed at the way she walked. She stumbled back toward me….Nobody would look at her—not even me. She sat down next to me on the ground and began to cry…and everyone pretended not to hear.

"So, you see, Mr. American," she said then, looking over at him, "that's why I protest. When people try to treat you like an animal, you have to make it clear you're a human being. You have to make it clear—or else, you're already as good as dead."

The soldier nodded inanely, cowed. She was alive and strong and resolute. He had been half-dead for months now—he saw that now. The woman's words were bringing him back from the nowhere place. He looked at her, again wondering if she could be the girl from his past—

She glanced over at him, startled by the intensity of his gaze. He had not realized it, but there was a smile on his face. "—What is it?" she asked.

He came back to his senses, but could think of nothing to do but laugh at himself. "…You're alive," he said at last, as if that would explain everything. Before she could reply, he blurted out, "I feel like we've met before."

She laughed. "Are you trying to pick me up, Mr. American?"

"What? No!" he protested, but she only laughed louder. She had perfect, white teeth. He could not help staring at them, even while he felt himself being undone by her laughter. He sensed himself blushing. Yet, after a while, her laughter died down, and she frowned:

"You're serious, aren't you? You think you know me from somewhere?"

He looked over at her in the same helpless way. He started to speak, but then stopped himself; after a few seconds of internal struggle, he began: "Don't I seem familiar to you?"

Her frown deepened. "This will sound weird, but you remind me of someone I used to dream about."

The soldier's eyes widened. The woman laughed at his reaction: "Don't get excited—it wasn't that kind of dream."

"I didn't mean…"

However, she only shook her head and smiled.

"What were your dreams about?" he asked eagerly.

"That's the funny thing: I can't remember. …I only know someone like you was in them. Sounds crazy, huh?"

He wanted to tell her everything then. He wanted to tell her about the pit in his wood and the dimension of light. He wanted to open himself to her and show her everything, but that was when he sensed something in his peripheral vision—a blur in the form of a man! The soldier turned his head abruptly—to an alleyway to his left. He instinctively wanted to reach for his gun—to drop the protester and grab his weapon—but there was nothing in the alleyway. He had stopped walking; the woman looked back at him:

"What's wrong?"

He was still staring down the empty alleyway, as if seeing a horror—

"Hey!" she called to get his attention; at the sound of her voice, he jumped.

"Huh?" he said, out of breath.

"Did you see something?"

"Just my eyes playing tricks," he mumbled. Nevertheless, his heart was thumping in his chest; and as he considered the blur in the form of a man, his mind returned to the revelation he had had while hiding in the bombed-out building: the blurred figure and the man with the shiny shoes were one in the same—

"Are you okay?" It was the woman again. She was looking at him uneasily.

He stared at her for a while—as if he had to remember who she was and how they had come to be there—then he nodded to reassure her. He looked around: the sandstorm was growing stronger. The woman had led him to a neighborhood the old regime had originally set aside for guest workers of the oil industry. Over time, students and the shadow classes of the society had adopted the area, because of the cheap rents and relative lack of oversight. The neighborhood had become the stronghold of black marketers, smugglers, bootleggers, and the like. The soldier had raided this area once—in a massive operation, with multiple units. They had rounded up about one hundred men, most of whom had been involved in an oil smuggling enterprise. They had raided apartments that were stacked to the ceiling with used-looking merchandise—everything from microwave ovens to expired medicine. Considering the state of the economy, and the country, the black market had been the only thing keeping the country going; but even in times of war, the men in power always had to get their cut.

The soldier nodded his head absentmindedly as he walked, then readjusted the unconscious protester in his arms. He was about to ask the woman how much longer they had to go when she turned into a stout building sandwiched between two of the cardboard-looking high-rises. When the woman opened the door, the soldier instinctively leapt back, because there were dozens of people there, waiting in the semi-darkness. Some of them rose as the woman entered. They went to her—women and children, mostly: the wretched people of the shantytowns. They surrounded her, pleading and holding out their hands. She nodded her head and told them something in the local language. This seemed to placate them, and they returned to their seats and positions on the floor. That was when the soldier looked around and noticed people lying on cots, with saline drips connected to their arms. Others were covered in bandages. There was an unsavory scent in the air: death and disinfectant. This was some kind of clinic. Everything was in one large room. There were two doors in the rear. One led outside—he could tell because it had a window in it. The other one probably led to an office or bathroom. He stepped in cautiously, closing the door with his heel. At the sound of the slamming door, the woman looked over at him. Seeing the unconscious protester in his arms, she gestured him toward a desk in the corner of the room. He had to step over people. Many had burns or gunshot wounds or freshly amputated limbs. A few of them had all three.

There were some papers on the desk, but the woman pushed them to the floor to make space for the protester. While the soldier placed the protester on the desk, the woman went to a cabinet and returned with some medical supplies and a candle. As was usually the case in the city, the power was off again. She handed the soldier the candle, and a box of matches, then she began putting on some latex gloves. The soldier lit the candle, and held it up so she could see what she was doing. The soldier stared at her, engrossed. Soon, she was stitching up the protester's head wound.

The soldier glanced over his shoulder—back toward the windows. The outside world suddenly struck him as a terror to be avoided. The sandstorm was picking up, and a menacing growl now lingered in the air, from the wind. Now that he was inside, the only thing he wanted to do was hide. In fact, in the woman's presence, he could not look beyond the next few minutes or hours or days, or whatever it would turn out to be. Maybe this was a new spell—another detour from reality, which would leave him stranded in yet another wasteland—but he did not care. He could not be concerned about a theoretical future when the present reality seemed like a respite from time, itself. He had probably been with the woman for forty minutes now, yet he felt as though hours had passed. He was not the same man he had been a few minutes ago; and in the face of all the new uncertainties of his life, he knew he did not want to go back to what he had been.

The woman was about halfway through the stitches when the soldier whispered, "You're a doctor?"

"Not yet," she said without looking up: "I was in my first year of residency when I came back."

"You were in England, right?" he guessed from her accent.

She nodded: "I grew up there. My mother never made it out of that refugee camp," she said grimly. "After she died, some relatives in England claimed me. After reports started to leak out about the government letting people starve, the UN sent some aide workers to manage the relief efforts. The UN workers got me out of the country."

The soldier did not say anything for about twenty seconds. Eventually, the obvious question came to him: "Why'd you come back?"

She stopped what she was doing and looked up at him momentarily, before going back to her operation: "I came to help my country," she said plainly, without any hint of self-sacrifice or self-importance—or even patriotism. He noticed she was sweating: he found there was something strangely erotic about the way beads of sweat formed on her long, slender neck. He stared at it longingly, then shook his head to free himself of the spell.

"...Too many lives have been wasted in this war already," he said after a moment of silence—a moment so long his statement seemed unconnected to anything.

She glanced up at him again and smiled, as though he had said something moronic. He felt self-conscious as she went back to her work. For a moment, she was silent, but then she continued:

"Why are you here?"

"I'm a soldier."

"No, I don't mean that. Why are you *here*? Why did you help me? Why were you walking alone on the street...dressed like that," she said, looking pointedly at his clothes.

"Oh...I'm through with the war," he said.

She smiled at first, then stood up straight and laughed, so that the candle's flickering light highlighted her perfect teeth. "Your president will be needing every able-bodied soldier soon. I don't think he'll like your going AWOL."

He looked at her anxiously: "You have to get out of this country—especially after what happened last night. They'll bomb everything...from the air. It was all a game before—pretending they were setting up a democracy—but Americans don't play when it's time to take revenge. As soon as the sandstorm clears, they'll level it all…say they were bombing terrorists."

She was looking at him with narrowed eyes, as though impressed by his honesty. "You don't talk like an American."

For whatever reason, he smiled. "What's an American supposed to talk like?"

She laughed. "You're the first one I've met who didn't believe he was over here to save us."

"I haven't saved anyone yet," he mused, looking off to the side.

She stretched her back now, getting out the kinks after bending over to do the stitches. She was finished with the operation. "…How do you intend to get back home?"

"You mean to America?"

"Yes. Don't you miss your family?"

"I thought I did," he began vaguely. "Lately, I needed to call them. …To hear their voices, as if I was addicted to them or something…but maybe all that was only a kind of war loneliness."

"War loneliness?"

"Yeah: war makes you lonesome," he explained. "You crave all kinds of things you wouldn't otherwise."

She nodded her head, understanding instinctively, but continued, "Your parents will still be worried about you—especially after last night."

He shrugged. "I want them to know I'm well—that I wasn't killed last night; but other than that, I don't feel as though I have a home. I don't feel as though there's anything to go back to…if that makes any sense."

She laughed whimsically. "Few things make sense in war."

He smiled. "What about you? Does your family know you're here?"

"You mean my English relatives?"

"Yes."

"It's not as though I ran away from home or something," she said with a laugh.

"…Well, they can't be happy about you being here—in this madness."

"You can't always go through life making people happy. You can't even make yourself happy most of the time."

He nodded, feeling suddenly melancholy.

At that moment, a boy on one of the cots began to groan; she took one step in that direction before stopping and turning back to the soldier:

"You can call your family if you want," she said, proffering a key from her pocket. When he looked at her quizzically, she explained, "My English relatives gave me a satellite phone when I told them my plan to come back here. It's in that cabinet over there," she said, pointing. He took the key, and she went over to her patient.

He put down the candle he had been holding, then went over to the cabinet. Once he had the cabinet open, he looked at the phone nervously. He did not know if he wanted to call his parents. He remembered how the strange lady had answered the last time. He was wary about something like that happening again. He felt he would be tempting fate. It was perhaps 2 a.m. in New York, with the time difference. The idea of calling them in the middle of the night was not really a palatable one, but he felt somehow obligated to the woman. If he did not call, she would ask him why, and he would be forced to tell her his insane stories and rationales. He began to dial the number, acutely aware he had no idea what he would say to his parents. How could he tell them he was a deserter? He would leave that out. He would only tell them he was okay, and that they should believe that, regardless of what the Army told them. He shook his head: that would worry them needlessly, and make them ask more questions. He wanted to put down the phone, and think through what he was going to say, but the phone was ringing, and that left him frozen—as if the chiming sound were another spell being cast on him—

Someone picked up the phone, but a few seconds passed before the person actually spoke into the handset. It was his mother. She made an indistinguishable noise—something between a yawn and a groan—then said, "Yes?"

His mouth felt dry: "Mom, it's me."

"…Who is this?"

"It's your son—"

The soldier could hear his father in the background. The man was asking who it was, and his mother was speaking to him, saying, "It's someone who says he's our son."

"Is it Our Senator?" his father asked. That was how he referred to the soldier's brother now, since he had won the election. It was a title, like Duke or Earl—

"No, he's got the wrong number," his mother explained to his father.

"Mom," the soldier said into the phone—

"You have the wrong number," she tried to explain, talking into the handset now.

"It's me, Mom!" he said so forcefully that all the conscious people in the clinic looked over at him—including the woman.

At that moment, the soldier's father took the phone from his mother:

"You've got the wrong number."

"It's me, Dad," he was almost pleading now—

"You're not listening, kid," his father said in annoyance. "You have the wrong number. We only have one son!" Then, the phone was slammed down, and the soldier was listening to the dial tone.

"What the hell…?" he whispered. However, there was no time to think, because it was then that the front door was kicked open. Besides the loud bang, the sandstorm's roar was like a freight train. When the soldier looked to the open doorway, there was a man with a gun there. The soldier recognized him instantly from the rooftop brick-throwing incident. The man's eyes were wild, searching for the object of his vengeance. Within seconds, he saw the woman crouched over her patient, and brought up the muzzle of his gun. And there were other men at his back—more insurgents with guns. Luckily, the soldier's gun was still slung over his shoulder. His reaction was lightning quick, and his aim was true. He had said before that he was through with war, but seeing the woman in danger made the killing easy. Soon, he was riddling the men's bodies with bullets. Those to the rear managed to dart out of the door, but the soldier knew they were only regrouping. He yelled for the woman to come to him, and she came. He remembered the back door, and was soon pulling her over to it.

Outside, the ferocity of the sandstorm was like the stuff of nightmares, but there was no choice but to go out into it. The back door led to a labyrinth of alleys. They had to squint from the stinging sand, and hold their hands before their eyes. Already, the soldier's eyes and nostrils and mouth had grains of sand in them, but he could do nothing about it now. He held the woman's hand, and they ran past shanties, and people sitting couched against walls because their shanties had already blown away. Eventually, they reached a major street. Pieces of clothing and buckets (and a never-ending river of trash) were swirling in a funnel in the middle of the street. As the soldier looked on, a chair tumbled past and promptly crashed into the windshield of a car parked on the curb.

They were running again—as much as anyone could run in such a storm. It was like wading up a powerful river, fighting against the current. The swirling sand stung their faces and hands and ankles—and whatever else had been left uncovered by their clothing. It was like being in a swarm of killer bees. There was nowhere to hide; and after a while, not even their clothes could protect them. For a storm like this, they needed armor, not cloth.

Eventually, the flight or fight impulse began to pass from the soldier's system. He tried to get his bearings and think through his next course of action; but with the sand in his eyes, he could barely see by now. His only solace was that the woman was beside him. Her hand was in his, and it felt good. Even though he had to squint in order to see her, he saw her clearly in his mind's eye. She was beautiful, and for her beauty, he would do anything—cross any barrier. He had a sudden flashback of the thing that had just happened with his parents, but forced his mind away from it. For now, the only important thing was the woman.

They trudged for about a block in this manner—and that alone took them perhaps five minutes. They would have to find shelter soon. The fleeting moments of intimacy he and the woman had shared within her clinic now seemed like things that had happened years ago. He had the feeling she was already lost to him, even though her hand was still in his. He grasped it tighter, desperate not to lose her—

Some sand went down his windpipe, and he coughed. He could not keep this up much longer, and he doubted the woman could either. He squeezed her hand again, needing the reassurance of her presence, but it was not enough. He had kept his eyes closed for long stretches of time, as to protect his eyes, but the need to see her made him open his eyes—

A bag of trash flew out of the nothingness and collided with him like a bowling ball. His hand slipped from the woman's, and he crumbled to the ground. For a moment, he lay disoriented on the sandy earth, before he came to his senses. When he did, and he remembered the woman, panic seized him. Holding her hand had had a calming effect on him. In a world of chaos and death, the woman had been the only thing sustaining him. Without her, it was like the end of the world.

"Hey!" he screamed as he searched the sandstorm for the woman. Of course, with his sand blindness, she was nowhere in sight. He went to take off running, but by now he had lost all bearings. Every direction seemed the same! His turban had partly unraveled after the collision with the garbage bag. In his haste and desperation, he wrenched it off. He took off running. He had no idea where he was going, but there was no time to lose. He ran with his eyes closed, taking glimpses of the swirling darkness every few seconds. In his mind, every step separating him from the woman was like a hundred miles. Maybe, in his disorientation, he was going in the opposite direction from her, but he would not allow himself to acknowledge this possibility. All that there was, was running; and as he did so, he told himself he was running toward her. In his mind, there was nothing else but the woman—

He banged into a parked car, screaming out as his shin collided with the front bumper. As he screamed, huge veins appeared on his neck. He screamed both from the pain and the frustration…and in the dim hope that the woman would hear his voice.

Maybe it was instinct that made him look at the car more closely—look inside the passenger compartment. He moved toward the driver's side window, cupping his hands over the corners of his eyes, so he could look inside the vehicle. When he finally did, he felt his innards knot themselves! Inside the car, he made out the face of the militant—the white-turbaned, bearded man who had been on top of the building when the protesters marched down the street. Maybe it was not the same man, and all the faces of his enemies had morphed into one barbaric archetype over the months he had spent in the war zone...but there were other men in the vehicle, and these men not only had guns, but the unmistakably belligerent faces of his enemies. Now that the soldier's turban was gone, there could be no doubt they knew he was their enemy. The white-turbaned man yelled something then—something that was lost in the fury of the storm—but the soldier felt those words within him, as if a bomb had exploded in his chest—

He was running again! His only hope was that they would lose him within the swirling darkness. It was not an impossible wish, since he had already lost the woman. ...And then, miraculously, he saw her. He saw her form. It was of course a vague etching in the chaos, but he knew it was her. She was coming straight toward him. Yet, the momentary relief of seeing her again was negated by the reality of the white-turbaned man—

He heard a bullet whiz past his ear—literally, millimeters from his ear. That was the only reason he heard it in the storm. He screamed for the woman to run, but she was waving her hand—

"Run!" he screamed—even though it was pointless in the storm; and then, when he was within reach of her, two bullets impacted with her chest, and she staggered back. He leapt to grab her before she collapsed onto the ground, but he missed. He scrambled up to her and crouched above her. She had wrapped the scarf over her face, to shield her eyes. He ripped it off, so he could look at her. Her eyes showed her shock and pain; her mouth sucked for air, which no longer seemed to reach her lungs. He wanted to scream, himself, but all the air seemed to have left his body. She seemed to be mouthing words to him. He stared at her bloody lips, but he could not decipher the mysteries she had to impart to him. And then, as he crouched there, clutching her to his body, he was amazed to find her body was being bathed in light. It was the same mesmerizingly beautiful light from the dimension of light—and as he looked at her, he realized she was again fading away. Though blinding, the light did not hurt his eyes. It was soothing and warm. There was no sandstorm anymore; he no longer had to squint to see, or brace his body against the stinging sand. He held the woman close, but it was as if the substance of her were disintegrating—as if she were a sand woman, flowing through his fingers. In seconds, she was gone, and his arms were empty. As soon as she disappeared, the light ceased, and all his fantasies came to an end. Instantaneously, he felt the swirling sand against his body once more. The blast made him topple to the ground and clamp his eyes shut. He lay there in the fetal position, incapacitated, as if the loss of the woman had taken the last of his soul. He was in this position when the militants came to capture him.

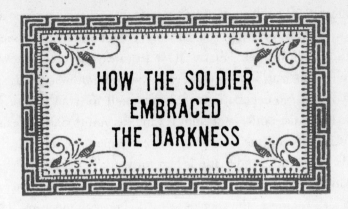

HOW THE SOLDIER EMBRACED THE DARKNESS

After an indefinite period of time, the soldier woke up in a dark, windowless room. He coughed after his first two breaths. A pestilential stench burned the back of his throat and nasal passages. He had a flash of the last thing he remembered: the woman fading away in the light. He groaned, as if the recollection had gutted him. He tried to take stock of himself. He had a headache, and his vision was blurry. He was lying flat on his back. Above him, there was a light of some kind—a lamp. Trying to focus his eyes on the blurry, shifting image, made his headache intensify. He grimaced.

Then, after a moment of confusion, it occurred to him there were men above him. One was holding the lamp. This man kicked him then—not with vehemence, but with the kind of annoyed impatience one had for a sleeping dog.

"Wake up!" the man screamed now. The man then nudged the soldier in the ribs a few times with his boot, until the soldier propped himself up on his elbows and grunted in a manner that was meant to placate his abuser.

Presently, the other man started talking in the local language; the soldier tried to see the man's face, but the sensation this caused was so sublimely painful that he almost felt drunk after the effort—

The man who had kicked him and screamed for him to wake up now began talking—in English—so that the soldier realized this man was translating for the other one:

"You have nothing we want," the man began in a rapid, almost indecipherable cadence. "We want no information from you. You have no secrets we desire to know. We keep you alive only so our men can see what an American is—how weak you are. If we torture you, it is to show our men that Americans can bleed and scream. Nobody knows you are alive—or where you are. No negotiations are being made for your release. Your only purpose is to exist until we deem it is time for you to cease to exist. This is the power that we have over you. As we are men, we tell you there is no hope for your future, and that it is best for you to consider yourself already dead. Do you understand?" the man concluded abruptly. As he waited for the soldier's response, the silence seemed almost thunderous. The soldier had been sitting there with his head bowed and his eyes closed, but he looked up now, defying the pain. Between the kerosene lamp's flickering wick and his blurred vision, his captors' faces seemed like something from a nightmare. He suddenly recognized the white turban of his enemy—

"Do you understand?" the translator asked again, after a pause of about five seconds.

"I understand," the soldier said simply; and then, when the militants nodded and prepared to leave, he whispered, "Thank you."

At this last comment, the translator looked back at him uncertainly, but then the men left, and the door was closed behind them, and the soldier found himself alone in the darkness. As he listened in the silence, it occurred to him the sandstorm had passed. At the very least, he had been unconscious for hours. In fact, as he lay there, he knew it was possible days had passed. He knew then that the last days of his life would probably play themselves out within the darkness around him.

Some hours later—or maybe even the next day, or the next—the soldier was taken to his first torture session. His captors burst into the hovel, so that the door banged against the wall. It was daytime outside. He cringed on the ground, putting up his hands to shield his eyes from the brilliant sunlight glaring through the open door. They jerked him from the ground as if he were a sack of garbage. The next thing he knew, they were dragging him outside. They wrenched him behind them—even though he would have walked compliantly. They screamed at him, even though he could not understand their language; they slapped him, and twisted his arm behind his back, causing him to fall to the scalding sand. Yet, no sooner was he on the ground, coughing on the dust, than he was wrenched up again, and kicked for having fallen. For most of the thirty or so seconds it took them to drag him from one hovel to another, he kept his eyes closed—in order to block out the blinding sun. Just as they were about to enter the hovel set aside for torture, he managed to turn his head and get a glimpse of the barren desert. He recognized the sand dunes, and the deceptively beautiful, cloudless blue sky. Only then did it occur to him this was the place he had seen when he touched the man with the bloodshot eyes. This was where the man was going to be shot in the head. The soldier trembled—not necessarily out of fear, but in awe of the cosmic forces that had brought him here—

And then, he was inside the hovel. The door was slammed shut behind him and his captors. As he looked around in the relative darkness, he saw there were perhaps ten men in the room, standing in the shadows. At his entrance, they cheered at the prospect of seeing how an American screamed and bled. The soldier was still in shock. He kept seeing the man with the bloodshot eyes being shot in the head. The scene played in a frenzied loop. Over his tour of duty in the war zone, sand dunes and deceptively beautiful skies had always been in the back of his mind. They had been an unconscious compass, guiding him to this place—

One of his captors yelled something in the local language; the others applauded. Next, someone kicked the soldier in the back, so that he stumbled forward and fell heavily to the ground. As the men cheered, he coughed on the dust and prepared himself for the suffering to come.

They hauled the soldier up by his armpits. A spotlight and a chair had been placed in the middle of the hovel. Soon, he was strapped into the chair.

In his dazed state, he was only vaguely aware of it. His audience laughed and screamed for the show to begin. He sat there silently—even after the torture began. To his amazement, he realized he did not feel a thing. With minimal effort, he allowed the pain to fade away—like all the other irrelevant things in his life. After a while, he did not even grimace anymore. It was as if the pain were a stray thought: a passing fancy. Instead of this torture chamber, hidden away in the searing expanse of the desert, he saw himself walking with the woman; and in this new, magical world, there was no discomfort between the woman and him. There were no words that needed to be said, because they knew one another. There were no actions that needed to be explained, or motives that were not immediately understood by the syntax of their love. Every once in a while, he would look up from his fantasies and see the sweaty, enraged faces of his torturers. However, these images—and the sensations he felt while viewing them—would always be like stray thoughts; and ever eager to focus his mind on what was important, he would quickly find himself alone with the woman, enjoying the tender comforts of lovers.

In time, he was returned to his hovel, where he continued his dreams and let the outside world fade from existence. When he regained consciousness, his body throbbed with the most unspeakable pain. Ribs had been fractured; they had kicked him in the face, loosening his front teeth. Blisters spotted his body, in the places where they had burned him with a cigarette. They had even ripped off one of his fingernails. Mercifully, his mind quickly sheltered him from the onslaught. In fact, his newfound powers amazed him. With practice, he realized he could transform the drab walls of his prison into wide-open spaces. Within seconds, he could be in fields full of blooming flowers, or secluded tropical beaches, or whatever his soul desired. In the first few days or weeks or months, while the other captured Americans grew unstable and despondent, the soldier turned the surrounding horrors into his own little slice of paradise.

One day, remembering what the girl of the pit had told him—about them being husband and wife—he willed his mind to consider how it would be to make love to her. She had told him her last memory: making love to him in the early morning, before he went to work. He now put his mind to constructing that scene. At first, it was like any other fantasy—contrived and artificial; but soon, the scene became self-perpetuating. Details filled themselves in so perfectly he felt as though he had been transported back in time. …The bedroom was cramped—a small, working class apartment in the city. The drapes were a gossamer fabric, allowing the early morning light to caress their bodies. The window was open: he could hear cars driving past and honking their horns. Somewhere, a mother yelled for a child to get out of bed. Yet, as they made love that morning, all the background noises and realities faded away. It was almost as if they were taken away to another world. As he touched her, everything seemed possible. Their bodies moved to a syncopated rhythm only they could understand. And when the moment of pleasure finally came, it was as if they had achieved something forbidden— something that had been set aside for the gods…

Even after the scene came to an end, the soldier lay panting in the darkness. The scene was like nothing he had ever experienced before. He did not know if it was a fantasy, a recollection of what had happened, or a vision of what could happen if he reached some forbidden metaphysical plane. The only thing he knew for sure was that he was willing to do anything to enter that place again—even if he had to lose his mind and soul to do so.

The days and weeks and months passed as he lay in the darkness dreaming of the woman. Every once in a while, one of his captors would enter the hovel to beat him and/or feed him. Sometimes, the one who spoke English would be there, translating a rant on how America was losing the war: how the sands of the Sahara were being soaked with American blood. The soldier barely acknowledged these things. In truth, with thoughts of the woman in his mind, the outside world fell away. Upon occasion, he would try to conjure a sense of urgency, and put his mind to escaping this prison camp. However, no matter how much he suffered in the prison camp, thoughts of the woman would always drag him away to a place beyond the concerns of the outside world, where nothing mattered but their love.

There was a latrine to the side of the hovel. Rather, there was a pit in the floor, which was covered by a slab of wood. The slab had a hole in it about half a meter in diameter. The stench was impossible to describe. As the soldier was locked in the hovel, baking in the desert heat, the odor grew into something that seemed tangible—something he could taste and chew and feel. Somehow, it was worse when he got a whiff of fresh air—when they dragged him out to the torture hovel or one of the jailors opened the door to shove in some of the watery gruel. Fresh air would revive his deadened senses for a moment. He would breathe hungrily, desperate to purge the latrine vapors from his system; but when the door was closed, it would always be a cruel reminder that he was locked in hell. The poison would seem thicker around him, suffocating him.

In this sense, maybe many of the things he saw while alone in the hovel were hallucinations triggered by the vapors. He did not only remember things anymore: he saw them and felt them, the way one would if teleported back in time. After weeks and months within the putrid darkness, the soldier no longer bothered to differentiate reality from what was only his mind's response to the unraveling of reality.

By now, he probably spent ninety percent of his time sleeping, or lying on his pallet with his eyes closed. After the first few weeks or months of torture sessions, his captors became wary of him. No matter what they did to him, he just sat there, staring blankly into space. To prove their theories about the weakness of Americans, they used the other captured Americans in their torture sessions, and left the soldier alone. The soldier would hear the other Americans screaming upon those occasions when he drifted from his dreams. The screams would make him want to kill his captors. They would fill him with dark, vengeful thoughts, until he felt his soul being choked by hate. At those times, thoughts of the woman would be the only things keeping him from surrendering to the darkness.

One day, after what seemed like an eternity in the hovel, the soldier woke up with the creepy feeling that something had changed. He sat up and looked around. In the darkness, there was not really anything to focus on, but he sensed something in the far corner; and as he looked closer, he saw what he could only conceptualize as a shadow in the darkness. The shadow seemed to have a human form, so he cleared his throat anxiously and said, "Who's there?"

There was no response; the shadow did not move, and as the soldier thought about it objectively, he knew nobody could have entered without him knowing. The shadow had to be an optical illusion. He lay back down, and closed his eyes, and returned to his dreams.

However, the next time he opened his eyes, the shadow in the darkness was still there; and as he listened more closely, he heard breathing—

"Who's there!" he whispered, terrified. The shadow in the darkness seemed somehow more tangible—more threatening to reality. …But there was still only silence. His heart was thumping so loudly in his ears that he could not tell if there was still breathing coming from the far corner. He strained his eyes in the darkness, but it was pointless. He was about to shake his head and go back to sleep when the shadow seemed to move! As the soldier jumped, a pleasant American voice said:

"I am here."

The soldier could not move for a few moments—could not even breathe. His mind darted about like a wild animal. But the voice was American. Something about that reassured him; his frantic heartbeat slowed down, and he sighed, saying, "Why didn't you say anything before?"

"You were having good thoughts just now," the pleasant voice said. "I didn't want to interrupt them."

"What do you know about my thoughts?" the soldier fired back irritably. His head had begun to ache again, and he rubbed his temples now.

"We all have good thoughts when we're alone in the darkness," the pleasant voice began. "It's when we're in the light of day that our thoughts turn bad."

The soldier did not say anything for a long while. The pleasant voice disturbed him. It seemed fresh—beyond the life-sucking horrors of this place.

"…How long have you been here?" the soldier asked, thinking his cellmate must be a new arrival to the camp.

The pleasant voice chuckled in the darkness. "Time doesn't matter to us anymore, my friend."

"I guess you're right," the soldier said vaguely, but there were still alarm bells going off inside of him. He looked across the darkness again: "You must not have been here too long. You don't seem like the others."

"I'm not like the others," the pleasant voice agreed, "—but neither are you."

"I guess not," the soldier said uneasily. And then, as something occurred to him, he spoke up again, saying, "How'd you get in here without me noticing?"

"You were dreaming when they brought me in," the pleasant voice replied. He said "dreaming" not "sleeping," as though he knew the soldier's dreams had nothing to do with consciousness. The soldier frowned. Maybe if he could see the man's face he would not feel so uneasy. He remembered the man with the shiny shoes. Was it the same thing? He was not sure he had the courage to find out.

While he lay there considering these possibilities, the pleasant voice suddenly asked, "Why are *you* still here?"

"What?" the soldier asked, confused.

"Why are you still here—in this prison camp?"

"I'm a prisoner," he said, still confused.

The pleasant voice laughed. "You're allowing yourself to believe your being here—in this prison—has anything to do with men with guns, or locked doors."

The soldier did not say anything for a few seconds. "What are you saying?" he started cautiously.

"Your jailors never had any power over you—that's why they don't even bother to torture you anymore. You're waiting for someone or something to come and free you from this place, when you already have everything you need to escape."

The creepy feeling came over the soldier again. He did not know what terrified him more: the prospect that he was imagining this conversation, or the prospect that the pleasant voice might actually belong to someone. He wanted to go to sleep and forget this had ever happened. Logic told him the pleasant voice would be gone when he woke up—just like all his other fantasies. He lay down flat again, and clamped his eyes shut, willing his mind to be still. Maybe five minutes passed this way. He kept telling himself the pleasant voice was only a figment of his imagination; but after five minutes of silence, his curiosity and weakness got the better of him, and he called across the room, saying:

"Are you there?"

"I am here," the pleasant voice replied.

The soldier nodded his head uneasily, then lay down flat again. After a while, he looked across the dark expanse once more. "A side of me doesn't really believe you're there," he started. "It thinks you're something my mind made up: a voice in my head..."

There was silence from across the dark expanse; after ten uneasy seconds, the pleasant voice laughed, saying: "What worries you more, the possibility that you might be talking to someone who isn't there, or not having anyone to talk to?"

The soldier shook his head nervously: "You're too calm—too thoughtful—to be real."

The pleasant voice sniggered, but said nothing.

There was another moment of silence. The soldier's mind seemed on the verge of collapse. Yet, "...I'm glad you're here," he said at last. It was the only thing he could think to say: the only thing that seemed honest and irrefutable.

"I know you are," the pleasant voice replied, as though the statement had not needed to be said.

The soldier wondered where all this would lead. "Will you be here when I wake up?" he asked at last.

"I'll be here for as long as you think you need me," the pleasant voice replied.

"Yeah, I guess you're right," the soldier said, thinking about it the way a psychiatrist might think about his patient's delusion.

An eerie cry came from the torture hovel, and the soldier awoke with a start. An American prisoner was screaming. The soldier looked toward the door warily. The POW's screams seemed to echo in his mind, so he shook his head as if to dislodge them. When the screams began to intensify, the soldier clamped his eyes shut and began the now perfected practice of blocking out the outside world. It was only when he remembered the pleasant voice—and the improbable conversation that had passed in the darkness—that he opened his eyes again. He looked across the dark expanse anxiously. There was still nothing definite there, and he squinted—

"I am still here," the pleasant voice said.

The soldier was both relieved and disturbed…but he did not want to explore either option too deeply. "Is it morning already?" he asked in a strange, breathless voice. As he asked it, he looked toward the door, which was on the wall to his left, and perpendicular to both himself and the pleasant voice. During the day, there was usually a telltale sliver of light beneath the doorway; but now, as the soldier looked, there was nothing there. It did not occur to him that sometimes the sand accumulated beneath the door, blocking out all light—

The tortured American's cries reached a sickening pitch. The soldier clamped his eyes shut.

Sensing the soldier's reaction, the pleasant voice mused, "I'm surprised that still bothers you."

The soldier said nothing. There was really nothing to be said.

"Have you met any of the other POWs?" the pleasant voice asked now.

"No," the soldier said distractedly, still trying to get the screams out of his head.

"Really?" he said, incredulous, "—in all the time you've been here?"

"No," the soldier said again.

"You never wondered why?"

"Not really."

"The guards are afraid of you," the pleasant voice revealed. "They think you're some kind of demon—since you only stare ahead blankly when they torture you. They say you don't have a soul. That's why they keep you locked up by yourself. They don't want you around the other POWs—since you've become their hero."

"Me?" the soldier said faintly.

"The other POWs think you don't scream because you're brave. They want to be like you. The guards should have killed you a long time ago—to break the men's spirit—but even they are secretly in awe of you. You've become the object of everyone's superstitions," he said oddly. Then, in a lower voice: "The guards say they're going to save you for last. After they kill the rest of us, they're going to find a way to make you scream." Here, the pleasant voice laughed in the same odd way.

The soldier looked up warily, but said nothing. The pleasant voice resumed:

"When I heard the others talking about you, I knew your silence had nothing to do with bravery. I know you don't scream because deep down, you know you're already dead."

"...W-what?" the soldier stuttered.

"Don't be afraid of the truth."

The soldier's mind worked slowly—like a truck straining up a mountain. "You're saying this is some kind of afterlife: hell...?"

"Isn't it obvious?" the pleasant voice said plainly.

The soldier thought about. Rather, he turned his mind to all the suspicions he had ever had about his strange life. He felt sick. A cowardly instinct told him to resist everything the pleasant voice was telling him. "What makes you so sure?" he said in a tone that was equal parts combativeness and desperation.

The pleasant voice was still calm: "I know because I remember dying. I remember living another life, then dying, then coming back to life as the person I am now. I know none of this is real—just like you know it, deep down."

The soldier's mind went to the woman—to his need for her. If what the pleasant voice had said was true, and they could go from life to life, then maybe there was a mechanism to get back to the paradise in his fantasies. He looked across the dark expanse of the hovel hopefully: "Do you remember who you were...before all this?"

The pleasant voice sighed. "Bits and pieces of it." Then, as the old memories were triggered, the story came flowing out of him—like blood from an open wound. "...I was a street kid in the South Bronx," he began, "—an animal. My parents had abandoned me as a kid, so I lived in a group home. I sold drugs: I can still remember the soulless way the crackheads used to look at me. I did the deals in an abandoned building. The women would sell their bodies. Sometimes, men would whore out their own daughters and wives for the drugs. The drugs took their souls, but they took mine too, and I hated myself, and hated the crackheads for making me hate myself.

"...I'd meet these young girls. In the beginning, when they had life in them, I'd want them to take the drugs, so I could have sex with them; but after a few weeks, when the life was gone from them and they were nothing but nasty, worn-out whores, I couldn't even stand the sight of them. ...I only had one friend. We lived in that group home together. He wasn't like me, I guess, 'cause he had love in him. There was this girl in our neighborhood: one of those Catholic school girls with those pleated skirts. My friend was like a zombie every time he saw her. I don't think he ever got up the nerve to talk to her. She was going places—was into school and all that—and guys like him and me, we knew, deep down, that we weren't going anywhere.

"...I saw her one Saturday. She was carrying about five grocery bags, and was straining, so I offered to help. Regularly, a girl like her would have walked on without saying anything; but that day, she was tired from the bags—vulnerable. She had ten more blocks to walk and knew she couldn't make it. We talked about school and so on. She told me how she got accepted to college. I tricked her. I offered her some candy after we had walked a few blocks. I guess by then she didn't want to seem rude, so she took it. It was laced with drugs, of course. After walking a short way, I could tell it was affecting her. She didn't know where she was—what was going on…I led her to the abandoned building. Once I got her in there, I started stripping her. She was out of it—dazed. I had her lying on the same pissed-stained mattress I used to fuck all the other crackheads. I had her down to her panties and bra. With the drugs in her, her face was peaceful. …That was the thing that got to me. She was like an angel. The sight of her turned my stomach—especially knowing how my friend felt about her. I saw her at last. She was beautiful, man—beautiful and clean…full of life and ambition, and I saw myself crouched over her like a vulture. I hated myself then: hated myself fully. I put her clothes back on, ashamed. And then I ran. I just ran out of there, leaving her on that mattress.

"When I couldn't run anymore, I walked—but I was still trapped in my ugly neighborhood. Burned-out buildings, crackhouses, slums. That was my life—my *future*. …And then I saw my friend on the next block. He saw me, and waved, but I knew I would never be able to face him again. I had ruined everything. There was a diner on that block. I ducked into it to avoid my friend. I wanted to die right then, and I guess it was fate, because the manager was one of those old-time gangsta niggas who kept a loaded shot-gun under the counter. There was a story in the neighborhood about how he had gunned down a kid who tried to rob him. I had a replica handgun—a pellet gun I used to scare the crackheads when they tried to act stupid. I didn't want to live anymore, so I pulled it out and waved it in the air. I figured the manager would blow me away on the spot, but he was stunned. Lots of times, reputations are mostly nonsense: myths. The manager was nothing but a helpless old man after all. He was practically crying when he handed me the money from the cash register, and so I hated myself even more.

"When I left the diner, my friend was still across the street. The entire robbery had probably taken less than thirty seconds. My friend was watching me curiously. When he saw me come out of there with that replica gun, he froze. I ran. All I could think about was getting away from him and every-thing. When I saw those police cars coming up the block, I saw my chance to escape. ...I waved the gun again, and they gunned me down—took my life—and I was happy for it.

"I *died*," he said for emphasis, "and then the next thing I knew, I was floating in light. Everywhere I looked, there were these scenes: glimpses of other lives I've had. The longer I stayed there, the more I felt my old life fading away. All my old memories began to disappear; new memories took their place. Instead of crackhouses and urban slums, I saw myself growing up in the suburbs. I had parents and a family: people who loved me... I should have been happy, but I still remembered what I had done to my friend and that girl, so I still hated myself. How I got here, to this war, is another long story, but behind it all is hate, and his will."

The soldier had been listening as if in a trance, but he came out of it as the pleasant voice said those last words. "*Whose* will?" he asked, his mind unraveling.

"The one who sent me here to find you."

"*Sent* you?" he said, frowning.

"Yeah: none of this is random. You realize that, don't you?"

The soldier nodded his head. Then, while a sense of panic built itself up inside of him, the logical question occurred to him: "Who sent you?"

"You really don't know?" the pleasant voice asked, genuinely surprised.

"No," he said, almost feeling ashamed of his ignorance.

The pleasant voice took a deep breath. "Think back to how you got here. Somewhere along the way, a man showed up to guide you. He popped out of nowhere, told you something, then disappeared."

When the soldier remembered the man with the shiny shoes, he shuddered. "...You're saying that man sent you here?"

"Yes," the pleasant voice said simply. "I met him a few weeks ago. My unit and I were on a mission. We raided a compound, capturing some militants. After we had secured the place and were winding down, I looked out the window and noticed a date tree in the backyard. There was a full moon out, and for whatever reason, the entire scene drew me in—called to me. I found myself going to the tree. When I was out there by myself, a man popped out of nowhere. I looked up and he was there. I stared at him for a while before I realized I couldn't see his face. I stared at it, but I couldn't focus. And then, the man started to speak. He said if I lagged back at our next mission, I'd find you. He said we needed one another."

"Why?" the soldier asked reflexively.

"I don't know. I guess I should have asked, but as soon as he was finished, he disappeared. I thought I was going crazy. I didn't tell anyone about it. I didn't know what to think…but at the next mission, I stayed in the back and watched the rest of the men in my unit run into a building. A moment later, it exploded with them in it. The blast threw me to the ground—knocked me out. …When I started to regain consciousness, the militants realized I was still alive, so they brought me here. Even then, none of it made any sense to me until I heard the other POWs talking about you. I asked the guards to put me in here with you. I guess they sensed we were the same."

The soldier lay there numbly. "Why is this happening?" he said at last.

"Are you a Christian?" the pleasant voice asked abruptly.

"I guess," the soldier replied, wary of where this might lead.

"Lately, I've been thinking about everything that's happened to me. It's like we're minor characters in a Bible story: the people who suffer and sin and sacrifice their souls so that Jesus can come off looking good."

Something about the words left the soldier queasy and anxious—

"We're God's playthings," the pleasant voice resumed, "—nothing but actors playing the roles he's picked out for us. He's watching us—feeding off our sufferings."

The pleasant voice's blasphemies made the soldier nervous. Even while he felt the truth within himself, he was desperate not to believe. His mind groped about for something to contradict everything the pleasant voice had told him. Desperate, he blurted out, "—But he saved you from the bomb that killed the rest of your unit. He saved me, too!"

The pleasant voice laughed at his stupidity. "Look around you. Is this what you call 'saved'? He saves us from death today so that we can suffer tomorrow. He only 'saves' us so that he can damn us."

The soldier swallowed to try to lubricate his parched throat. His mind went back to the man with the shiny shoes: "You're saying that man was *God*?"

"I don't know if he's *the* God, or just our God. The only thing I know is that he controls all this. We're jumping from one life to another, and he controls where we go and what we remember. That's how he damns us—by controlling what we remember and what we know. Showing us the future and the past is only another way of controlling us."

"But *why?*" the soldier said in frustration, still unable to grasp the grand picture. "Why is he doing this?"

"I already told you: We're the minor characters in a Bible story—"

"But *what*—"

The pleasant voice shushed him. "...Do you remember the Last Supper from the Bible, when Jesus realized He was about to die, and He told the Disciples one of them would betray Him?"

"I guess," the soldier said, struggling to keep up.

"Jesus said the man who betrayed Him would be damned, and I always found that strange. Why would Jesus, Who came to earth to save us from damnation—and Who forgave even those who crucified and mocked Him on the cross—damn His own disciple? His premonition wasn't really a warning to the betrayer, because He knew His words would not change Judas' act. His actual words were '...woe unto that man by whom the Son of man is betrayed! It had been good for that man if he had not been born. (Matthew 26:24, *King James Version*)' I looked up the words, myself—*memorized* them. There was no other purpose to Jesus' prophecy than to plant the seed of damnation in Judas' mind. Remember how it turned out?" the pleasant voice asked rhetorically. "When Jesus' premonition came to pass, all that was left to Judas was death—suicide. By showing Judas the future, Jesus damned him. Yet, without Judas' betrayal, there would be no Christianity: no crucifixion; no resurrection. To be the Savior of the human race, Jesus had to damn Judas; and just like Judas' betrayal of Jesus was the lynchpin of Christianity, our sins give strength and power to our God.

"The more he gives us glimpses of our future and past lives, the more we hate ourselves. Remember what I told you about my life as a drug dealer? He *let* me remember that. He let me take that with me into this life, so I'd continue to hate myself. The more we hate ourselves, the greater his power... just like Jesus and Judas."

"…How can you know these things?" the soldier said feebly.

"Maybe I only know them because he wishes me to know. It's likely the only reason he sent me here was to push you down the path—to damn you further. On the other hand, maybe together, we can outwit him. We can succeed where Judas failed. Judas was trapped by time. He listened to Jesus and allowed himself to be damned. That's the key to it all: God doesn't strike down people on the spot anymore: He sets them on the path to damnation. He gives them glimpses of heaven and hell, and manipulates them into damning themselves. But if we ignore His premonitions, and get off His designated path, we can outwit the grand designs of God!"

The soldier instinctively shuddered at the heresy. He felt queasy and exhausted. He wanted to lie down again, but:

"Now is the time for us to act," the pleasant voice encouraged him.

The soldier's mind felt shredded; he groaned—

"Even if you sit here in the darkness, waiting for your turn to be shot in the head, it won't end," the pleasant voice revealed. "You'll start this all over again, in some stranger's body, thinking someone else's thoughts."

"What do you want me to do?" the soldier said in frustration.

"It's all simple," the pleasant voice began. "I figured out the hole in his trap," he said excitedly. "When we die, and switch lives, we forget everything. That's when we're free from him. Maybe we're already damned, but when we die and forget it all, at least we don't *know* we're damned!"

The pleasant voice began to laugh now. It was a horrible, cackling laugh: the laugh of a madman. The soldier shuddered, bewildered that he had allowed himself to believe in the man's madness. He again wanted to close his eyes and forget everything that had happened, but the door suddenly banged open. The sound was like an explosion; the soldier jumped back, terrified…and the sunlight was so blinding that he could practically feel the pain in his brain. Out of the glare, two jailors appeared. The soldier reflexively put up his hand to shield his face. However, when he looked up, he saw the jailors going toward the other side of the hovel; and as he stared in amazement, he saw the jailors haul up the man who was there. The pleasant voice actually belonged to someone. The pleasant voice belonged to a living, breathing human being. The soldier and the man with the pleasant voice seemed stunned when they saw one another. Rather, they were stunned when they recognized one another. Somehow, the pleasant voice belonged to the man with the bloodshot eyes! Before the soldier could say anything, the jailors dragged the man out of the hovel, slamming the door behind them. The soldier's heart beat mercilessly. He realized this was the moment he had been reliving since the man with the bloodshot eyes touched him in the wood. The man was going to be shot now. Outside the hovel, the man began to scream. All the other times this scene played in the soldier's mind, the man's scream had been a reflection of unimaginable terror. Now, as the soldier lay in the darkness, listening to the scream, he suddenly discerned the defiance within it. The man with the bloodshot eyes was going through with his plan to outwit the grand design of their god—*whatever it was*—

The lone gunshot echoed through the camp…and then the horrible silence. …The soldier could not move—could not breathe. By then, the only thing he could do was stare blankly into the darkness.

Outside the hovel, there was still the same horrible silence. The man with the bloodshot eyes had actually been there! That impossible fact exhausted even more of his energy and will, and he lay down flat on the ground to rest. He had to remember what the man had tried to show him, but he could not get his mind around what had just happened! If the man with the bloodshot eyes was real, then nothing was impossible. If the things the man had said were true, then nothing was keeping the soldier within this hovel but the limits of his imagination. Moreover, if death was irrelevant, then the woman was still out there, somewhere. Suddenly hopeful, the soldier tried to will himself to be somewhere else—anywhere else. He tried to will his secret wood to appear; he conjured thoughts of his family with a newfound desperation…but nothing happened. He felt weak and frustrated after his strange efforts; and just then, another tortured American began to scream elsewhere in the prison camp. After a gunshot interrupted the American's screams, there was again the horrible silence. The soldier remembered: he had to die before he could switch lives; the jailors were going to kill all the other prisoners, then they would come to him, and torture him until he screamed…and then he would die. He prepared himself.

That was when he saw something in the far corner. It was like an illuminated puff of smoke. He blinked deeply, hoping to clear up his vision, and then he saw it for an instant: the cat! It was briefly in focus, and then it faded back into the darkness. The soldier's head ached from the effort required to focus, but he forced himself to concentrate. Amazingly, after a few fitful starts, the cat appeared in the corner once more. It was the same white cat: so white that the darkness was no match against it. He was crawling up to it now: over the slab of wood covering the latrine, and toward the corner of the hovel, where the pleasant voice had been.

It was actually the cat! He could hardly believe it. He was stretching out his hand now. Even in the darkness, he could see the clear blue of its eyes. He was amazed when he actually touched the cat. He was expecting something to happen—an explosion or some other contrivance—to keep him from touching the thing that had been systematically guiding his journey through this wasteland. The cat's fur was so soft it seemed slick. Its purring intensified as he sat there petting it. Logically, he knew the cat could not be real. The only thing that could allow the cat to be there was his imagination. As he went to pick it up, his hand touched the wall; and to his astonishment, the wall crumbled as his hand brushed against it. The wall was incredibly brittle in that corner. He could shove his fingers into it and pull away whole handfuls of earth. The third time he shoved his fingers into the wall, he saw a small aperture of light. He had already dug through the wall! Astounded, he bent down and looked out of the aperture, at the outside world. It was the same limitless expanse of desert, with the heat waves rising off the sand dunes in the distance.

Remembering the cat, he turned from the aperture and again looked around the hovel. However, the cat was gone. He tried to will it to reappear, but the trick would not work this time. At first, this disturbed him, but nothing could really surprise him anymore. He returned to the crumbling wall. He used both hands to dig now, so that the hole was soon big enough for him to crawl through. He was not actually thinking about freedom as he slipped through the hole. In a sense, he was acting more out of curiosity than anything else. He wanted to see what was going to happen next: what new adventures and horrors his imagination was going to reveal. Even if there was no cat, he wanted to see how far his delusions and hallucinations would take him into the abyss.

Either way, the fresh air called to him. He breathed deeply and felt it cleansing him. For those first few moments, when he was outside of the hovel, shielding his eyes from the blinding afternoon sun, he just lay there taking deep breaths. A side of him was content to stay there—even at the risk of the prison guards spotting him—but then he heard one of the prisoners of war screaming out from the torture hovel. Something about those screams called to him, so that he got groggily to his feet. He moved as if being guided by an invisible force. The POW's screams started out low, and then reached a pitch that made the soldier think a jagged stick were being shoved into his own eardrums. After a few moments of rest, during which time the soldier could hear the torturers laughing in the background or screaming taunts, the prisoner started screaming again, and the soldier had to brace himself as that implausible pitch was reached. He had to walk around to the other side of his hovel in order to get to the torture hovel; as he was about to turn the corner, he first smelled cigarette smoke, and then he heard someone laugh. He darted back. It was a guard. The man was leaning against the hovel leisurely, smoking a cigarette and laughing at the prisoner's cries. Something about this realization outraged the soldier, so that before he was even aware of it, he charged around the corner. He had lost weight and power over the months of his imprisonment, but an unknown force gave him strength. He balled his hand into a fist, slamming it into the guard's face. The man had gasped in surprise; as a consequence, the cigarette was shoved down his throat. Even as the man crumbled to the ground, the soldier's hands were already around his neck. The man tried to cough—to do anything to bring the burning cigarette up his throat—but the soldier's grip was unbreakable—

"Stop laughing!" the soldier whispered as he strangled the man. He was not whispering because he feared being overheard, but because he was dehydrated. He was amazed by his strength. He probably crouched there strangling the guard for a minute or two; but in his disjointed mind, the entire thing passed in seconds. And then, when the guard lay dead on the ground, with his mouth hanging open, and the cigarette smoke wafting out of his throat eerily, the soldier took the man's Kalashnikov in hand, and walked toward the torture hovel. He walked boldly—without trying to hide. He kicked the door in, so that it banged open, and then he fired the gun at the torturers. There were two of them over the screaming American. The men yelled something at him, but he did not notice as he dispensed his justice and allowed his senses to be ravaged by the ever more disjointed passage of time. When the torturers were dead, he freed the disoriented prisoner. Unfortunately, as the man was unable to differentiate friend from foe at this point, he merely scurried into the corner. The soldier left the man to his demons, and went for the door. When he got outside, he saw more militants running toward him. They fired at him, and he fired back at them. Maybe two or three minutes passed like this. After he managed to kill them, he hobbled around to the remaining hovels, freeing his fellow captives. Most of them were so wild with freedom that they set off for the sand dunes at once, not even bothering to look back, or to thank him. Even the man he had freed from the torturers was revived by now. The man limped behind his fleeing countrymen, leaving the soldier standing alone.

The soldier watched them disappear over the sand dunes, then he looked up and saw the vultures; and then the cat was there, reminding him of everything that had happened and everything that was possible. However, in the end, he realized he had been shot, and that death was near, so he lay down flat and closed his eyes. Remembering everything the man with the bloodshot eyes had told him, he embraced death and willed his mind to take him to the woman.

—Book Two—

THE END OF TIME

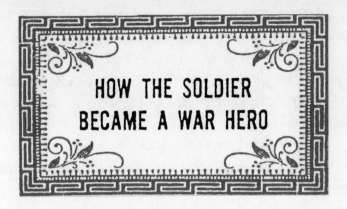

HOW THE SOLDIER BECAME A WAR HERO

The soldier entered the dimension of light. It was exactly as he remembered, and exactly as the man with the bloodshot eyes had told him. Looking around, he saw all those scenes of his past lives and past sufferings. Soon, he felt his old memories leaving him. His life in the cul-de-sac, and his parents' faces, and the wood…everything began to leave him. It was like being eviscerated. He told himself to let it all go, and to concentrate on holding onto the truths that would help him in the next life. He willed the woman to be with him. He conjured the paradise he had experienced with her; but as the old memories left him, he still felt as though his guts were being torn out. He tried to keep it together, and concentrate on the woman, but he was being ripped apart. He could feel tendons snapping, bones cracking…

And then, strange memories began to fill him up. He saw himself growing up on the streets of the South Bronx. The surrounding neighborhood was a sinkhole of poverty and hopelessness: a gray world, where darkness and light had come to a horrible stalemate. After a few seconds, he realized he was the friend the pleasant voice had described when talking of his previous life. They had grown up in the group home together, and fought side-by-side, until the man with the bloodshot eyes gave in to self-hate and provoked the police into gunning him down.

The soldier saw it all now: the sickening scene of his friend's death. His mind rebelled against the new memories—as if his soul were trying to vomit up a poison. But one of the memories called to him. The girl had been in the gray world with him—the same girl from the pit. From time to time, he would see her waiting at a bus stop in her Catholic school uniform. Even in the gray world, he had always loved her—even though he had never actually talked to her. Day after day he would see her at the bus stop. With her prim uniform and beauty, she had always seemed beyond him. She had seemed driven and ambitious, whereas his own life had seemed pointless. ...He had tried to approach her once, but the bus had come just as he was about to make his move. She had stepped onto the bus without even looking in his direction, and a side of him had been relieved. She had ignored all the other boys in the neighborhood. More than that, she had crushed them with her eyes and silence; and in time, the boys had learned to leave her alone, and to turn instead to the droves of "hoochie mamas," who switched their hips to devastating effect when they sensed the eyes of a potential lover...

The day his friend committed suicide, he had gone back to the group home as if in a trance. Everyone had been talking about it; and then, a few hours later, when the soldier was already on the edge of an emotional precipice, a new story had begun to circulate the neighborhood. A girl's body had been found in a crackhouse. Some crackheads had come upon her while she was unconscious, and they had had their way with her, until the only thing to be done was to stick a knife in her and put her out of her misery. When the young soldier allowed his mind to accept the fact that the girl they found was *his* girl, he had plunged over the edge of the precipice—

The pain in his gut intensified. He screamed out again; but as he looked about desperately, he saw he had re-entered the darkness. Either way, he still felt himself coming apart—as if the cul-de-sac and the gray world were fighting for supremacy within him. It was a bloody civil war, with no clear winner. Years seemed to pass. When he was beginning to think he would be trapped in this nowhere place forever, he opened his eyes and saw he had been returned to the real world. At first, he was so stunned that he looked out on the world without seeing it; he listened to the sounds in the air without hearing them. Nothing was really registering in his mind. ...Then, as if a switch had been flipped, and his nerve endings were suddenly turned on, he found himself gasping from the most excruciating pain he had ever felt.

It was as though his body had been hacked into pieces, and then sewn back together. He could feel the stitches holding his flesh together; his bones felt shattered; he instinctively tried to look and take stock of his body, but the surrounding glare was too powerful. His eyes burned and watered, so he clamped them shut and lay there twitching involuntarily from the pain—

"Shut up!" a crazed voice screamed. In fact, someone had been screaming those words all along. That was what had awakened him. Each word seemed like an explosion, so that he began to believe the crazed man was screaming directly into his ear. The screams were coming from his left, but the soldier was too incapacitated by pain to move. After a few seconds of preparation, he opened his eyes again. The glare did not seem as overpowering as the first time. Still, he grimaced and had to blink rapidly in order to soothe the pain and accustom his eyes to the light—

"Shut up!"

The soldier turned his head to the left, staring blankly as he watched a man squirming on a bed. The man seemed to be covered with bandages. As the soldier looked closely, he saw the man was missing his lower left arm, and was flailing the bandaged nub in the air. The man's face was not bandaged, but it was a bright orange color—either from some kind of allergy or a burn…most likely the latter. Considering the way the suffering man's eyes roamed the room, he seemed insane. Something about looking at the man seemed indecent, so the soldier looked away—

"Shut up!"

The soldier had a flashback of all that had happened in the war zone—all the improbable things the pleasant voice had revealed to him. He closed his eyes again, and grunted—

Several people ran into the room, and up to the suffering man's bed. The soldier opened his eyes and looked at it all uneasily. He had to reacquaint himself with notions like "room" and "bed"…and "doctor" and "hospital." All these things came back to him. The emergency medical team did not notice him as they tried to calm the suffering man. The soldier looked at them for a while, but as watching the suffering man again seemed unseemly, he looked elsewhere. His bed faced the door. As the upper half of that wall was composed of glass, he could see into the hallway. Nurses and orderlies were wheeling patients down the hall. It occurred to the soldier this was a military hospital: all the nurses and doctors were in uniform; the wretched-looking patients seemed to be soldiers and marines.

Now that the soldier's eyes had gotten used to the glare, he looked at his body for the first time. He, too, was covered with bandages. Complicated equipment was connected to him—intravenous tubes and sensors. As his mind reeled, he remembered his final moments of consciousness: lying down on the sand to have his last fitful dreams of the woman. It all came flooding back, and his mind struggled to digest what had happened. As far as he could tell, he was still alive—still living his old life. Somehow, he must have been rescued from the desert. He did not know how it was possible, but he could see no other explanation.

The suffering man was still screaming for someone or something to shut up. The medical team was screaming as well—either at the man or amongst themselves. Orderlies held the man down gruffly, so that it almost seemed as if they were throttling him; and then, after the sedative had been administered, the man's cries faded away to whimpers, before there was at last silence. Everyone seemed to sigh in relief. On his bed, the soldier closed his eyes. There was nothing more to see, and he was tired of seeing. He took stock of his body again. The saline drip, or whatever concoction of drugs they were feeding him intravenously, felt cold as it entered him. He could feel it within his veins, gradually losing its cold edge as it dissipated in his blood stream. The places where he had been shot were now hypersensitive. As he still feared the slightest movement would cause all his stitches to burst, he tried not to breathe too deeply, or to move too abruptly—

Someone else burst into the room, causing the door hinges to squeak. The entrant stopped after he took two steps into the room. There was a moment of uncomfortable silence; and then, "They said someone in here was having 'an episode.'"

"Yes, Colonel—we sedated him."

"Again?" the Colonel said in an annoyed tone.

"This isn't a psychiatric hospital," the doctor retorted. "My first priority is to keep these men safe and alive."

"Every military hospital is a psychiatric hospital, Captain," the Colonel corrected him, "—that's the nature of war." And then, after the tense silence, "How am I supposed to treat him if you drug him every time he regains consciousness?"

"He was ranting again."

"...Still yelling for someone to shut up?"

"Yes, sir."

The Colonel sighed. "How long will he be unconscious this time?"

"The rest of the night."

"When he wakes up, call me."

"Understood."

Through all this, nobody noticed the soldier had regained consciousness—probably because he kept his eyes closed. For hours afterward (or so it seemed to him), he replayed the words of the conversation in his mind. In time, he again turned his mind to the woman. Like before, he saw himself making love to her in the cramped apartment, experiencing the pleasure that had been set aside for the gods...

"Shut up!" the suffering man screamed. The soldier opened his eyes momentarily—a reflex action. However, remembering where he was, and knowing there was nothing in the room he needed to see, he closed his eyes and lay there, drifting on the current of pain. Even after the emergency medical team ran into the room again, he kept his eyes closed—not out of subterfuge, but because he was not really interested. The suffering man's yelling was an annoyance in the background—like the screams of the American prisoners of war had been before. In passing, he wondered what had happened to the POWs he had freed into the desert. He concluded the men must have made it to safety and sent help back for him. That was a good enough explanation for him, so he let all his unanswered questions fade back into the nothingness—

The Colonel ran into the room once more. The soldier's eyes were still closed, but he recognized the man's voice. The Colonel began to ask the suffering man a series of inane questions, like, "Whom do you want to shut up?" To each of his questions, the suffering man would only scream "Shut up!" louder; and after listening to this for a few minutes, the soldier felt like screaming "Shut up!" himself.

In time, the Colonel/psychiatrist made his diagnosis, and the sedative was administered to the patient. As the suffering man's screams began to subside, the soldier realized if the doctors knew he was conscious, they would give him something for his own pain. He merely had to ask, but that would have taken too much effort somehow. On top of that, the thought of the psychiatrist asking him inane questions made his blood run cold. The only thing he wanted for now was to revel in the nothingness for a while.

Eventually, he slept. In the dream, he was with the woman, making love. His tongue went to her bare breasts, tracing the edge of her pert areolas. He liked the taste of her sweat, and the way she moaned when he did things to her body. Everything about her tuned him on, so that he felt like a hungry animal, ready to devour every inch of her. Her thighs were strong and taught. The smell of her when he parted her thighs was like a sea breeze. He inhaled deeply, his body already trembling from the anticipation of pleasure. When he lowered himself onto her, they both gasped at the sensation. Her body rose to meet his, and they became one—

But the dream or recollection ended abruptly. When he was returned to the real world, the hunger was still in him. It was like a kind of madness, blinding him. Initially, he had no idea where he was. It was only after ten or so seconds of looking around that he realized he was in the same hospital room as before; but even then, his hunger for the woman was like a madness within him. He checked the corners of the room, searching for her—

A nurse entered the room to check his chart. She gasped when she saw him sitting up. The soldier ignored her, and continued to scan the room for the object of his love.

The nurse ran up to him. "Can you understand me?" she demanded. There was a euphoric grin on her face. He groaned in annoyance, because she was blocking his view of the room. He craned his neck to see around her, still hoping that the woman of his dreams and fantasies might be there to satisfy his hunger…but at last, when he saw the woman was not there, he looked up at the nurse. By now, she had put her hands on his shoulders and seemed on the verge of shaking him in order to get his attention. When she again asked him if he could understand her, he sighed and whispered that he could. The nurse's grin broadened, and she ran out of the room.

The soldier sat back in bed. At first, he merely felt frustrated, but when he realized the nurse had gone to fetch others, a wary feeling came over him. He would be forced to interact with people again—to defer to the wills of the men who had power over him. He wondered if spending so much time alone in the hovel had made him antisocial. His eyes went to the glass portion of the opposite wall. More dazed men were being wheeled past; one skeleton-looking man shuffled by, pushing his intravenous drip before him on a stand, as if the thing were a dance partner.

…And then, the nurse came running back, leading what seemed to be a stampeding herd of officers/doctors. They burst into the room, all wearing amazed grins. Charts and vital signs were consulted. Frenzied questions were asked, most of which the soldier did not have the patience to decipher. The news of his awakening spread throughout the hospital, like an infectious disease. Through the windowed portion of the far wall, the soldier saw other patients and soldiers congregating in the hallway, in order to get a look at him. Generals and colonels came running into the room like little boys desperate to share in a secret. When they saw the thing was true—that their war hero was conscious—they laughed amongst themselves and shook hands with one another. As the soldier lay there, their faces all blurred into one grinning monstrosity.

Once the chief doctor had established his health, a general took over the commentary, rambling on about the soldier's heroism, and the hunger of America to find out more about him. The general's skin had a leathery consistency, and was of an unlikely complexion—somewhere between gray and green. The man said something then, and everyone burst into applause. Even in the hallway, they were applauding. As the soldier watched them, he grimaced at the prospect of all he would have to endure—all the things still hidden in the shadows. He remembered the man with the bloodshot eyes, and the things the man had said about their damnation. The soldier did not know how much of that he believed, but he instinctively knew something horrible was on the horizon. In fact, as he looked around, he saw he was not merely a soldier anymore—*he was a war hero*. Their cheering ate away at him. The people around him were supposedly his friends and countrymen, but for some unknown reason, he was terrified—

"Don't worry, son," the general with the unlikely complexion said, seeing the war hero's expression. "You're safe now. You're in Germany. We're just stabilizing your wounds before we send you home to America."

The war hero stared at him blankly, but then nodded his head. He was finally away from the war zone. *...Home to America*. The phrase stuck in his mind. He thought about his parents and the cul-de-sac. His life in Long Island did not seem real anymore; but at that moment, he wanted it to be real. He wanted something that would not fade away or be changed by the vicissitudes of his imagination. He wanted a loving family and a home over his head. He was tired of wandering wastelands and chasing after fantasies. The woman was still everything to him; but like all fantasies, she was frustrating and unreliable. For once, he wanted to turn away from fantasies and dreams, and embrace the mundane, everyday blessings of life. He took a deep, cleansing breath: maybe the nightmare was over at last. He would be home with his family soon, and then maybe he could put all this behind him, like all the delusions of war. When he smiled, the people in the room began to cheer once more. Even in the hallway, people were clapping. The war hero surrendered to it. His smile grew wider, and he found himself chuckling—despite the pain this caused in his chest and abdomen—

"Okay, let's give him some rest," a commanding voice suddenly yelled above the celebration. The man had stood on the periphery all that time, observing the war hero. While everyone else had cheered and grinned at the blessing of their war hero's awakening, the man had stood staring at him, devouring every last detail of his movements. The man's eyes were a unique shade of blue—a kind of opalescent purple; and even though he only seemed to be in his mid-forties at the most, deep rivulets of wrinkles shot out from the corners of his eyes, as if he spent all his time squinting. The man's jet-black hair was unusually long for a military officer, actually touching his collar; and from the man's commanding voice, the war hero immediately recognized him as the Colonel—the psychiatrist who had diagnosed the suffering man. At the psychiatrist's order, all the commotion within the room ceased, and the well-wishers began to file out grimly, like children who had been told to go to bed. The psychiatrist stood by the door until everyone else had left, then he closed the blinds on the far wall, so the people in the hallway could no longer gawk at the war hero.

"We'll talk in the morning," the psychiatrist said at last, smiling abruptly, so that all the rivulets at the corners of his eyes stood out prominently. The effect was ghastly, and the war hero nodded absentmindedly before closing his eyes.

In the morning, the suffering man was taken away—more likely than not, to a better-equipped psychiatric hospital. In his place, they put a comatose man whose legs and eyes had been lost in an explosion. The soldier woke up at the sound of the commotion. A nurse came to change his bandages. Somehow, her youthfulness reminded him of the woman from the desert, and this disturbed him a little—since he was still desperate to put his fantasies behind him. The nurse kept smiling at him, and making comments about how he was healing well.

After the young nurse left, he was left in peace for a moment; but within minutes, an orderly wheeled in a tray containing an unidentifiable gelatinous swill. The war hero ate it slowly, amazed by how heavy his arms seemed: how weak he was. After the swill was cleared away, and the war hero began to think he would sleep at last, the young nurse returned to take him to his physical therapy session.

Getting out of bed, and into the wheelchair, was so arduous that a side of him wondered if he would ever be able to walk again. Maybe it was only then he considered the extent of his injuries. The pain alternated between dull aches and sharp pangs—which grew more intense when he moved the wrong way. As such, his first movements were tentative: he had to discover what the right and wrong movements were. He was seeing stars before his eyes by the time the young nurse was finally able to maneuver him into the wheelchair.

All he needed was to get his strength back. That was what the young nurse kept repeating. In the hallway, he saw the devastation of war for himself: more soldiers with missing limbs; wards with bed-ridden wretches, who stared into space blankly, seeing all that was lost to them. The soldier tried conjuring images of home. He needed something real and good to counter everything he saw. He asked the young nurse about calling his parents, but she only looked at him oddly, before telling him the doctor would take care of it...

The physical therapist was a middle-aged woman with muscular arms (but an otherwise plump body). He asked her about calling his parents, but she only gave him a strange, noncommittal smile and told him he should talk to the doctor about it. After that, she exhorted him to torture himself for two hours. Joints and limbs that had grown stiff over the months were flexed and twisted. "Pain is the key to life!" she kept repeating: he could either challenge and defeat the pain now, or become a victim of it for the rest of his life.

By the time he was wheeled back to his hospital room, this time by an orderly, a layer of clammy sweat covered him. He felt butchered: parts of his body were either numb or hypersensitive, as if in shock. Yet, as the physical therapist had said, the promise of life seemed to lie beyond the pain...

He closed his eyes as soon as he was back in bed. However, as he was about to doze, the door burst open. The psychiatrist and the general with the unlikely complexion entered the room. After these men, there were two junior officers, who wheeled in a stand with multimedia equipment. The sight of their uniforms (and their smiling faces) brought him back to the reality that he was still a soldier in the Army—and that his life and dreams were to be deferred to other men's wills.

While he was thinking this, the general with the unlikely complexion went on another of his long rants about courage and the American way of life. The war hero wanted to ask about his parents; but by now, the question made his guts clench, so he kept silent and waited for the thing to reveal itself. The psychiatrist was still staring at him with those opalescent purple eyes.

At last, the multimedia presentation began. The soldier was shown some footage from American television networks. The story of his heroism and awakening was being talked about like a sign from God. The commentators in the media were awed by fact he had single-handedly killed five prison guards and freed twenty prisoners of war. These things had all been relegated to the back of the war hero's mind—with all the other useless information. He searched his recollections now, trying to corroborate the things he had done with the things being praised in the footage. He remembered how he had killed that first guard: how the man's laughter had awakened an insane impulse in him. He remembered how his hands had felt around the man's neck; he remembered how he had gone around as if in a trance, killing the other guards. ...As much as he wanted to believe his murderous outburst had been triggered by some sense of justice, or by courage, he knew it had merely been a soulless act. After freeing the other POWs, he had not run along with them, because their freedom had meant nothing to him. He had not shared in their joy at being released, nor had he had dreams of returning to those he loved. The only thing that had driven and sustained him was death.

Presently, as the footage from America played, the general began talking about how much America needed him—especially as things were not going so well in the war zone. The men he had freed from the prison camp had arrived in America a week ago. There were images of them waving to crowds of hundreds of thousands as they had parades in their various towns. They were the emissaries of a new religion, in which the war hero was the guru and holy warrior all combined in one. In a war that had gone horribly wrong, he was to be an emblem of hope for Americans. An uneasy public, which could no longer believe in the myths of spreading democracy and rewriting civilization in their own image, could easily believe in him; and maybe, as they cheered for him, their misgivings would fade away. He would be like a mother's lullaby, chasing away the scary dreams of little children. He saw all this in a moment of clarity, and lay there frozen by the weight of the thing.

...He missed the woman. The idea of her—and the idea that she was still alive somewhere, waiting for him to come to her—was a panacea for all his wounds and newfound burdens. Maybe such thoughts were unhealthy—in the same way that an alcoholic's yearning for a drink was unhealthy—but the key to getting well was acknowledging his needs and yearnings. ...He had been thinking about her all day; a side of him had been asking for his parents so they could drive her away. In their absence, the woman had been taking over—reclaiming her place at the center of his universe. And would it not be great if she were out there somewhere—if she were beyond death and the effects of time? Yes, such things were impossible, but what was the point of being sane when one was unhappy?

On the screen, the people of America were still celebrating—still allowing themselves to believe the bestial acts committed in their names were things to be praised, rather than evidence they had all lost their minds. As he watched the screen, there was something in the cheering that made him panic inside. He sensed a dark power at work. With every cheer, he felt himself fading away, as if they were draining his soul—

He clamped his eyes shut. He felt doomed. Soon, he would be back in America—just like the other prisoners of war. He, too, would become a puppet in the farce, jumping about ridiculously as his masters pulled his strings. When his eyes returned to the screen, there was footage from a morning talk show. Several prisoners of war were talking about their miraculous rescue. The war hero tried to remember the men's faces, but they were strangers to him—even as they described the details of his act. One of them was supposedly the man he had freed from the torturers. As the man described how the war hero had burst into the hovel and killed the torturers, the man began to cry. The beautiful interviewer patted him on the shoulder and hugged him—as did his fellow POWs. The war hero grimaced and averted his eyes from the screen. When he looked up, he saw the psychiatrist was still staring at him intently. The man had been watching him all that time; when the war hero made eye contact with him, the psychiatrist smiled his ghastly smile once again—

What the hell you looking at! the war hero thought. A side of him wanted to spring at the man and claw at those penetrating eyes...but he knew this impulse was only a by-product of his powerlessness. His body and soul belonged to America. Even though he was a war hero, he would still have to be a good soldier. With this awareness, he nodded his head.

The presentation came to an end. The general and junior officers clapped at its conclusion; the psychiatrist went over to the equipment and ejected the disc. The general shook the war hero's hand again; the junior officers followed suit, then they exited the room, leaving the war hero alone with the psychiatrist. The man was still standing by the multimedia equipment, staring at the war hero.

"Now it's time to get you prepared," the psychiatrist announced.

"Prepared for what?" the war hero asked.

"For the media—for America."

The war hero thought about it for a few seconds. Then, as if some conclusion had been reached in his mind, he nodded. "I understand, sir."

"Good. Before we get started, is there is anything you would like to talk about?"

"Nothing in particular, sir."

"Let's talk about your stay in the prison camp."

"Okay, sir."

"How long were you held captive?"

"I don't know, sir."

"You have no guess?"

"Some months?"

"Oh?"

The war hero shrugged.

"How many months, by your calculations?"

"...I don't know," he said, suddenly annoyed with this game, "—six, maybe?"

"I see." The man sighed dramatically then, and a sorrowful expression came over his face. "Loss of time is one of the after-effects of captivity."

"Sir?"

He sighed again. "As best as we can figure, you were only in that prison camp for three weeks, soldier."

"Oh," the war hero said, his face blank. He looked down at his arm: examined a tube feeding drugs into his veins.

"Everyone else in your unit died on the night the base was bombed. That was five weeks ago," the psychiatrist explained, "—and you've been in this hospital for two weeks. That leaves a gap of three weeks. The base bombing was a big story in the news. The enemy won a victory over us that night, managing to kill thousands of soldiers. It was assumed everyone in your unit was killed. Naturally, when we learned you were not only still alive, but had freed your fellow prisoners of war, America began to celebrate."

There was silence. The psychiatrist was expecting him to say something, but he only stared ahead.

"…You have nothing to be ashamed of, soldier," the psychiatrist went on, taking the war hero's silence for embarrassment. "Life in a prison camp can make anyone lose track of time," he went on. "The torture must have been horrible."

"I guess so, sir," he said, still staring blankly into space.

"You guess so?" the psychiatrist said with an incredulous laugh. "The torture was the only thing the other POWs could talk about. They dreaded those sessions. You didn't mind them?"

"It was torture, sir—of course I minded."

The psychiatrist stared at him for a while. A frown was there for a moment, making more ghastly rivulets form on the man's face. "…Did you meet any of the other POWs before you freed them?"

"No, sir," he said. He remembered the pleasant voice, but his mind again rebelled against the impossibility of it.

"Why didn't you meet any of them?" the psychiatrist pressed him.

"The jailors kept me locked up by myself."

"Don't you find that strange?" he asked with a frown. "They kept all the other POWs locked up together, four men to a cell. Why did they keep you in your own cell?"

"I guess they didn't like me, sir," he said. When the psychiatrist laughed, the war hero made an effort to smile. He wanted to go back to sleep.

"…Okay," the psychiatrist began again, after another moment of uncomfortable silence. "I have something I want you to look at, soldier. I want you to look at it and tell me if you have any explanation."

"I understand, sir."

The psychiatrist put another disc into the equipment, and then he stood by the side, watching the war hero again. For the first time, the war hero noticed the psychiatrist was holding a folder in his hands. Something about that seemed ominous, but the show began then. On the screen, there were now images of the war hero lying in bed, tossing and turning—

"As I told you before," the psychiatrist began, "you've been in this hospital for two weeks. However, even as your body healed, you remained locked in a deep, unconscious state. It wasn't even that you had head trauma that would explain this unconsciousness. [On the screen, the war hero started to groan, as if in the midst of a nightmare.] Our equipment recorded frenetic mental activity," the psychiatrist went on, "some of which lasted two or three days at a time. As you can see," he said, pointing to the screen, "during these episodes, your face expressed a wide range of emotions—everything from profound joy to pain. Drugs had no effect on you—sedatives, muscle relaxants…none of it made any difference. Then, the last couple of times, you began to scream out garbled sentences: pleas to people, whom you now seemed to think were lost forever. You kept talking about your parents… and a woman."

The psychiatrist stopped the presentation shortly thereafter, then turned to face the war hero—who was looking on in stunned disbelief. "Who was this woman, soldier?" the man asked then.

The war hero's mind felt like it had been shredded; he panicked instinctively, knowing the things he had experienced were beyond any plausible explanation. Yet, he would have to explain something, so his mind groped for a plausible lie. The psychiatrist's eyes seemed unyielding. The war hero looked away, his gaze going to the closed blinds. Behind them, he imagined hundreds of patients passing by in a grim procession—

"Who was she?" the psychiatrist asked again.

"I can't remember, sir," he lied. Lying was the only escape route he saw. "I guess it was someone I was dreaming about," he went on.

"Okay," the man said in a tone that said he was unconvinced. "…Tell me about your family, soldier," the psychiatrist continued. "The nurse tells me you were asking about calling your parents."

The war hero looked over at the man uneasily, then he stared at his arm once more. "…Yeah, I guess I miss them."

"Tell me about them."

"There's not much to tell, sir," he began cautiously. "We're just an average family."

"Where did you grow up?"

"Long Island, sir."

"Had any siblings?"

"Yes, a brother and sister."

"Tell me about them."

"My brother's a U.S. Senator, and my sister is an agent in Hollywood."

"Really? That's impressive. Tell me about your parents. What does your father do?"

"He's a doctor—a urologist."

"What about your mother?"

"She used to be an office manager."

"Used to be?"

"Yes, sir—she's retired now."

"I understand. …Where did you go to high school? On Long Island?"

"Sure, sir."

"Were you a good student?"

"I suppose. I got into Harvard."

"…I understand." He sighed again, and seemed genuinely perplexed for once. He was looking down at the folder in his hands now—the way someone looked at something so irreconcilable that it was disturbing. "What troubles me about what you say, soldier, is that according to Army records—these records I had sent over—you have no parents or other relatives. You grew up in a group home, as a ward of the state. [The war hero sat up straighter!] You didn't even have any next of kin on your Army application" the man continued. "You were an *orphan*."

The war hero closed his eyes and lay back on the bed, forcing himself to take deep, calming breaths.

The psychiatrist spoke up after about ten seconds of silence; he had been staring at the war hero, dissecting his reaction. "I have something I want you to see," the man started again. The war hero looked at him warily as he walked over to the bed. The man then opened the folder and placed it on the war hero's lap. "I did some checking, myself," he went on. "You were abandoned as a baby. You were found outside a church: you still had your umbilical cord attached. It was a famous case. It was in the news, see," he said, pointing to the first document in the folder. "I managed to get this newspaper article emailed to me."

The war hero picked it up uneasily. He read the headline: "Baby Found Abandoned Outside Church." After that, he read the first two lines before folding up the article and putting it to the side. "Okay," he said at last.

"Do you have an explanation?" the psychiatrist asked, still lurking by his bed.

"Of what?"

"Of the things you yelled out while you were unconscious: of what you just told me—about having a family?" Then, stepping even closer to the bed, he pointed out the next form in the folder. "Here is your Army application," he began. "You put the orphanage as your address; you joined the Army right after high school. On the application, you put no next of kin; there is no one to contact in the event of an emergency or death. …So, coming from such a background, don't you think that maybe you found some kind of relief in the fantasy of a loving family—"

The war hero shook his head—either to deny the psychiatrist's conclusion or to block out the man's words entirely. "I was just confused, that's all," he said, staring ahead blankly. Then, glancing up at the psychiatrist with those same blank eyes, "I guess that family was from a dream I had…that's all."

"So you no longer believe you have a family?"

"That's what the records say, don't they?" he said peevishly. Then, in a calmer tone, "I was confused, that's all. I forgot."

"…I called up the orphanage and asked about you. You had a traumatic upbringing. They told me you saw your best friend gunned down."

"…Yes," he whispered, staring ahead blankly.

"You signed up with the Army a few days after that. I talked to the recruiter who signed you up. He says he remembered you because it was as if you weren't even there. Those were his exact words."

"I understand, sir," the war hero whispered. His throat was dry, and he swallowed deeply—

"How did you get to that prison camp, soldier?" the psychiatrist asked abruptly.

"What?" the war hero blurted out to buy himself some time.

"Everyone in your unit was found within blocks of that ambush. Weren't you with your unit when they were attacked?"

The war hero instinctively panicked at this question; he kept his response vague, saying, "I must have been captured and brought to the prison camp."

"…When exactly were you captured?" he said, frowning.

"Some time after the ambush," the war hero responded. He was not really thinking anymore: the words came flowing out of him, and this alarmed him—

"Why would militants capture you, but kill everyone else?"

"How should I know?" he said, panicking inside. He was like a criminal who realized his story was falling apart; to push things to their conclusion, he continued, "…They captured me, that's all. They captured me, but the others died. …You think there's another explanation?"

"There are always other explanations, soldier," he said, returning the article to the folder. Next, he walked back over to the multimedia equipment, and placed the folder on top of it. "…Tell me what you remember about being captured."

He sighed. "I can't remember, sir." He was staring straight ahead again.

"You can't remember?" One of his thick eyebrows rose, mirroring his doubts.

"I only remember being taken by some militants. I have no details for you. …Everything's a blur. I can't even tell you how I got here."

"So, you don't remember anything?"

"Nothing beyond what I told you."

"I see." Then: "You're a national hero now," he said, as if asking the war hero if he understood his position.

"Yes, I know."

"You single-handedly saved twenty POWs from a prison camp. The media are eager to interview you. They will want to ask you the same questions I asked you. What will you tell them?"

"I'll tell them what I told you: I can't remember. I have *amnesia*." And then, to deflect further questions, "I'm sure the rest will come back to me in time, sir."

"Yes," the psychiatrist said. He picked up the folder from the television, then moved toward the door, saying, "…that's the nature of secrets, soldier: they tend to come out eventually." He left after that, and the war hero closed his eyes. He tried to conjure images of the woman, so he could return to the paradise of her arms; but when he closed his eyes, the only thing he saw was the huge, flag-waving crowd. He shuddered.

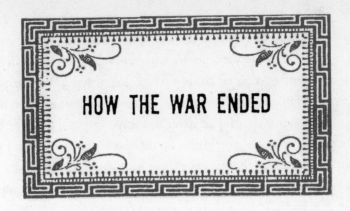

HOW THE WAR ENDED

The New York City subway car was packed and sweltering. The young woman stood with her back pressed against the door, wondering how much more she could take. The hot, sweaty bodies of half a dozen strangers were pressed against hers. One of them—an elegantly dressed man—was squeezed against her so closely that she could feel his heartbeat. His high-priced cologne would have been pleasing under normal circumstances, but now it only made her light-headed and sick. Then, as the train rocked unexpectedly, the man's aluminum attaché case was jammed up into her stomach; her left shoulder joint, which was shoved against the door, exploded with pain; and as her discomfort reached these new, unsustainable limits, she hugged her huge handbag to her chest as a kind of defense mechanism.

Fifteen minutes later, the train was entering the final stop. By now, the young woman's need to escape had escalated to a full-blown mania—

She coughed and grimaced: the air conditioner was broken, and the musky sweat of all the other tired, irritable passengers hung in the air. On top of that, there was a deranged homeless man across the aisle from her, and it was as though his stench were eroding her nasal passages. Beyond the homeless man's matted gray beard, his face wore an odd expression of contentment as he sat there licking the hair of a Barbie Doll. All the saliva in the doll's hair acted like mousse, making the hair stick straight up. After a few cat-like licks, the homeless man held the doll at arm's length, observing his handiwork. He seemed pleased, because he began chuckling to himself. The young woman tried to ignore it all; but as the homeless man continued to mutter to himself, some teenage boys began making crude, unimaginative jokes about his urine-stained pants—which happened to be unzipped. The young woman felt the laughter attacking her—drilling into her head. The madness made her strong. The need to escape left her muscles quivering with the power required to rip the doors open. She turned and faced the door; she was so eager that it was almost as if she were fighting with those around her. Some of her neighbors grumbled and sucked their teeth at her rudeness, but by then she was incapable of caring. Through the window in the door, she saw the blurred, drab, confines of the last stop. The train was still decelerating, yet she felt as though it would never stop: as though they would all be trapped in here forever. As this was the terminus of the subway line, all the other passengers prepared to disembark as well. Many of those who had been sitting now stood up—even though there was no space for them to do so. Those who were already standing now inched closer to the door, so that they literally pressed the woman into the metal and glass—

The train ground to a jarring halt; but even then, the doors remained closed—as though the conductor were taunting them. Soon, ten seconds had passed and the doors had yet to open. Some of the passengers began to grumble and suck their teeth. The teens, who had been merrily taunting the deranged homeless man only moments before, began to curse. The young woman being crushed into the door was at the vanguard of all those irritable people. She felt like a lightning rod for their mounting restlessness and frustration. After the day she had had, she felt that if she did not get outside and breathe fresh air soon, then she would explode. Her hands clenched, as if she were preparing to rip the doors apart—

Then, all of a sudden, the doors finally burst open; the great multitudes surged forward. She sprang out of the train like a terrified animal fleeing from a predator. She was in the first car of the train, and the stairs leading to the outside world were directly in front of her. She ran up the stairs without realizing she was doing so. It was as though the thousands of other passengers were chasing her—were on the verge of stampeding her. Even when she was out of the subway station, she continued running. Dusk had just fallen on the Brooklyn streets, casting the world in a somber, slightly sinister light. Yet, she hardly noticed as she ran.

It was only the red light at the upcoming intersection (and the impenetrable crowd of waiting pedestrians) that made her stop. She stood confusedly on the curb while the traffic zoomed past. Even though she was outside now, she felt as though she were still trapped on the train. She breathed deeply again, instinctively trying to calm herself, but the air was a soupy mix of car exhaust and the grease from the street's vast array of fast food joints. …She realized she could still smell the homeless man—as if his molecules had infected her, and were even now becoming part of her—

Somewhere, an ice cream truck was blaring a music box rendition of "Pop Goes the Weasel." As her senses were in a jumble, the song seemed out of tune; the notes had a haunting, airy quality, which transformed the darkening streets into something nightmarish. When she looked around in bewilderment, a cabbie took her searching expression as a sign she might require his services. He banged on his horn more urgently, as to get her attention, but she shook her head timidly when she made eye contact with him. She was still hugging her huge handbag to her chest.

It was then that the elegantly dressed man from the train tapped her on the shoulder. He and many of the other passengers had caught up to her. She looked up to see him smiling at her. "Have a good day," he said as he turned to the left and joined the stream of pedestrians going with the flow of traffic. "—Remember what I said," he reminded her as he waved his hand. Before she had time to think, he was gone and she was left with an unsettled feeling in the pit of her stomach.

The elegantly dressed man had whispered something to her during that bizarre train ride. Somehow, those whispered words had been brutalizing her all that time. A side of her had been trying to block them out—to erase them from her memory. She shook her head…

Even before she got on the train, she had felt herself coming apart. She had spent the day waiting on lines at the Department of Labor, trying to get an extension on her unemployment benefits. All day, she had gone from bureaucrat to bureaucrat, until an elfish little man with a rumpled shirt put her out of her misery. His office had been small, with an aroma of mildew and dirty socks; his desk had been stacked high with folders—people's lives, she had realized. He had told her to sit down without looking at her. Her folder had been in his hands. His fingernails, she had realized with sudden fascination, had been unbelievably filthy—as though he were purposely cultivating a fungus beneath them. She had looked on, amazed, and yet appalled that those fingers should be touching something connected to her. That folder had been her life; his diseased fingers had roamed over it with impunity. She had forced herself to avert her eyes; but after perusing the contents of her folder for about ten seconds, the man had told her that her appeal for an extension of unemployment benefits was denied. When she sat there staring at him in shock, he had told her to leave, and to not come back.

All that had happened thirty-five minutes ago. She had walked out of his office in a trance. She could not remember how she had gotten to the subway, or any of the other things that had happened; but two stops from the end of the subway line, the loud ping that preceded the closing doors had brought her to her senses. She had looked around like a startled sleepwalker. The reality of her ruined life had hit her then.

With no more unemployment benefits, she had known it was only a matter of time before she lost everything. The reality of unpaid bills and mounting debts had come down on her like a stack of bricks. She had been out of work for about a year now. She had just started her career when the terrorists blew up the White House. The economy, already weak, had buckled. Things had gone steadily downhill, until she and her entire department were "downsized" a few months later.

When she first got laid off, she had thought it would only be a matter of days or weeks before she got another job. The outside world, with its talk of war and terrorist bombings, had been irrelevant to her. The reasons for the stock market crash had been beyond her. She had tried to find work, but with the recession deepening, few employers had been hiring. She had considered working as a waitress—or anything that would allow her to bring in some money—but the pay would never have been able to cover her expenses and student loans.

She had needed those unemployment benefits. They had been the only thing keeping her afloat. After being out of work so long, it was as though she had never worked: as though she had always been adrift in this city—and always would be.

The subway ride had continued. Suddenly anxious, she had scanned the faces of the people around her, perhaps searching for something human and comforting; but in true New York fashion, everyone's face had worn a blank expression.

It had been then she looked up to see the elegantly dressed man. His peculiar smile had made her immediately ill at ease. He had stared at her intently—as though he knew her. The good manners her mother had tried to instill in her had compelled her to stare at him in an effort to place his face. There had been something strange about him—something she had been unable to place. He could have been anywhere from thirty to fifty. Although his face had been wrinkle-free, there had been a few specks of gray in his wavy hair. Objectively speaking, he had been handsome, and yet there had been something about him that disturbed her. It had been an aura—something anachronistic and inscrutable—

"You look like you've had a bad day," the man had said then. The young woman had looked up at him in shock, because even though he had whispered the words, she had felt them inside of her. Something had told her to flee—to block out the man and anything else he might say to her. She had grunted noncommittally, hoping he would take the hint and leave her alone; but even then, she had trembled inside—

The subway car had swayed unexpectedly, causing the tired, irritable passengers to bang against one another; the elegantly dressed man's attaché case had jammed into her stomach. Growing more restless by the second, the young woman had stared off to the side. Eventually, she had noticed the homeless man, and his stench. To distract herself, she had thought about taking a long, relaxing bath when she got home. This self-hypnosis had worked for a while; but at the penultimate stop, the rowdy teens had shoved their way onto the train. One had stepped on her foot as he entered; she had yelped like dog, clamping her eyes shut in an effort to block it all out.

And then, when the packed train began to rumble toward the final stop, the elegantly dressed man had leaned in closer to her, his lips practically touching her ear lobe as he whispered, "Most people can't see what's right in front of their eyes." She had felt herself on the verge of screaming at him— of telling him to leave her the hell alone—but there had been a sudden commotion within the car as the teens made sport of the homeless man. Their raucous laughter had filled the air like a demonic presence. She had gritted her teeth and clamped her eyes shut again, wondering how much more she could take.

…And now, she stood on the Brooklyn streets, wondering how she had gotten to this place….The light at the intersection changed to green, and she stepped tentatively into the street. By now, many of the other subway passengers had caught up to her. They rushed past her now; a few of them bumped into her in their haste, but she was too numb to care—to even acknowledge them.

After her outburst of energy, she moved lethargically. In a way, it was as if she had nowhere to go. Her co-op was about five blocks away; but considering everything that had happened today, she did not feel as though she had the right to return. Two and a half years ago, when she moved from Kentucky in order to embark on her "glorious career," she had been ambitious and focused. After what had happened today, she knew that side of her was dead.

Over the months of her unemployment, she had gotten into the habit of walking to Prospect Park and sitting on a bench, by the lake. Sometimes, she would feed the ducks; but mostly, she would only sit there, staring blankly into space. She considered going there now—even though it was getting dark. She suddenly wondered if the elegantly dressed man had been trying to pick her up. It would be good to have sex, she thought, but there was no lust or longing behind it. She suddenly wanted to be romanced: to have one of those storybook relationships—not because she found any of that worthwhile, but because it would be something to do. She sighed.

She had a lover—not a boyfriend, but a lover—whom she called when the yearning for sex came over her. Every time she gave in to her urges and called him, it had been a new milestone—a new threshold of desperation.

She had met him at a park playground, where he had been playing basketball. He had been a horrible player, but the movements of his body had amazed her. He had come up to her afterwards, and she had not resisted him. The scent of his sweat had made her head swim; he had talked and made jokes, but she had not really listened. On her face, there had been a meditative expression—like on the face of a gymnast preparing to perform a complicated maneuver. And then they had been at her place, having sex. At first, she had lain there, petrified as the thing came to fruition; but then, when she clamped her eyes shut and allowed her imagination to roam, she had found herself experiencing something pure and good. It had been like paradise; she had been transported away from the concerns of her everyday life, to a plane of existence where the pleasure seemed godlike and forbidden. In the aftermath of the pleasure, she had been amazed—especially when she opened her eyes and saw her lover snoring. She had known the godlike pleasure had nothing to do with him. She had known it came from something hidden deep within her. Nevertheless, she would call him every time her soul cried out for the forbidden pleasure. For a moment, she considered calling him when she got home; but in the end, she only sighed and walked on.

As she ambled past a newsstand, she noticed the day's newspapers all had pictures of the war hero on them. The great hero had returned to America yesterday. On the front page of the newspapers, he was standing at attention while the president pinned a medal on his broad chest. The war hero's face called to her for a reason she had never taken the time to reason out. There was an earnestness to it that was almost unsettling. This reaction had been troubling her for the last few weeks—since the first announcement that the man had saved twenty prisoners of war. Luckily for her, she had never paid much attention to the war…

After she crossed the next intersection, she turned to the right and entered a quieter residential block. Her pace was slower now—not only from the enervating effects of the day and the heat, but also from the feeling of being weighed down by her thoughts… The block was dark and silent—especially in contrast to the blocks with the subway station and eateries and rushing traffic. She felt suddenly lonely, and this annoyed her. She wondered how many messages her mother had left for her today. Her mother, who had been deeply proud of her during her years of success, seemed to be taking her ruination worse than she was. The young woman did not want to listen to any more pep talks—nor did she want to hear any more advice on "finding a good man."

Her pace had slowed to a weary shuffle by the time she entered the block of her co-op. When she looked up, she became aware the ice cream truck's song was still echoing down the streets. In the summertime, "Pop Goes the Weasel" always seemed to be in the air: the same notes repeated over and over again, so that it became an invitation not only to ice cream, but to madness.

While she was thinking about ordering Chinese food for dinner, something darted from beneath one of the cars parked on the curb. It leapt into her path; she jumped back. A muffled shriek escaped from her throat, but she was too terrified to scream—too shocked to do anything but stare and tremble. It took her a moment to realize the thing that had leapt into her path was only a cat. Yet, it was a cat the likes of which she had never seen before. It was white: so white that it seemed to glow. Something about its gaze was brazen and commanding. She felt uncomfortable. Its eyes were huge; by the streetlamp, she saw they were aquamarine. The more she stared into those eyes, the more a sense of panic seized her—

She clamped her eyes shut and shook herself to free herself from the spell. She took a deep breath; then, opening her eyes again, she looked around the block uneasily before returning to the cat. The cat was too clean to be a stray. More likely than not, the owner had let it out for the night…but it was still staring at her intently, and standing in her path, demanding her attention—

It's only a cat, she chided herself. She stepped to the side, then walked past the cat. She did so timidly, never taking her eyes off the creature. It turned its head and watched her; but otherwise, it did not move. She looked hopefully toward her building and began to walk faster; when she looked back, she was relieved to see the cat was still in the same position. For some unaccountable reason, she was walking even faster now—almost jogging—as if fleeing from a monster. Unfortunately, when she was about two doors away from her building, there was the same blur of white fur past her. This time, the cat ran all the way to her building and sat down in front of her door!

What the hell! she thought as she stood there frozen. Once again, she and the cat stared at one another, but then she shook her head. *Get a grip*! It was only a cat. More likely than not, it belonged to someone in her building. The cat had probably seen her before, and knew she lived there. What other explanation could there possibly be? Buoyed by this piece of logic, she moved toward her building. Her first few steps were again tentative ones; but then, as a sense of defiance grew within her, she stepped up to the building boldly, pounding the heels of her shoes on the pavement. A side of her had hoped this would scare the cat away, but it only sat there patiently, waiting for her. As she approached it, she realized it was making a sound— not purring exactly…it was as if the cat were projecting a humming sound into her mind. Despite the defiance she had tried to evince earlier, she could not get over the feeling the cat was inside of her….

When she reached the entrance, she got out her keys from her suit pocket. The cat was still staring at her with those beautiful aquamarine eyes. She stood before the door for a moment, staring down at the creature. It was still making that sound. A side of her wanted to reach down and pet it, but that seemed like a sacrilege somehow—as though her hands would soil its fur. Also, even for a cat, there was something unusually aloof about it— something not quite right. It was direct, but it did not rub against her leg like cats usually did; it did not meow. It just sat there waiting for her. She felt her doubts and fears growing again, but she fought them off by inserting her key and unlocking the door. When the door was open, the cat darted into the foyer, where the mailboxes were situated to the right. There was another locked door beyond the foyer; but just then, the door opened and the cat slipped into the doorway. When she looked up, she saw the super-intendent of the building emerge.

The superintendent was a man of middle age. Even though his constitution seemed firm, she always suspected there was some hidden deformity about him. He walked in a slouching, shambling manner, and some latent maternal impulse made her want to box his ears and tell him to walk straight. He emerged from the doorway clad in his usual soiled overalls. When he saw her, he grinned—which was to say, his lips twitched over his discolored teeth.

"You just coming from a job interview?" he asked as his eyes roamed the contours of her suit.

"Something like that," she said. She wanted to rush off, but he was still standing in the doorway.

"Is your intercom working?" he said, gesturing to the console on the outer wall of the building.

Her first impulse was to scream: *It hasn't worked since I told you it wasn't working six months ago*! However, still eager to move on, she merely shook her head.

"I'll stop by to fix it tomorrow, if you wish."

"That's fine." She again prepared to leave, but—

"Is it hot enough for you out there?" he ventured with another twitching smile.

Even on the best of days, she would not have wanted to have this conversation. "Yes, it's hot enough," she said, a confrontational edge entering her voice.

He stood there for a moment, as though compiling more trivial questions to ask her; then, perhaps sensing the growing antagonism within her, he nodded shyly. At last, there was an awkward moment, in which they both had to maneuver inside the cramped space of the foyer, like two crabs facing off against one another. Once that was over, and they had switched positions, he gave her one last twitching smile and rushed off. She was relieved. Yet, when he was gone, her mind returned to the cat. As the superintendent had not noticed it, she began to wonder if it had only been a figment of her imagination. She smiled for once, and shook her head at the strange thoughts coursing through her mind. She took a parting glance out of the window in the door, looking at the darkening world. Faint echoes of "Pop Goes the Weasel" could still be heard, but the door was closed—and all of that seemed to be behind her. She would take a long bath and go to bed early, and sleep the way people slept when there was nowhere to go in the morning.

Before going up to her apartment, she decided to check her mailbox. She did not really expect anything good; and as expected, she found nothing but a credit card bill (which she did not bother to open) and a brightly colored letter, which declared that a fantastic offer was in store for her if she responded by a certain date. She grunted in annoyance. Thoughts of a warm, soothing bath returned, and she moved on. It was a four-story building, and her apartment was on the fourth floor. She walked slowly, but with the satisfaction of knowing she would soon be able to close her door behind her and forget the tribulations of the day (at least for a little while). The only respite she had left was forgetfulness. She saw that now. Tomorrow, the horror would be there again; but tonight, snuggled under the covers, she would forget, and find peace in her dreams.

This burgeoning sense of peace probably accounted for the blow she felt when she got to the top of the staircase and saw the cat waiting in front of her door. She froze at first, but then she took a deep breath and continued on. The strange purring noise—or whatever it was—intensified as she approached. It was not exactly unpleasant, but the weirdness of the sound—and of the situation, itself—disturbed her. Her mind churned out some fanciful theories—like maybe the cat was not a cat at all, but a loved one's spirit returning to show her something. Her thoughts went to her mother—the only living relative with whom she had any ongoing connection. She felt suddenly guilty about her earlier thoughts; new, superstitious terrors gripped her. She again considered the cat's unusually white fur, its piercing aquamarine eyes and its obvious intention to be with her. It had not merely followed her home: it had known where she lived. As simpleminded as such thoughts seemed to her, she could not deny them.

She put her key in the lock, and opened the door; before the door was fully open, the cat entered her apartment. She froze, but it was too late now to turn back. She pushed the door open wider, but stayed outside, as though afraid of being alone with the cat. She reached her hand in and turned on the light. The kitchen opened up before her; to the left, there was a hallway, which she stared down in awe, seeing the cat walking toward her bedroom. When the creature reached the open doorway of her bedroom, it again stopped, turned toward her, and sat down to wait.

A tingly feeling spread over her skin now. She went back to hugging her handbag. After a few moments of indecision, she entered the apartment timidly—as though she were the intruder. She always locked her door upon entering her apartment, but she hesitated now. The thought of being locked in with the cat made her tremble inside. She closed the door but did not lock it. The cat was still waiting by her bedroom door—

"Get a grip, girl!" she whispered to herself. However, the more she reminded herself it was only a cat, the more irrational she felt. She wondered why she had even allowed the cat into her house. She had a sudden impulse to get a broom and shoo it from her apartment. She wanted to do something brutal to it, in order to prove her dominion over it.

The cat entered her bedroom as she drew near; her steps faltered. It was only a cat. She took a deep breath, cursing herself. Nevertheless, she was again tentative as she reached her hand into the darkness and turned on the light. The cat was lying on her bed, licking the fur on its haunch with long, slow licks that reminded her of the deranged homeless man on the train. The cat lay there as though that were its bed. Her mind was so dazed she found herself considering the possibility that this was her cat and she had only forgotten somehow. She again shook her head to drive away such thoughts. The impulse to grab a broom and chase the cat away—or at least off her bed—came over her again. She had to do something to exert her will before the cat took over completely. That was the thing that disturbed her: the feeling that the cat was taking over and she was powerless to do anything about it. The cat seemed fully content now. It did not even bother to look at her anymore. It just lay there, purring and cleaning itself.

On the nightstand, her answering machine's red light was flashing. She knew there would be more calls from her mother…and maybe a few more collection agencies had left threatening calls about her unpaid bills. She looked around her room anxiously. Even though her bedroom window was closed, she could still hear "Pop Goes the Weasel" echoing on the streets below. Like the cat's purring, the song seemed to be projecting itself into her mind. Thus, maybe it was merely for reasons of self-preservation that she retreated from the room. In the hallway, she leaned against the wall, taking a deep breath. Then, like a drunkard, she clambered toward the kitchen, sliding her hand against the wall to maintain her balance. She had to clear her head…and she was hungry. Except for a bagel for breakfast, she had eaten nothing all day.

In the kitchen, she made herself a salami and cheese sandwich. She put down her handbag for the first time, and ate standing at the kitchen counter. Actually, she left all the ingredients strewn before her on the counter; after devouring one sandwich, she literally threw another one together. She drank from a carton of orange juice, not even bothering with a glass. It occurred to her she should make something for the cat to eat, but she defiantly decided against it. She liked the idea of the cat being dependent on her for food. That was the proof she was master and it was beast. She wanted it to come and beg her, and meow plaintively for her to throw it a few scraps… She realized she could still hear the cat's purring. It had not decreased in volume when she left the room. She looked about the kitchen anxiously, checking to make sure the cat was not there. She was alone in the kitchen, but that only made her wonder if the purring, like the cat, were only a figment of her imagination. Maybe she was in the middle of a nervous breakdown. She remembered her crazy grandaunt, who had had a nervous breakdown after her husband died, and turned to a life of prostitution. Maybe she was going through the same thing.

She left the cheese and bread and salami and juice on the counter, and meandered back down the hallway to her bedroom. The purring intensified as she did so. The cat was sleeping on her bed, balled up into a white mound of fur. This relieved her. Seeing the cat like that reassured her she could shoo it off the bed when she was ready to sleep. For now, she felt as though she had been given a reprieve; and suddenly remembering her plan to take a long, hot bath, she sighed. There was an adjoining bathroom. She went to it now. She closed the door behind her; and as she did so, she felt silly— since she was the only one there. Yet, the thought of the cat wandering into the bathroom while she was bathing brought an anxious feeling over her— as though the cat were a man. It was a silly feeling to have, and she knew this, yet she still closed the door and locked it.

She turned on the water to fill the tub, then began to undress. There was a radio on the windowsill: she turned it on and tuned it to a jazz station. Outside, it had grown darker. "Pop Goes the Weasel" was still playing down the block, so she pulled her blinds shut and continued undressing.

The war hero was at a packed banquet in the Capitol building. His mind was still whirling from yesterday's medal ceremony. All the politicians and high dignitaries had been there. The president had taken pictures with him—just as his one-time brother had done before he was shipped out to war. Some of the prisoners of war he had freed from the prison camp had been there as well, patting him on the back and laughing with him as though they were old friends. While this was going on, dozens of photographers had clamored around him, yelling for him to assume contrived poses. His story about having amnesia had only added to the spectacle, making him more of a romantic figure.

Now, one day after the medal ceremony, he felt as though the entire world were rewriting itself in order to accommodate the myth of his heroism. At the moment, two dignitaries were talking to him (they had in fact been talking to him for about five minutes now). He suddenly became aware he had not heard a word they had said. His periodic nods—which had become instinctual over the last few days—had somehow duped them into believing he was paying attention. Over the last few days, the nation's most powerful men and women had seemed desperate to be his friends. Business cards had been pressed into his hands; appointments and dinner dates had been suggested. The war hero went where the Army told him to go, and did what they told him to do, but he did not feel personally connected to any of it.

He was beginning to tire of it all—and there were still weeks to go in his national tour. Muscles that had begun to heal were beginning to ache again. He took stock of his body now. In his right hand, there was a flute of champagne. In his left hand, there was a hideous trophy. There had been a ceremony earlier, and the Speaker of the House had presented the trophy to him. It was a bayonet stuck in a block of marble. Supposedly, it was the bayonet from the gun he had used to free the other POWs (even though he could not recall there being a bayonet on that gun). The pointy, serrated end was sticking up threateningly, so that the only way to hold it safely was by the marble bottom. The names of all the men in his unit were engraved on the blade. The trophy felt like lead in his hands. He wanted to throw it away—dump it in the nearest garbage can, along with the evolving myth of whom he was supposed to be.

That was when the war hero looked up to see his brother—the senator. He had to remind himself his brother was not his brother anymore. The thought was insane, like everything that had happened since he woke up in Germany. Either way, his one-time brother was across the room, charming a group of politicians. As the war hero stared at his brother, he wondered if the man recognized him, because the man's eyes kept wandering over to him. At the same time, everyone was staring at him. He was the center of the celebration—

An old southern senator came up to the war hero then, and clapped him on the back. The two dignitaries had still been talking to the war hero, but the southern senator elbowed them to the side, where they stood morosely, sipping their drinks. The southern senator had a tumbler full of whiskey, and was one of those cloying drunks, who had a need to touch those with whom he conversed. The man kept calling him "Son," and the war hero had a sudden impulse to hit him with the hideous trophy—to ram the serrated edge of the blade into the man's jowls. The image made him wince; realizing he was drawing near the limits of patience and sanity, he turned his mind to thoughts of escape. He made up a lie about having to use the bathroom, and then he fled. When he glanced back, the southern senator had fastened onto the two dignitaries he had previously elbowed to the side, and was spilling whiskey on one's tuxedo while he swayed and held the other by the shoulder.

The war hero ducked behind a decorative column, and then he made for the door. Outside, in the hallway, the guards saluted him; he returned their salutes half-heartedly. Before him was a spacious marble hallway. Besides the guards, and a young aide who was yelling something into a cellular phone (either in anger or because of bad reception) there was nobody else around.

The war hero wanted to escape—to run out of the open door and never look back. Later tonight, he was heading to New York; tomorrow, he would be on all the morning talk shows…and then, there would be a parade eventually—down Broadway, with confetti heaved from the windows, and cheering crowds lining the roadway. The image left him with the same creepy feeling he had had since the psychiatrist showed him that presentation in Germany—

There were footsteps behind him. When he looked, he saw his brother walking toward him! The man was smiling at him; the war hero looked at him helplessly and hopefully—because there seemed to be a note of recognition in his brother's eyes. The man was putting out his hand to be shaken now; the war hero took it automatically:

"I meant to talk to you earlier," his brother said with an apologetic laugh. The war hero could only stare; he seemed dazed. "…Are you okay?" his brother asked.

The war hero sighed, and looked around absentmindedly, as if he had lost something. Finally, he looked at his brother soberly: "I need to talk to you."

"Okay," his brother said after the uneasy pause. "Would you like to talk in my office—it's down the hall?"

"Okay."

His brother began to lead the way. "…I meant to ask you if we could do some events together," his brother began, "—since I'm your senator."

"You mean a photo op?"

His brother looked back apologetically—

"Don't worry about it," the war hero said with an exhausted wave of his hand. "Just talk to the Army guys—they're in charge of my schedule."

"Thanks."

Things were moving quickly. The war hero felt his heart beating fast. For those few moments, he was merely allowing himself to be led—like a man heaved off a cliff allowed gravity to bring him to his fate. Eventually, his brother stopped in front of his office, and got out his keys. His brother looked back at him again, instinctively trying to smile and put him at ease: "What did you want to talk about?"

The war hero spoke as if speaking to himself: "...I have to know if it's all a delusion," he whispered.

"Pardon?" the senator asked as he opened the door.

"I'm going to ask you some questions, Senator," the war hero began, "—but all I want is a 'yes or no' answer."

"Okay," his brother said, disturbed, but still trying to smile and act at ease. He ushered the war hero into his office. The office was posh and spacious. The war hero noticed a picture of his family on the desk—his father, mother and sister...but he was not in that picture. He remembered the day the picture had been taken. He stared at it in bewilderment, and stretched out his hand, brushing his fingers over it. His brother closed the door then, and walked up to his side while he stood staring at the picture.

"Uncle Alvin took that picture," the war hero began.

"What?"

"...You have an Uncle Alvin, right?"

"Oh, yeah, but—"

"He's not a biological uncle, just a friend of your father's—another urologist your father used to know."

His brother looked at him uncertainly. "You know Uncle Alvin?"

The war hero ignored him: "He took the picture after Christmas dinner, when everyone was exchanging gifts. Mom..."—the war hero caught himself and shook his head—"your mother was always complaining that she didn't have enough pictures of the family, so Uncle Alvin said it would be his gift to the family."

His brother frowned. "How—"

"Just yes or no for now," the war hero interrupted him. "Is everything I said true?"

"Yes," his brother responded uneasily. He walked around and sat behind his desk. The brother offered the war hero a seat, but he shook his head, preferring to remain standing. The war hero continued:

"In high school, you had Mr. Livingston for English. He called you 'Brutus' after you played the role in a school play."

His brother nodded, his expression strained.

"...In your room—your boyhood room—there's a place in your closet where there's a loose plank. You used to store things in there."

His brother had to scour his mind, but then he looked up suddenly when he remembered.

"You hid your porn there," the war hero continued, "—and some condoms that you never got around to using."

"How could you know that?" his brother whispered, his face pale.

The war hero only nodded his head, because he saw, by the senator's reaction, that it was all true. "Thank you, Senator," he said then. "I'll see you when I get back to New York." He turned to leave then. His brother put up his hand to get him to stop, but he realized his hand was trembling; the man opened his mouth, but for once he found no words. The next thing he knew, he was alone in his office, staring at the closed door.

The ex-convict had always felt uncomfortable lurking around this block, on which so many million-dollar brownstones stood shoulder-to-shoulder. He was sure someone would notice him, and call the police. It was obvious he did not belong here. The free clothes they had given him at the halfway house were beginning to fray at the seams; his sneakers were encrusted with mud and worn down—since he walked everywhere; and his face was a hideous mask of scars. A crazed inmate had practically filleted his face with a rusty razor blade, and then kicked out his four front teeth. His face was now crisscrossed from the hundreds of stitches it had taken to sew his skin back together. Because of nerve damage, he could not really smile anymore. He could not frown, or convey any other emotion—which was just as well, since he felt hollowed-out inside.

He had spent the last three years behind bars for storing stolen goods for a friend. The so-called friend had absconded when he heard the police had raided the house, leaving the ex-convict to stew in prison. Before that, the ex-convict had spent about four years in various youth homes and reformatories for crimes that mostly involved being around the wrong people at inopportune times. One-third of his life had already been spent in prison, and he was only twenty-two years old. After all those years, he had finally been regurgitated by the prison industrial complex—but into a world that despised him. Everywhere he went, people regarded him with disgust and horror. He wore partial dentures now, to compensate for his lost teeth, but with the nerve damage to his lips, his words had a sloppy, sibilant quality. New York State had gotten him a job as a stock boy in a supermarket, but all the customers had stared at his face; a little girl had cried, and the manager had fired him, saying he was too much of a distraction. With all that, the thought of returning to prison did not really terrify him anymore—as it had when he was released two months ago. More and more, he thought of prison as an oasis. He did not belong in the world of free men. Freedom was destroying his soul. He needed prison bars—not because he was a criminal—but because the bars would keep the world at bay.

When he saw the elegantly dressed man enter the block, it was as if God were showing him the way back to Paradise. The ex-convict knew if he attacked the man and robbed him, he would go back to prison—and receive a harsher sentence as a repeat offender; but again, he could not help thinking that doing it would save his soul, somehow: would be some kind of stand against forces he could not quite articulate, but which he could feel around him.

And now, feeling everything had been decided, the ex-convict moved faster. He clenched his jaw to build up the all-consuming hate that would allow him to commit the act. Soon, he was across the street, stalking his prey. However, when he was about ten paces away, the elegantly dressed man turned and faced him, smiling as he said, "I see you've reconsidered my offer."

The ex-convict froze, but then walked up, looking drained. When he reached the man, he stood there with lowered eyes, like a child awaiting punishment. The elegantly dressed man was still smiling at him; remembering the man's question about reconsidering his offer, the ex-convict nodded.

"Good: come this way. My house is right around the corner."

The ex-convict now walked with an inner sense of panic; when they stopped in front of the elegantly dressed man's brownstone, he was trembling slightly. Somehow, he felt compelled to speak—to say something that would aver his humanity. Yet, the only thing he could think to say was, "You do this often?"

The elegantly dressed man laughed before shaking his head. "It all depends on what you consider 'often.'" Then, in response to the follow-up question in the ex-convict's eyes, he continued, "I like meeting new people. Have you ever walked down the street and looked at someone, and imagined everything about him? ...his past, what his parents did for a living, who his first crush was on...?"

"That's an interesting hobby," the ex-convict said obliquely.

"No, not at all: it's not a hobby—it's what I do for a living."

When the ex-convict looked at him confusedly, the elegantly dressed man smiled and started walking up the stairs. The ex-convict followed with a halting gait; he held onto the handrails, like an old man. As the elegantly dressed man looked back at him, he smiled again—both at the sight of his enfeebled ascent and in response to the question. He explained: "I am a man of business: a venture capitalist, you might say. I make money by figuring out what billions of people around the world want out of life. I sit on various boards and councils. I dispense advice on how profits can be made; I introduce like-minded individuals (individuals who need one another, whether they know it or not). I am one of the catalysts for the American way of life," he said, gesturing over his shoulder, where a huge American flag dangled from a pole. The ex-convict looked at the flag as if just noticing it. Indeed, now that he looked, he noticed the front door was littered with a dozen or more stickers and ribbons, which decried "Support Our Troops" and "God Bless America," and a raft of other patriotic slogans. In fact, every house on this block had flags and ribbons displayed, as if these things were modern-day talismans, meant to appease the gods.

They entered the elegantly dressed man's home soon thereafter. The inside was cool and fragrant; the ex-convict felt even more ill at ease. He did not want to step on the man's fine, oriental rugs with his filthy shoes.

"Do you want something to eat?" the elegantly dressed man asked.

The ex-convict shook his head with lowered eyes.

"Very well then. There is a shower down that hall," he said, pointing. "You'll find a towel and robe hanging there for you."

The ex-convict stared down the hall as though seeing a horror waiting at the end of it; but then, wordlessly, without further acknowledging his host, he walked down the hall with the unsteady carriage of a man whose fate was no longer in his hands.

After the plane landed at New York's LaGuardia Airport, and taxied to the terminal, the war hero pretended to be asleep—as he had for most of the one-hour ride, in order to avoid talking to the businessman next to him. The businessman had tried several times to tell him his life story, and the war hero was tired of listening—both to people's stories and the constant praise that came with his newfound status. He was still in his dress uniform. The various medals were still on his chest, where the president had pinned them. …And the episode with his brother had left a dull ache within him. At least he knew he was not mad: he really had lived another life. At the same time, as he had thought before, what was the point of being sane in a world like this? He wanted to get away from everything. He wanted to strip off his clothes: the entire myth of whom and what he was supposed to be. He did not want to be congratulated anymore; he was tired of hearing applause every time he entered a room. He felt like a walking fairy tale: everywhere he went, reality seemed to morph into myth….

The loquacious businessman tapped him on the shoulder to awaken him. The war hero remained silent and still, hoping the man would lose interest and join the throng streaming out of the plane. Nevertheless, the man shook him again, this time harder, and the war hero felt himself possessed by the urge to break the man's neck. This intention must have been in the war hero's eyes when he opened them, because the businessman gasped and grinned nervously. As the war hero glared at him, the man grabbed his carry-on bag and moved on. Sighing, the war hero glanced out of the window, where night had entrenched itself.

He took a deep breath, and closed his eyes again—not to sleep, but in order to regain a little of what he had lost. He felt drained. Thoughts of the woman suddenly flooded his mind, and he did not resist them. The old scene reconstructed itself in his mind once more: he and the woman making love in the cramped apartment, their bodies entwined in the early morning light. He smiled. Maybe the woman had always been an escape hatch from the burdens of his life—a way to avoid un-faceable realities. Whatever the case, the stewardess eventually came around to ask him if he was okay. He opened his eyes and saw the plane was empty. He told her he was fine, and rose from his seat. He must have seemed frail to her, because she got his carry-on bag from the overhead compartment. He took it from her with a certain amount of resentment—as though emasculated. Yet, the stewardess was still smiling at him: not the phony smile they were paid and trained to maintain, but the genuine, heartfelt smile of a sexually receptive woman. She seemed to be appreciating the way his body filled out his dress uniform. She knew who he was: the captain had announced his presence to everyone; his fellow passengers had applauded him, while he sat fidgeting in his seat, wishing they would shut the hell up. Now, as he watched the stewardess, it occurred to him he could use her hero worship to his advantage, and take her back to the high-priced hotel room the Army had booked for him. For a few moments, he considered the merits of seducing her; but on second thought, the entire enterprise seemed too cumbersome. He needed to rest.

He thanked the stewardess and walked away, limping slightly. He was back in New York—his supposed home—but that did not really mean any-thing to him. He reminded himself he was an orphan—that he had to give up the idea of a home in the suburbs, and a family. He had to let go of all the things that never were. As he walked out of the plane, he felt like a con man trying to get his story straight.

These were his thoughts when he walked into the terminal and was met by a huge, cheering crowd of well-wishers. He jumped back. By then, he had gotten his military-issue duffel bag from the luggage belt. He had placed it (and his carry-on bag) on a cart, and was heading toward the exit when the crowd confronted him. Within seconds, he was in the midst of them—engulfed. People were patting him on the back; reporters were shoving cameras into his face. He heard none of what they were saying, but he kept repeating, "Thank you." The crowd seemed like one soulless entity to him now. All he wanted to do was get away. As he watched them, he sensed something horrible was approaching on the horizon. He wanted to flee before it got here. He was looking around for the quickest exit when his eyes came to rest on the ex-convict. He froze.

By now, the ex-convict had showered and changed into a suit the elegantly dressed man had given him. It was not only the scars on his face that made the ex-convict stand out from the crowd, but his grim, dignified silence. He was not cheering like everyone else. He merely stood on the periphery of the crowd, staring; and then, when the war hero made eye contact with him, he nodded in a way that seemed to convey some hidden meaning—as a signal between conspirators, perhaps. The war hero stared at the ex-convict's scarred face hopefully—

A reporter shoved a microphone in the war hero's face, causing the ex-convict to disappear from his field of vision. When the war hero looked to that spot in the crowd again, the man was gone. An unsettled feeling came over him. It was strange: as though he had lost his one chance to understand everything. Just when the feeling seemed on the verge of becoming full-blown panic, the war hero looked up to see the ex-convict standing before him. In the ex-convict's eyes, there was still something conspiratorial. Seeming to confirm their association, the man took possession of the war hero's cart and wheeled it through the crowd, so that the war hero could travel unmolested in its wake. The next thing the war hero knew, they were both in a nook by themselves—away from the crowd. He looked at the ex-convict as if he had just performed a magic trick.

"You need to use the bathroom?" the ex-convict asked then, in his sloppy, sibilant way. As he said it, he gestured over the war hero's shoulder, where there was a bathroom. "I'll hold off the crowd," the man went on. "You go ahead."

The war hero nodded again, then entered the bathroom. It was empty, quiet and relatively dark. He looked around it confusedly, realizing he did not really have to use the facilities. However, the silence was good. For a moment, he thought about locking himself in a stall for an hour or so, until everyone left. He went to the sink, but only stared at his reflection. He stared for about thirty seconds. He looked good in his dress uniform, with all its medals and commendations. Yet, as always, none of those things seemed real.

He looked about the bathroom absentmindedly. In retrospect, he did not like the idea of hiding in here. It did not go well with his heroic war image—which he felt duty-bound to protect, even if he did not feel personally connected to it. He turned from the mirror and headed toward the exit. That was when the ex-convict entered. The man had gotten rid of the cart and was holding the war hero's bags in his hands. They stood staring at each other again.

"What happened to all the reporters?" the war hero asked.

The ex-convict put down the bags: "I told them you'd hold a press conference in the terminal upstairs."

The war hero frowned: "Am I?"

"No—it will give you time to make your escape."

The war hero nodded and sighed, and once again looked about the bathroom absentmindedly. The ex-convict was staring at him with the same strange intensity once more. When the war hero looked at him, he said:

"You really don't remember anything? You don't know me?"

"...Should I?" the war hero said, unsure. He wondered about the scars—about the face beyond the mangled flesh—

"I guess it makes no difference," the ex-convict said, deep in thought. He took a deep breath then, saying, "My master told me to come for you."

"Your master?" he said, frowning at the strange term.

"Yes."

"And who is your...your master?" he said, again stumbling over the phrase.

"He is a man you will want to know. He spared us when we were young."

"Spared us?"

"You and I...you mostly."

"What's this about?"

The ex-convict thought about it for a few seconds—as though having to digest the recollections, himself. "...We robbed him when we were kids," he started. "...Got a few hundred dollars from him. I held the knife on him, while you got the money from his pocket—"

"Wait…what?" the war hero protested, fighting to understand. "We used to rob people as kids?"

"Yes."

"How old were we?" he said, dubious.

"I was about thirteen—you were younger…maybe nine or ten. We did it all the time—it was a game, I guess: a stupid childhood game. But when we robbed my master it was different. He just stood there, smiling at us, as though we were his kids, playing cops and robbers with him… Afterwards, he tracked us down somehow. We were both in that group home and he showed up saying he was from Children's Services. That's when he made the deal with us: said if we stayed out of trouble then he would watch over us—take care of us."

"Take care of us?" the war hero mumbled, still fighting to understand.

"He would buy us things. Stuff would show up in boxes, addressed to us: shoes and clothes and games…all kinds of things. It was like he knew our thoughts—or really was watching over us like he said. It was weird—like, one day I was playing basketball and I ripped my sneakers…you know, those old canvas sneakers. I ripped them, then, the next day, a new pair of sneakers arrived. It was like we had our own private Santa Claus…but I just couldn't get it out of my head. Every time I went outside, I kept looking around for him—or one of his spies. I guess you didn't mind as much, but it drove me crazy.

"…I stole from that store just to prove to myself that he wasn't every-where. I can't even remember what I took now—I went in there to steal something, so I could prove to myself that he wasn't everywhere. I got away clean—I'm sure of it…but when I got home, the cops were waiting for me and that was the last time you and I saw each other."

The war hero stood staring at the man. "Wait, you said this guy sent you to get me?"

"Yes, he wants you to stay at his place. He has a huge brownstone."

The war hero laughed. "Look, thanks, but the Army already has a hotel room booked for me. I'm sure they have a ride waiting outside for me."

"Then come for dinner. He's waiting now."

"…You bullshitting me with this, man?" he said skeptically. The man's story was plausible; but in this version of reality, the kid with the bloodshot eyes had been his only friend. His mind flashed with all those memories: the horrors of the orphanage; the nightmare images from when the kid got himself blown away by those police officers. Granted, there were huge gaps in his memories, but the ex-convict's story just did not seem right. On top of all that, the ex-convict's paganish awe of his "master" left the war hero uneasy. "Is this some kind of game?" he said at last.

"—Nah, man," the ex-convict pleaded.

"You really knew me?"

"Yeah, we used to hang out together…all those years ago. It's strange how things turn out," he said, looking meditatively at the war hero's commendations and medals. "Now you're a great war hero. I remember when I used to kick your ass for your dessert," he said with a slurping sound that was supposed to be a nostalgic snicker.

"Yeah, well…" the war hero could not think of anything else to say, so they just stood there uneasily. And then, looking up, his mind again went to the hideous scars on the ex-convict's face. "What happened to your face?" he asked without circumspection.

"My cellmate did it to me while I was in prison."

He was intrigued: "Why?"

"His face was bandaged when he came in. The police had shot him about ten times…literally blown his face off. He had robbed some diner with a fake gun, trying to get himself killed—"

The war hero instinctively shuddered; the ex-convict looked at him uncertainly, but then went on with his story.

"Anyway, he came to jail with his face bandaged. He didn't say anything for weeks. Everyone figured he couldn't speak. Being a quiet man in prison is either a good thing or a bad thing. People fear quiet people, and leave them alone. Those bandages added to it. …When the bandages came off, everyone started calling him Scarface…like in the movie. He didn't have front teeth, and his face didn't heal well. The cuts started to ooze pus… that's when they started calling him Scumface. When they saw he didn't stop them from joking, they only teased him more. After a while, even I started calling him that. I didn't think he minded. Everyone was doing it. But then, one day, he snapped. We were in the cell, and I called him Scumface, and he snapped. He kicked me in the mouth right there, and then he had that shiv out…sliced up my face. Then, he started screaming about how Jesus had damned him…something like that. They hauled him away—took him to the psych ward. He killed himself the next day."

The war hero was trembling. He retreated to the sink again, and gulped down some water…but it made him feel sick. He wanted to lie down—to close his eyes and forget.

The ex-convict stared at the war hero as he stood with his back turned. "…You okay, man?"

"No, not really."

"You really don't remember anything?" the ex-convict asked again.

"Nah."

"…Maybe that's for the best."

The war hero looked up at him via the mirror. The ex-convict explained: "Sometimes I wish I could forget it all. If I could flip a switch right now and forget everything I went through, then I would. It's not as though there were many good memories—for either of us."

The war hero had been watching the man via the mirror. He now turned to face the ex-convict. "How long did you know me?"

"All our lives, until they took me away."

"…So, you could tell me things about my past?" the war hero ventured.

"If you wish to know, then I can tell you—but my master will be able to tell you more than I can."

"Your master?" he said with another frown. "Why do you call him that?"

"He doesn't make me call him that or anything. I call him that so I'll remember what our relationship is."

"And what is your 'relationship?'"

"I sold myself to him today."

"What?" The war hero laughed uneasily, hoping it was a sick joke, but the ex-convict's face remained grave.

"I'm his property," the man continued. "…But it's not as bad as it sounds.

Most of us sell ourselves to people and things all the time—it's just that we're unconscious of it. I made a conscious choice to be his property."

The war hero put up his hand to stop the man from speaking. He did not want to hear anymore. "What does your…boss want with me? He's expecting me to sell myself to him, too?" He said this last part with a sarcastic air that reassured him.

"No, he could never buy you—that's why you were always his favorite."

They were both silent for a moment.

The war hero shook his head: "Look, this is all a little too weird for me—"

"Just have dinner with him tonight. There won't be huge crowds there. I could see in your eyes how much you hate them. His place is quiet, and I have the car waiting. Like I said, my master will be able to tell you things about yourself."

"…Maybe I'm tired of people telling me things about myself."

"You will want to hear what he says. …He has a way of saying things."

The war hero sighed—

"Just spend an hour with him," the ex-convict urged him, "—or five minutes, if that's all you can stand. Either way, you'll never forgive yourself if you miss this opportunity."

"Five minutes?" he said, thoughtfully.

"Yes, if that's all you want…but you'll want more."

The war hero groaned and shook his head. He was exhausted—mentally worn down. The ex-convict was still staring at him like a dog waiting to be thrown a morsel of food; the war hero stared at the man, wondering if they really had been friends, and if the man were a nightmare version of himself.

"You didn't tell me what your name is," the war hero said then.

"No, I didn't. My name doesn't make a difference. It won't make me any more of a human being—or any less."

"Maybe not," he said, lost in his thoughts. Then, "Five minutes, you said?"

"Yes," the ex-convict repeated, "but you'll want more."

The young woman lay back in her bathtub and smiled to herself. Her body was drifting off to sleep, and she did not resist. She felt weightless as she soaked in the warm water. The floral aroma of the bubbles left her feeling intoxicated and free. On the windowsill, the radio was still playing softly, adding to the soporific effect of the bath. She needed this...

She fell asleep with a smile on her face. After an uncertain period of time, she became aware she was underneath the water. Her lungs were filling with the perfumed fluid of the bath. Instinct told her to panic—to flail about wildly until she somehow managed to fling herself from the tub. Yet, even then, the carefree feeling had a hold of her. There was neither pain nor discomfort as the fluid filled her lungs. If anything, she felt even more at peace now, so she lay back and allowed the nothingness to take her.

She was content to let that be the end of it. Still, after two or three minutes, it occurred to her that her body was still sinking. Instead of being in a bathtub, it was as if she were in the ocean. She sank deeper and deeper into the darkness. The longer it went on, the more she felt her calm exterior cracking. She had wanted her end to be quick and painless, but she sensed something gathering around her in the darkness. It was like a taunting predator, having its fun before it devoured her. She had been sinking for what seemed like minutes now. Common sense told her she should already have been dead, but she was still conscious. Maybe this was some kind of dream—

A blinding light appeared out of nowhere. She clamped her eyes shut to protect her senses. It took about ten seconds for her eyes to adjust; but when they did, she saw she was in the dimension of light; all around her, there were the scenes. She saw herself throughout history. She stared, amazed, but then concluded this had to be a dream.

Then, when she looked up, she saw she was on a collision course with one of the scenes. She tried to avoid it, but it was no use. The instant she touched it, everything went black. She was falling now—toppling through the darkness. Whether this was a dream or not, she could not care by now. She screamed, flailing her limbs wildly. Then, as she continued to fall, she heard a sound that was like a rumbling train. She twisted her body, trying to see which direction it was coming from. When the air began stinging her, she became aware the rumbling was from the wind, and that she was in the middle of a sandstorm. Before she had time to make sense of it, she was standing on the ground, in the midst of it. The swirling chaos seemed like a monster, devouring her. She wanted to run—to flee—but it was everywhere. As she was about to surrender to the hopelessness, she saw a man approaching through the chaos. With the stinging sand, she saw only his form; but for some unknown reason, she was relieved. She found herself waving to him. She took a step in his direction; and as she did, something impacted her chest—

Her body convulsed from the shock, crumbling to the ground. The pain was like nothing she had ever felt before. Blood spurted from her chest—with the sandstorm, she felt it more than she saw it. And then, the war hero was there, holding her, staring down at her in horror. She stared into his face—despite the stinging sand. Something in his eyes called to her—spoke of a connection she had not thought possible. There were intimate stories reflected in his eyes, and she suddenly wanted to spend a lifetime listening to them. …But death dragged her away before she could say or do anything.

Everything went black again. For a moment, she did not have a definite body. She was like something in the primordial stew, waiting either for evolution or a Divine will to decide her destiny. She waited in this nowhere place for an unquantifiable period of time; then, all at once, she was on the streets of New York City. She looked around in shock. It was night outside. There were missing streetlamps and a few abandoned buildings across the street. It was the gray world—the South Bronx—but she had no idea where she was.

At first, the streets were bare; everything seemed indefinite. Then, miraculously, people appeared on the sidewalks and street corners. She gasped as she saw them appear out of the nothingness. Cars materialized on the streets—not in great numbers, but enough to give motion and light to the darkness. She looked around in a daze; when she glanced down, she saw she was in a Catholic school uniform. On her shoulders, there was a bag of schoolbooks…but this was all wrong; and at that moment, she had the sense something was behind her. She felt a hot, foul breath at the nape of her neck.

She screamed, letting the bag drop from her shoulders, then she ran for her life. She darted past the other pedestrians, who looked at her as if she were insane. She did not hear footsteps or anything tangible, but she could feel the thing behind her. She dared not turn to look; and as she ran, she could not understand why the others were not screaming and running as well.

She sprinted through an intersection blindly, so that an oncoming car had to slam on its brakes to keep from hitting her. She did not stop. She was entering a busier block, with more stores and more pedestrians. She was running at full speed now. Yet, no matter how hard she ran, she felt the thing gathering about her, like a mist. And then, when she was in the middle of the block, she felt the thing flitter across her skin, like a wet tongue. She convulsed reflexively, and tripped. She hit the sidewalk hard, and lay there balled up, waiting to be ripped apart by the thing she could still feel gathering around her. Some people congregated around her to help. They kept asking her what was wrong, but all she could think was that this was all wrong. When she looked up, she saw there was no monster behind her; nevertheless, she still felt the thing out there. She sat up on the sidewalk, and began to cry. Some people asked her if they should call the police, but she ignored them. The only thing she knew was that this was all wrong. She got to her feet now; and then, while those gathered around her continued to question her, she pushed past them and wandered off.

Home: she had to get back home. She remembered how minutes ago she had been in a bathtub. The entire sequence of events flashed in her mind again. She saw the scenes with the war hero; she remembered the sensation of drowning and sinking. She shook her head, knowing there was no sense to be made of it. The only thing to do now was go home—lock herself within the comforts of her apartment. Once that was done, she would figure out what had happened. For now, she felt too vulnerable out here on the streets.

She saw a subway stop on the next block, and went for it.

By the time the ex-convict pulled up in front of the elegantly dressed man's home, it was after ten o'clock; but as the war hero had said he would go through with it, he felt obligated. He was just getting out of the car when the front door of the building opened, and a man appeared in the doorway.

"That's my master," the ex-convict announced. He had gotten out of the car as well, and was taking the war hero's bags from the trunk.

The elegantly dressed man walked down the stairs. Now, he was extending his hand to the war hero. They shook hands and the elegantly dressed man gave him a hearty pat on the back. After that, the war hero was led up the staircase, to the building. The war hero looked at the elegantly dressed man's face, trying to see if he remembered the man; he tried to reconstruct all the things the ex-convict had told him, but there was nothing but a vague sense of malaise.

The elegantly dressed man had been talking all that time. As had been the case over the last few weeks, the war hero found himself nodding to the man's words—even though he had no idea what the man was saying. There was a side of him that did not want to hear. He wanted to ignore everything, so he could rush away unaffected by the words. The huge flag in front of the doorway cracked in the wind then, like a whip. The elegantly dressed man made a joke that the war hero did not have time to decipher, and then they were inside the man's home.

The doorway to the house seemed like a portal to another world and time. The décor was from the gilded age of the early twentieth century. The war hero could practically smell the wealth. There were hardwood floors and vaulted ceilings and glittering chandeliers.

Within seconds, he was whisked away to the man's den. The den was filled to the ceiling with leather bound books—maybe five thousand books. The elegantly dressed man seated him in a deep leather chair before going to pour some drinks. The soldier sat there uneasily, looking around. Besides the books, and the bar, there was a huge mahogany desk with neat piles of papers; and behind the desk, there was a bulletin board with tacked-up pictures.

The elegantly dressed man returned with the drinks, and sat in the leather chair opposite the war hero. The man still had not stopped talking all that time. The war hero now made a conscious effort to hear what his host was saying. He frowned, trying to concentrate; eventually, he heard the phrases "defending America" and "keeping America strong." Instinctively, he wanted to block off his senses again, but the elegantly dressed man made his pronouncements so forcefully that for a moment the war hero almost believed. For a moment, he believed in the promise of America, and the proposition that freedom could be spread through bombs and missiles. For a moment, he loved America, and had his faith in war restored…but then, he remembered the woman he had met in the desert. While the elegantly dressed man talked of American power, the war hero remembered how the woman's mother had been slapped by men drunk with the illusion of power. He nodded his head then, knowing that he loved the woman. As always, she was a vessel of life, protecting him from death and madness—

"No more, please," the war hero interrupted his host. He said it the way someone begged an attacker to stop hitting him.

"Pardon?" the elegantly dressed man said.

"I don't want to hear any more," he said. "I don't want to hear how much you love America. I'm through listening to that shit." As he said it, he felt relieved. He felt free for once; when he looked over at his host, he saw the man's confusion, and felt compelled to explain himself. "…That's all I've heard for the last few weeks," he said in a calmer voice. "I didn't mean to be rude, but I'm sick of hearing it. No one can love a nation," he said, as if hoping to appeal to the elegantly dressed man's sanity. "Love was meant for flesh and blood—for *people*—not for governments. All you people who claim to love America don't know anything about love."

The elegantly dressed man smiled. "So, you're an expert on love?"

"I know love was meant for human beings—for flesh and blood. Everything else is fake—a con game. When people go out to fight for their loved ones, they don't need patriotism to keep them going, because the love is real. Patriotism is fake love—that's what I know. When the danger is real and imminent, there's no need for patriotism, because people will gladly fight for what they love: they don't need to be reminded. When cavemen were fighting for their tribes, they didn't need patriotism. It was when powerful men began to construct empires that patriotism was needed. When soldiers were sent to fight halfway across the world, that's when patriotism came into being—because they needed something fake, to fool people into believing their loved ones were still in danger. When Caesar and Alexander built their empires, they brought patriotism with them to their newly conquered lands, in order to make people love (and be willing to die for) something they had no way of understanding and benefiting from. Patriotism asks people to forget why they love, and what love is, so they'll be tricked into accepting their own pointless deaths—or the deaths of those faraway strangers they're forced to kill." The soldier was out of breath—panting. He had never talked like that before: it felt good. It reminded him of how the woman had talked, and he felt proud of himself somehow. Looking down, he remembered he was holding a snifter of the elegantly dressed man's brandy. He gulped it down. When he looked up, the elegantly dressed man was smiling at him:

"You have advanced from when I saw you last."

He looked at the man with a kind of uneasy curiosity: "When did you see me last?"

"You were only a street kid then, but you have advanced beyond all that. Your analytical skills have improved. I'm proud of what you've become."

There was something condescending about the man's compliment, and the combative side of the war hero wanted to scream at him; but he frowned then, disarmed by the prospect of his past. "You really knew me?"

"Yes, I knew you," the elegantly dressed man said with a smile. However, there was something unnerving in the man's eyes—a gleam that made the war hero feel a chill spread over his skin. Maybe it was to distract himself that he got up and pretended to read some of the books in the library—or at least their spines. The elegantly dressed man sat looking at him. The smile was still on his face—

"Are you still an avid reader?" the man asked.

"Still?" the war hero said, looking back at his host.

"You used to be before you left."

"Oh."

"I guess it's true what they say on the news: you lost all your memories.

You were a good kid—even if you were a bit unfocused at times," he said with a smile. "Still, that's all understandable, considering what your living situation was."

"Your..." he didn't know how to refer to the ex-convict. "Your servant said he and I lived together in a group home, and that you used to watch over us."

"You seem doubtful."

"...I'm only trying to gather information—corroboration."

"I'm sure your amnesia will pass," the man reassured him. "The brain is a mysterious thing. Once new connections begin to form, you'll begin to remember. That's why I wanted you to live here for a while. I figured it would bring back old memories."

"...Did I used to come here?" he said, looking around with awe.

"Yes, all the time. You liked this library in particular."

The war hero looked about the room, trying to remember, but there was nothing. He began to walk again, sometimes brushing his fingers lightly against the books. The elegantly dressed man began to talk about what a great honor it must have been to meet the president. The war hero tuned out the man's voice. He was beginning to think his five minutes were up, and that he would head to the hotel the Army had booked for him. However, he was coming upon the huge mahogany desk; and as he neared it, and looked up, one of the pictures on the bulletin board beyond the desk caught his attention. He moved toward it as if pulled by a gravitational force. He could feel his heart speeding up in his chest; then, as he looked up at the picture, the pathways of his mind seemed to slow, so that he had to stare at the picture for what seemed like minutes before he was able to conclude that the woman in the picture was the woman from the desert...the same woman he had been dreaming about all his life.

His throat was dry. He glanced back at the elegantly dressed man, who had gotten out of his chair during his monologue on the president, and was now walking up to the war hero. When the man reached the war hero's side, he looked up at the picture with an expression of deep appreciation on his face—

"Who is that woman?" the war hero asked. His voice was hoarse and eager.

The elegantly dressed man stared at the picture dreamily: "You ever look at a stranger on the street and imagine everything about his life—where he was born, who his parents were, where he went to school…?"

"Only when I look in the mirror," he said. The elegantly dressed man chuckled at the remark, and the war hero smiled as well—albeit uneasily. He looked back at the picture, still trying to reconcile the reality that that was the woman from the desert. Once again, he knew it was pointless to ask himself how it was possible. All he knew was that it was so. Indeed, he could no longer believe in chance developments anymore—in coincidence. The elegantly dressed man was suddenly part of the cosmic plan—an emissary of fate.

The elegantly dressed man smiled again, and gestured to the picture, saying, "She's magnificent, isn't she?"

The war hero nodded cautiously. He felt light-headed, but he fought the sensation. "Do you know her? Did you take that picture?"

"Yes, I took it. I was walking through the park one day last spring when I saw her sitting on that park bench, deep in thought. It was by the lake: children were feeding the ducks; as she stared at them, it was as if she were seeing something beyond them—some essential truth. There is an aura of honesty about her—you see it, don't you?"

The war hero nodded as though mesmerized.

"I look at her picture when I want to be reminded of what honesty is."

"So, you've never met her? You don't know her?"

The elegantly dressed man chuckled strangely, saying, "I will be knowing her soon… And I talked to her today: just some passing words to prepare her for our eventual meeting." He stood staring at the picture with a smile; as the war hero looked over at the man, he felt a tremor go through him. Suddenly uneasy, he looked away from the man. However, the picture called to him. There was no doubt that she was the one from the desert— no doubt whatsoever. The war hero felt himself coming undone—

"You look at that picture as if you've seen her before," the elegantly dressed man said then.

"…Yes," he said helplessly. And then, with as much circumspection as he could muster, "I feel as though I know her."

"Good, good," the elegantly dressed man encouraged him, "—you're catching on to the game. That's the same feeling I had the first time I saw her. I felt I knew her, even though it seemed impossible."

The war hero nodded equivocally, then looked back at the elegantly dressed man. "When do you think you'll be seeing her again?"

"Any day now."

"And what will you do when you meet her?"

"Talk to her—just as I'm talking to you."

The war hero laughed uneasily, saying, "Is my picture taped to one of your walls as well?"

"Better than that—your picture is within everyone's heart," he said with the old patriotic fervor rising in his eyes.

The war hero felt another surge of discomfort, but it was then that the ex-convict entered the chamber, saying, "What are your orders, master?"

The elegantly dressed man seemed to come out of a trance. He smiled and took a deep breath, before he looked at the war hero hopefully: "That depends on our guest—if he wants to spend more time with us or not."

The war hero stared at the woman's picture with the same helpless expression, then he looked up at the elegantly dressed man. "I guess I can stay a little while longer," he said at last.

It was an hour-long subway ride from the South Bronx to Brooklyn. By then, the woman's mind was like mush. She reached the subway terminal she had run from only hours ago, and walked up the steps to get to the Brooklyn streets. She did not run this time. As rush hour had long passed, the crowds had thinned considerably. She walked slowly. After the long subway ride, home was within distance at last, but she still felt lost. She knew this was not a dream, so she did not waste time allowing her mind to be fooled by such thoughts. She only had to look down and see her Catholic school uniform to know something amazing had happened. She had not been sleepwalking either—or anything else that seemed rational. She had stepped beyond a forbidden barrier, into something she had no way of comprehending.

Ten minutes later, she walked the last few steps to her co-op, and stood looking up at the building. She was relieved to be home, but she could not help thinking that this was all wrong. "Pop Goes the Weasel" was still playing in the background somewhere. She shook her head, but the song was like an unshakable burden, wearing her down. As she began to walk toward the door, she realized she did not have her keys. There was only one thing to be done, and she grimaced when she saw no alternative. She would have to ring the superintendent and ask him to let her in. She took a deep breath, rang the bell, and waited.

The superintendent's apartment was on the ground floor; after a few moments, the curtains of the window to her left were pushed to the side. The superintendent's face appeared. He looked at her uncertainly for a moment, then opened the window. "Yeah?"

"I forgot my keys. Can you let me in?"

"Let you in for what? You know somebody here?" There was a note of gruffness in his voice; as he stared at her, she became aware he had no idea who she was!

"It's me," she said.

"Is that supposed to mean anything to me?"

"...Don't you recognize me?" It came out in a whisper. She felt light-headed and sick.

The superintendent stared at her for a while; then, all at once, his eyes grew with recognition, and he laughed out uneasily. Yet, the situation was so inexplicable that his laugh faded away quickly First, he looked at her strange clothes, then back at her face. Unable to make sense of it, he laughed uneasily once more, and said: "I must be getting old: for a moment there, I forgot everything about you."

Those words disturbed them both. He looked at her as if trying to reconcile something impossible; she looked away from his searching eyes—

"Wait there," he said at last, "—I'll be right out."

He disappeared then, and she was happy for the respite. She took a deep breath.

When he came out to open the door, he stared at her for a while, as if to make sure it really was her. She stood there compliantly; and as he saw this, he realized she needed him. She had never needed him before—had never been anything other than dismissive toward him—so he felt a sudden sense of power. He was like a vulture swooping down on a fallen lioness.

For once, he was not in his discolored overalls. Instead, he was in a pair of shorts (which unflatteringly showed off his knobby knees) and a T-shirt that had huge perspiration stains around the armpits and neck. He was still grinning at her; her Catholic school uniform seemed to excite him.

"Coming from some kind of costume party?" he ventured.

"Something like that," she responded in her usual way.

As he let her into the building, he made more small talk about the weather. He walked ahead of her and kept looking back at her. She wished he would walk quicker—especially as his slouching gait again made her want to box his ears. On the final flight of stairs, he seemed to slow down his pace further. He was making allusions to her unpaid building fees now—but his voice was chipper as he mentioned it.

"Some of the others in the building were talking about throwing you out," he said with a strange smile, "but I refused." He stopped on the stairs and looked at her, his pose heroic, as if he expected her to bask in his greatness. She stared at him impassively, thinking about how easy it would be to bring him into her apartment and kill him: bang his head with a saucepan or slit his throat. …She groaned, a little disturbed by her thoughts, but mostly annoyed by this fool, who was still standing there, posing for her. She felt suddenly tired. The events of the night, supernatural or not, were forgotten now—and seemed too far back in her past to be relevant anymore. She wanted to go to sleep. The only impediments to that goal were the superintendent and her locked apartment door. When she came in earlier that evening, she had not locked the front door, but because she had a dead-bolt, it could not be opened from the outside without a key. Eager to move things along, she continued to walk up the stairs, in hopes that the super-intendent would come out of his pose and open the door for her. The man eventually moved along begrudgingly, but she could sense his mind working, trying to find a way to exploit this situation.

He began to search for her key on a ring that had dozens of keys. He fingered each key deliberately, and the entire process began to exasperate her—especially as she suspected he knew exactly which key was hers.

"Your maintenance fees are $2,000 in arrears," he mentioned with the same affected nonchalance. He kept searching through the key ring and did not look up at her. She stared at him, wary of where this conversation would head, but intrigued somehow by the thoughts that might be sputtering around in his head.

"And?" she inquired as his statement lingered in the air.

"...Well," he started, after a moment of reflection, "there are ways that that sum could be...relieved."

She laughed. "Ways like what?"

"...Like if you were nicer to me."

"Hmm..." She saw it all in her head: the various scenarios. She stood frozen for a while, imagining his skin against hers, his tongue in her mouth, with its taste of cigarettes and stale beer; she imagined him huffing and puffing on top of her—she doubted it would take him long to avail himself of her body and turn over to go to sleep...but she saw countless nights of this. She saw her deepening desperation forcing her into further misadventures and compromises. She saw the last of her essence being eaten away... and she shuddered. She took the ring of keys from him—not angrily or gruffly, but with resoluteness. She recognized her key within seconds, and had the door open. The kitchen light was still on; the bread and sandwich materials were still lying on the kitchen counter—along with her huge handbag. She gestured for the superintendent to come in, then she went to her handbag. In her mind she had seen her entire course of action. She would write him a check for the $2,000. That would practically empty out her bank account, but at least she would have made this last stand and preserved her soul for a little while longer. However, it was when she opened her handbag that she saw $5,000 in $100 bills. She knew it was $5,000 because the bank slip was still fastened neatly around the bills. She held the stack in disbelief, and fanned the bills with her fingers—the way crooks and blackmailers did in movies to make sure the money was real. She had forgotten about the superintendent, who was standing just inside the door, wondering if she was going to offer herself sexually or not. He had not been able to gauge her intentions when she took the keys from him; and as she stood there with her back turned, his confusion began to mount, so that he called:

"Hey?"

She gasped as she turned. She was still holding the stack of bills. She was trembling slightly—like a thief. Yet, seeing the superintendent, and remembering his proposition, she ripped the bank slip open and handed him what seemed to be half of the bills. She did not even bother to count. She only handed him the bills; then, with her eyes, she told him to leave. After he slinked away and closed the door behind him, she stood staring at the door. She was breathing shallowly—almost wheezing. Once again tonight, something inexplicable had happened. She looked down at the bills in her hand, wondering what all this could mean. For a moment, she asked herself if she had robbed a bank: if she had perhaps blacked out during the day and committed a crime. After what she had experienced tonight, anything seemed possible. She fanned the bills with her fingers again. Maybe God had listened to her prayers (even though she had not actually been praying to Him). She was willing to consider anything; but then, as she reflexively fanned the bills once more, a business card fell from the stack. She stared at it for a while, then reached down and picked it up. It was the elegantly dressed man's card. There was no name on it, but she identified the card with the man because it was inscribed with the words, "Most people can't see what's right in front of their eyes." Below that, there was a phone number. The elegantly dressed man must have slipped the money into her bag during that bizarre subway ride. ...*But why?*

She stared at his card in shock, wondering what this new thing could mean—

A sudden noise made her scream and leap. The noise seemed like thunder in the silence. She felt it reverberating within her, tearing her to bits. When she looked down, she saw the cat; and when she thought more deeply about the noise, she realized the cat had merely meowed. Before she had time to make sense of it, the cat started walking down the hallway again. It took about five steps before stopping and looking back at her in the manner that told her she should follow. She did as directed, still holding the stack of bills in one hand and the elegantly dressed man's card in the other. Her steps were feeble; she felt unreal…She followed the cat down the hall and through her bedroom. The cat stopped in front of the closed bathroom door, and looked back at her with those eerily beautiful eyes. It was waiting for her to open the door, and she shuddered. Within the bathroom, she could hear the radio playing on the windowsill. A haunting Charlie Parker solo was playing. She shoved the money and card into her pockets, then she reached out her trembling hand and tried to open the door. It was locked. Nonetheless, the cat was still there, staring up at her—and its disconcerting purring was beginning to fill the room (and her head). The purring brought a strange kind of urgency to her actions and her thoughts, so that the next thing she knew, she reared back and banged her shoulder—and all her strength—into the door. The flimsy lock gave immediately, and the young woman almost tripped over the plush bathroom rug as she rushed into the room. The floor was a little damp—since the tub always leaked a little when she bathed. As a consequence, she slid across the tiles before tripping over the rug. Luckily, she managed to maintain her balance. Yet, when she looked at the tub, she saw the body—*her* body—floating in the water. Somehow, she really had drowned: her waterlogged corpse was staring up at the ceiling.

The war hero and the elegantly dressed man were eating dinner together—at an oblong dining table that could perhaps seat twenty people. The two men sat at the polar extremes of the long table. The ex-convict had served their food previously, and had hovered around, in order to carry the gravy boat and other serving dishes from one side of the table to the other; but once the serving phase was complete, he retreated to the kitchen.

At the moment, the elegantly dressed man was in the middle of another patriotic diatribe. The war hero tried to ignore it. To him, the man was nothing but another evangelized patriot, who spoke in glowing terms of war and death, when he had seen no battlefields; who made decisive proclamations on the war effort, when he had nothing to corroborate those claims but the empty rhetoric of politicians and generals. He wanted to laugh in the man's face, and go about his business, but something warned him to retreat from such thoughts. There was something in the elegantly dressed man's eyes that was like the triumph of a great hunter. As the war hero sat across from the man, he suddenly began to wonder if he had stumbled in a trap.

Indeed, as he stared across the table, one realization settled like a cold mist around him: everything that had happened since he arrived in New York had been a cleverly laid trap. The ex-convict's story, the woman's picture... all of it had been an elaborate trap. He still could not grasp the reason for the trap, but he could sense it. His host's smile had a netherworldly coldness, as if the man were a well-mannered grim reaper. And there could be nothing coincidental about the placement of the woman's picture in the man's library. The story behind that picture was plausible, but it nonetheless jangled alarm bells within him—

The doorbell rang.

The elegantly dressed man stopped talking in mid-sentence. After a moment of silence and uncertainty, the ex-convict emerged from the kitchen, walked through the dining room, and went to open the door. The elegantly dressed man resumed his speech. The war hero tried to wall himself off from all that was going on around him, so that he could think. At the door, words were being exchanged between the ex-convict and another man. The words were low at first; but then, after about fifteen seconds, the man talking to the ex-convict seemed to grow enraged. The man was yelling now; when the war hero recognized the voice, his skin crawled.

Soon, there were footsteps—two pairs. The war hero could not think for a few moments. Before, he had felt like a beast lured into a trap; now, he felt like a beast cornered by two hunters. When he looked up, the ex-convict was standing there with the man—the psychiatrist from the hospital in Germany. The elegantly dressed man and the psychiatrist exchanged greetings. About those greetings there was a gentlemanly façade, but the most horrible threats were implied in the tone. The psychiatrist kept his voice calm; the elegantly dressed man was gracious—he even offered the psychiatrist a seat, so that he could share in the feast. Nevertheless, about the two men, there was the sizing up that happened when two dogs came upon a bone, and each growled at the other, in order to warn his rival away from his prize.

All that time, the war hero had not said a word; while the beasts growled in their gentlemanly way, he only sat there, staring at his plate. Arrangements had been made, the psychiatrist said. A hotel room was waiting for the war hero, and he had to be at a television studio the first thing in the morning. Accordingly, he would have to get his rest. To all this, the elegantly dressed man made gracious apologies. Soon, the war hero was standing beside the psychiatrist. They both shook the elegantly dressed man's hand, then they walked away. Some military police officers were waiting outside the house. The ex-convict handed the war hero's suitcases to the MPs. They saluted the war hero. He could not acknowledge them in his benumbed state. There were two government sedans double-parked at the curb. The psychiatrist, the war hero and the two MPs began to walk down the brownstone's stairs.

"…How'd you find me, sir?" the war hero asked as they descended.

"The Army sent a driver to pick you up from the airport. When he saw you leaving with another man, he followed you and reported back to us."

"I understand, sir," the war hero said vaguely.

"What do you know about that guy?" the psychiatrist asked at the bottom of the steps, gesturing back toward the elegantly dressed man's home.

"Not much, sir."

"Then why did you go with him?"

"His…his servant"—he still didn't know how to refer to the ex-convict— "…he said he knew me."

The psychiatrist groaned. "I told you of your importance to the nation, soldier," the man chastised him. "You can't go marching off with everyone who shows some interest in you, like some kind of lovesick puppy."

"I understand, sir."

"You'll be on national television in the morning," the psychiatrist went on. "You will need your rest."

"I understand, sir."

They walked along in silence for a while, then, just as they reached one of the double-parked sedans, the war hero ventured:

"Why are you here, sir?"

"What do you mean?"

"Does the Army think I'm crazy?"

"As I told you before, soldier, you're important to America. You are about to enter a very stressful period—media interviews, parades…lots of travel. You will need all the help you can get."

"I understand, sir," the war hero said again, as the psychiatrist opened the car door and gestured for him to enter.

The doorbell rang. The young woman jumped up from her couch at the sound—like someone who had received an unexpected shock. She had been lying there with a dazed expression on her face. She had fled to her living room, since it was the farthest point from the thing she had seen floating in her bathtub. When the doorbell rang again, she suddenly remembered she had telephoned her lover. Desperate for someone's company—for something real to hold onto—she had called the last person with whom she had had the pretense of intimacy. She had called him fifteen minutes ago. The phone was still lying beside her—discarded.

She ran to the kitchen now, where there was an intercom and a buzzer to let people in the building. The intercom did not work of course, so she only pressed the buzzer. She opened her apartment door after pressing the buzzer, and felt a sudden sense of relief at first the sound, and then the sight of her lover ascending the staircase. She had never loved him, or allowed herself to believe their lustful sessions had anything to do with love. However, behind all love there was the awareness of need for another human being, and she knew she needed him. She needed something: someone to corroborate that she was still alive. There was madness in the entire proposition, and perhaps dishonesty, but she was still relieved beyond reason as he climbed the last few steps to her apartment door. She was still wearing the strange clothes from the gray world, and he smiled when he saw her. Before he could say anything, she reached for him, and held him. She was trembling slightly, and he laughed softly at her unexpected show of vulnerability.

They entered her apartment; but now that he was inside, she did not know what she wanted from him. Usually, they went straight to her bedroom—without fanfare and pretense—but she was terrified of that wing of the apartment now. She lingered in the kitchen; he looked down at her uncertainly, but then laughed again—perhaps thinking her strange behavior was some new escalation of their sex. Maybe the Catholic school uniform was a new role-playing fantasy. He liked the thought of it, so he reached down and caressed her breast. He was pulling her to him now. Soon, his tongue was in her mouth. …She pulled away from him. When she looked up at him, there was a confused expression on his face.

"Can you just hold me?" she said. She took a step toward him, to hold him, but he caught her by the arms and held her at bay.

"What kind of game is this?" he said with a frown.

"…What?"

He shook his head, thinking of how he had gotten out of his bed and rushed over there, just to be rebuffed. "I'm tired of these games," he said at last. He let go of her arms, which fell limply at her side. "Every time I was with you, you acted like I was beneath you—like you were slumming with me or something. Every time I tried to talk to you, your eyes clouded over. You never cared what I had to say. You just wanted to be sexed up with no questions asked."—She shook her head absentmindedly; he continued—"I was fine with that, but now you come with this, 'I just want to be held' bullshit, as if you've ever allowed anything between us but mindless fucking—"

"Things are complicated for me, that's all," she protested.

"Things are complicated for you?" he mocked her, "You're the only person in the world with problems? Your problems are so much deeper than everyone else's?"

"Yes," she said, thinking of the corpse in the bathtub, "—that's exactly what I'm saying."

Her response seemed grandiose and self-important, and he stared at her, amazed by the extent of her ego. Eventually, he chuckled. His face was mean—nowhere near the fantasy she needed. A side of her wanted revenge. She wanted to drag him to the bathroom and watch his shock when he saw the corpse. She wanted to laugh and gloat over it, then throw him out. In any event, he was walking away now. Soon, he was at the front door, and the door was closed behind him. Indeed, it was closed so softly that after a few moments it was as though he had never been there. She listened for the sound of retreating footsteps, but there was nothing; and after a while, she found herself wondering if any of it had really happened.

The war hero's dream seized him completely. The events of the dream had been buried in his mind—not forgotten, just misplaced in the chaos of war. …He and his unit had been riding along in three Hummers, cautiously navigating their way through a sprawling shantytown. The community had been built in what used to be the city's garbage dump. It had been countless square kilometers of trash and human decay; and the roads, likewise, had only been narrow corridors through the trash. The war hero had been in the second Hummer. It had been about midday, but it had always seemed dark in the refugee camps. The wretched people of the desert had been all around him—men who had been butchered over years of war and ethnic strife; women who had been raped; children lying around with distended bellies, who were in the process of dying from starvation. The odor of the place had been like a heavy, pungent poison. He had felt it filling his lungs: pure death and hopelessness. The war hero had glanced out of the window just as they were coming upon a shack. A boy, maybe about ten years old, had emerged from behind the rag covering the entrance, and gestured with his index finger in the universal way that people had come to tell others they were going to shoot them. The look on the kid's face had been that of a murderer. The war hero had turned in his seat to corroborate what he thought he had seen—to reconcile the expression of a murderer with a ten-year-old. …And then, the bomb had gone off. The vehicle ahead of them had been lifted into the air—into a burning cloud of trash. From the force of the blast, the war hero's vehicle had capsized as well. The fire had engulfed them; all the shacks within fifty meters had been flattened. Indeed, all around them, there had been people screaming and dying in the sudden inferno—women and children, mostly. After a moment of shock or unconsciousness, the war hero had regained his senses. He had roused the soldiers beside him, and they had clambered out of the vehicle. Outside, the fires had raged; the men had all coughed on the smoke. The Hummer they had seen fly into the air had been lying on its side, fully engulfed in flames; and then, looking down, the war hero had seen the kid—the ten-year-old who had made the universal gesture with his index finger. There had been a piece of shrapnel stuck in his head. The kid had died instantly; but on his face, there had still been the brutal expression of a murderer…

The war hero opened his eyes after the dream. He did not burst upright; he was not panting. He merely opened his eyes and stared up at the ceiling. He was in the hotel room—he remembered after a moment of disorientation. He was lying on top of the covers, in his dress uniform, with his shoes still on. The television was playing—tuned to a twenty-four-hour cable news channel. He propped himself up on his elbows and looked at the television, which was directly in front of him and the bed. There was a story on him: a montage, where he was shown receiving medals from the president. Other images of the war were shown as well—heroic images with backdrops of the American flag. The sight of these things filled him with the usual sense of panic. He felt doomed, in fact. He groaned, crawled out of bed and shuffled to the adjoining bathroom. He was numb—as though his limbs were somebody else's.

When he turned on the bathroom light, he checked his wristwatch: it was three in the morning. He washed his face and neck once more—just as he had done in the airport bathroom. Life was beginning to enter his limbs; maybe sense and cogent thoughts were beginning to enter his mind as well. He had to escape: that was the first thought that came. He had to get away—at least for a little while. He had to flee from elegantly dressed men and Army psychiatrists and cheering multitudes. He had to breathe some fresh air for a while. This is what he thought as he undressed—as he pulled his tie free and loosened the buttons on his uniform. Soon, he was standing there in his underwear. He thought about taking a shower, but he knew that would not cleanse him the way he needed to be cleansed. He was restless; he wanted to have sex. He put his hand to his crotch, but his penis was flaccid—numb like the rest of him.

He left the bathroom. His army duffel bag was at the foot of the bed. He opened it with intentions of getting some civilian clothes and sneaking out of the hotel. However, when he shoved his left hand into the bag, he instantly felt steel slicing through the soft tissue between his thumb and index finger. Strangely enough, the sensation was not exactly painful. He pulled back his hand calmly and stared at the gash in his palm. He had forgotten about the bayonet statue. He had placed it in his bag before leaving Washington D.C. He stood up now, still staring at his hand. The blood first pooled in his palm, and then flowed down his arm, and onto the carpet and bedspread. He watched the streaming blood dispassionately as it splattered the carpet. The patterns intrigued him. He felt no pain from the wound—experienced no alarm at the sight of his blood leaving him. …But there was so much blood. Soon, the carpet was bright red with it. A voice told him to staunch the flow of blood, so he stumbled toward the bathroom, trailing blood as he went. He rolled some toilet paper around his hand, but only splattered more blood on the bathroom walls and floor in the process. The blood was not stopping. The wound was deep: the wad of toilet paper was already disintegrating from the spurting blood. He pulled the bloody wad off and flung it in the sink. His hand felt warm; he could feel it pulsing as the blood flowed. He grabbed a towel and wrapped it around the wound—wrapped it tightly. That worked better. He stumbled back toward the bedroom. He felt a little giddy and had to rest his bloody hand against the doorway to maintain his balance. He still had to get away for a while. He moved to the bag again. This time, he took out the hideous trophy with care, then he began to dress. He was still getting blood everywhere. The blood had already seeped through the towel. Everything he touched became bloodied. When he put on a white T-shirt, his bloody hand left red hand patterns all over it. It occurred to him

he needed stitches to close the wound—that he should go to the hospital…
but he had to flee…at least for a few hours. He did not want to be surrounded
by doctors and concerned Army officers; he did not want reports of this to
end up on the news, in between stories of celebrity gossip and fairy tale
reports from the front lines of the war. He pulled the towel tighter. However, the towel was too big to be a bandage. Besides, it would be too conspicuous to walk out of the hotel with a bloody towel around his hand. The
best option was to cut the towel. The hideous trophy came in handy for
once. He put it on the nightstand, then cut off the excess fabric of the towel.
When that had been completed, he balled his hand into a fist, so that the
wound was closed through the combination of the fabric and the pressure
of his fist. Next, he put a windbreaker over the bloody T-shirt, and pulled
on his jeans using one hand. His Army dress shoes had to do, since he did
not have any other shoes.

He was ready to leave now. He looked around the room to see if he had
forgotten anything. There were bloodstains all over the room; he had flung
his clothes elsewhere, and left the room looking like a total disaster area.
The hotel maid would probably pass out when she saw it, but he had to get
out of this place. He was just about to take a step toward the door when his
eyes came to rest on the hideous trophy. He felt he needed a weapon against
all the undefined dangers of the world, so he walked over to the hideous trophy and picked it up with his good hand. He realized it was too conspicuous
to carry in the open, so he put it down, pulled a pillowcase off a pillow, and
put the statue in the pillowcase.

With this final preparation, he moved toward the door. In his mind, he
was still telling himself he would return to do the morning television show
in a few hours. For now, he had to get away from the confines of this hotel
and everything it seemed to represent. He wanted to walk for a while—
burn off some of his restless energy…and of course, the woman was in the
back of his mind. Even as he moved toward the door, he felt like he was
moving toward her.

There was a wake-up call at 04:30 in the morning, but the psychiatrist was already awake and getting shaved when the call came. This left him with a sense of pride. Of course, his body was still on German time, so he would have been up anyway. He returned to the bathroom and finished shaving. He looked at his face in the mirror and was pleased. He smiled and flexed his pectoral muscles in the mirror in a manner that reassured him. He was just heading out of the bathroom when the phone rang again. It was the same woman from the hotel's wake-up service. He frowned as he listened to her:

"What do you mean there's no response?" he said.

"He's not picking up, sir," the woman replied.

"Well, never mind," he said in annoyance. "He's right down the hall from me: I'll go wake him up. Good day," he said at last, in a tone that made the phrase seem more like a curse than a benediction. He was not in a good mood anymore. He put on some pants and an undershirt, and got out the extra key he had for the war hero's room (he had accounted for all contingencies).

His annoyance grew as he left his suite and walked down the hall to the war hero's room. He was going to knock on the door, but he decided he would storm in and reprimand the war hero. He wanted to see the man's stunned expression as he was roused from sleep. The psychiatrist would yell at him like an old drill sergeant. Soldiers had to be kept in their place—even if they were war heroes. This was the psychiatrist's mindset as he stormed into the room.

The television was still on. Some of the war hero's clothes were dumped on the bed; and for a moment, the heaped clothes produced the illusion of a body.

"Wake up!" the psychiatrist yelled as he stepped up; but after three steps, he saw the bed was empty. ...And the sickly sweet smell of blood was in the air. The psychiatrist felt slightly sick—either from the smell of blood, or the ill omen that the blood triggered within him. That was when he looked toward the foot of the bed and saw where the blood had stained the carpet. He was seeing all this by the flickering light of the television, so he had to step up to make sure. When he saw it was blood, he noticed the trail from the foot of the bed to the bathroom. His innards churned. He turned on the light and looked around the entire room. There was blood on the sheet, blood on the clothes... The room looked like gladiators had used it for a death match. As his gaze returned to the trail of blood leading to the bathroom, horrible thoughts again filled his mind.

He approached the bathroom as if expecting to find the war hero's corpse—his butchered body. When he turned on the light, he did not know whether he was relieved or shocked. The blood was everywhere—and seemed starker against the white tiles of the room—but the war hero was not there. New, unsettling possibilities filled his mind: a kidnapping, perhaps. He was like a parent who had lost a child in a crowd. He thought about his career in the Army. His superiors would punish him for this. He felt sick to his stomach, and had to sit down on the toilet to keep his head from spinning. In half an hour, a car was supposed to pick them up and bring them to the television studio. When that time came, everyone would know he had failed, and there would be dire consequences.

Somehow, the young woman slept. After her confrontation with her lover, she had retreated back to her living room and lain on the couch. She had balled herself into the fetal position, and succumbed to a torturous, dreamless sleep. The nothingness of the sleep seemed to devour her as she lay there. By the time she awoke in the morning, she felt even more depleted. It was perhaps about five o'clock in the morning. A sticky film of sweat covered her. Her first impulse was to go and take a shower, but then she remembered the corpse.

A childish terror filled her; she wanted to run crying to a parent figure—

The cordless phone was still lying on the couch. Instinctively, she picked it up and dialed her mother's number. The number was on speed dial. Yes, her mother annoyed her, but she had nowhere else to turn. As the phone rang, she thought of leaving the city this day. Kentucky was the last place where things had seemed right—

Someone picked up the phone.

"Hello! Mom!" she screamed.

"Who you want?" an old white man drawled in the irritable way people had when just roused from sleep.

"…Mom?" she said, her mind able to produce nothing but that word.

"Ain't no mom here!" the man screamed. Before she could ask another question, the phone was slammed down, and she was listening to the dial tone. She pulled the phone away from her ear and stared at it, as if the problem lay with it. Her mind moved at a crawl; she trembled. …Obviously she had not dialed the wrong number—since she had used speed dial. The only other possibility made her put her trembling hand to her mouth. She did not know how it was possible, but she knew her mother no longer existed—that her entire life in Kentucky had been erased. She could feel her fragile heart thumping in her chest. She sat up on the couch and grasped her head in her hands. Now that she no longer had the delusion of a comforting mother to shield her, her mind returned to thoughts of her corpse floating in the bathtub. A side of her rebelled against the madness—rejected it. Maybe the corpse had only been a bad dream—an elaborate nightmare. Maybe the phone lines had gotten mixed up somehow. People did not see their corpses floating in bathtubs. She had to get a grip before she went over the edge. But the only thing to do was return to the bathroom and check for herself…

She stood up. Since she had slept in an awkward position, her back ached. She had a slight headache, and had to lean against the furniture for a few moments, in order to regain her balance. She took a deep breath, and continued walking. In the kitchen, she saw the bread and cheese and salami were still on the kitchen counter, where she had left them the night before. Her stomach tightened, because it was proof that she had not been dreaming. She remembered the cat—everything that had happened…Her bag was there as well, resting on its side; she looked down and saw she was still in the Catholic school uniform. When she shoved her hand into her pocket, the elegantly dressed man's money was there.

After another deep breath, she began to walk down the hallway. Soon, she was at her bedroom door. She faltered. She peeped into the bedroom: the blinds were drawn, and most of the room was cast in shadows. However, the bathroom door was ajar, and she had left the light on when she fled. The radio was still on; a disjointed trumpet solo grated against her nerves. ...She allowed her mind to be still, and began to walk across her bedroom. Within seconds, she was at the bathroom door, staring at her corpse. Maybe she stood there for a minute or two, trying to digest the impossible thing. There were no thoughts to think—no conclusions to be drawn. All there was, was an acceptance of the impossible.

In time, she shivered. Looking down, she noticed the floor was wetter than before. She was standing in water. She remembered the bathtub always leaked. That was another of those chores the superintendent had never gotten around to completing. Typically, after she took a bath, there would be a few puddles on the floor, which she would have to mop up. However, her corpse had been floating in the bathtub all night. The water was now dribbling into her bedroom. The prudent course of action was to drain the tub and mop the floor. She should get the body out of the tub before it became so waterlogged that it began to disintegrate. ...But her corpse's eyes were still open, staring up at the ceiling. The corpse's mouth was open in a silent scream. The young woman found herself backing away. She turned off the light and closed the door. She was trembling uncontrollably. Soon, she was in the hallway, groping against the walls as she fled. She felt dizzy again. In the kitchen, she instinctively grabbed her huge handbag and shoveled some of the food into it—not all of it, just what was lying open. She tapped her pockets meditatively: the elegantly dressed man's money and card were something else she would have to deal with in time—another sinkhole in reality—but she had to get away for now. She had to get out of this zone of unreality—this pocket of insane space—so that she could breathe for a little while and figure out her next course of action. At the front door, she glanced back at the kitchen. The counter was a mess. A voice deep within her badgered her to go back in and clean up, but she was like someone running from a tornado. For now, all she could do was try to outrun the storm. Later, after the swirling chaos had passed, she would see what could be reclaimed from the wreckage. She rushed out. She was giddy. She pulled the front door behind her, but did not know if it locked or not. At this point, she could not care. In her dazed state, she almost toppled down the staircase, but managed to grab the railing. Her hands were clammy with sweat, and slid disconcertingly. At the same time, she was escaping, and a sense of relief filled her. Out there, in the real world, things would make sense once more. That was all she could think as she fled from her home.

The elegantly dressed man sat on his living room couch, perusing the morning newspaper. The television played in the background; and on the coffee table, there was some fresh fruit. The ex-convict had placed it there before returning to the kitchen. The ex-convict was just returning with some toast and coffee when the story on the war hero's disappearance came on. The ex-convict put the tray of food on the coffee table, but lingered to watch the story. The elegantly dressed man was watching it as well. The ex-convict looked at his master and ventured:

"Did you…?" but he found he could not finish the sentence—either out of tact or fear.

"No," the elegantly dressed man said with a laugh. And then, with a coy smile, "I can't be responsible for everything." At that, he put the newspaper to the side, then reached down to pick up a slice of the buttered cinnamon toast.

The ex-convict continued to hover about, and the elegantly dressed man looked up at him enquiringly.

"…Why are you doing all this?" the ex-convict asked at last. The question had been in his mind for days now—since the elegantly dressed man first made his proposal. He had never had the courage to ask the question before.

"Are you getting cold feet?" the elegantly dressed man asked.

"No, I've given you my word…and life has nothing left for me—nothing to hope for. I'm just curious why you're doing this to him—why you made me tell him that story about being in an orphanage with him."

"I have not 'done' anything to him. All I've ever done is offer people options. People always decide for themselves."

"It doesn't matter to you what they decide?" he asked skeptically.

The elegantly dressed man smiled: "You're right. I do care, but you think my offering him options damns him. People damn themselves by choosing."

"Yes," the ex-convict said at last. He saw that now.

The doorbell rang then. The ex-convict looked at the elegantly dressed man as if to ask if he were expecting anyone at that early hour. When the man shrugged and returned to his newspaper, the ex-convict went to open the door.

After a few seconds, yelling could be heard from the front door. The elegantly dressed man chuckled to himself; and then, after a commotion at the door, angry footsteps could be heard approaching the living room. The elegantly dressed man did not even look up when the psychiatrist stormed into the room. He only sat there reading his paper; in time, he turned the page of the newspaper, as if nothing had happened.

The psychiatrist was breathing heavily. The ex-convict was behind him, waiting to see if his master wanted him to throw the man out or not. The psychiatrist found the silence unnerving. After his show of bravado by forcing himself in the door, he felt inept—

"Well?" the elegantly dressed man said at last, "can I offer you some coffee, or are you merely here to psychoanalyze me, doctor?" The man smiled.

Something about the smile was disturbing; strange thoughts went through the psychiatrist's mind again, but he beat them back by reminding himself of the matter at hand. "For now, I'm looking for a missing soldier," he said.

"And what about later?" the man teased him.

The psychiatrist ignored the word play. "I know you had something to do with his disappearance," he said in a way that seemed to hold a veiled threat. The elegantly dressed man laughed at the ridiculousness of it. He put down the newspaper and looked up at the man who had invaded his home. He looked at him earnestly, and then smiled again:

"Men get into trouble when they start mistaking their unfounded suspicions for facts, doctor."

"—Look," the psychiatrist began, his voice rising, "I don't have time for you and Igor here," he said, gesturing to the ex-convict.

"That was mean," the elegantly dressed man said with a laugh. "I think you've hurt my servant's feelings. Besides, why do you think I'd know where your soldier is?"

"I don't know what your game is, but I can smell bullshit all around you. I don't know who you are, or what con game you're trying, but the U.S. Military does not let people fuck with its soldiers—"

"Are you questioning my patriotism, doctor?" the elegantly dressed man said in a manner that was either sarcastic or defensive.

The psychiatrist scoffed: "Your patriotism is like the rest of you: all show."

The elegantly dressed man sniggered to himself, then returned to his paper, waving his hand dismissively in the direction of the psychiatrist. The ex-convict put his hands on the man's shoulders, but the psychiatrist swung around and punched the ex-convict in his mask of a face. The ex-convict staggered back; he was about to charge, but the elegantly dressed man put up his hand to pre-empt him.

"You're not going to blow me off!" the psychiatrist yelled then. He was huffing and puffing again.

The elegantly dressed man smiled at him, as if captivated by the extent of his stupidity. "Sometimes answers aren't worth having, doctor."

The psychiatrist scowled; the elegantly dressed man laughed at the man's expression, shaking his head in disbelief. At last, he mused, "In your ignorance, you actually think your feeble mind can handle the truths I have to share."

"Enough of this!" the psychiatrist screamed.

"Hmm...Fair enough," the elegantly dressed man conceded with a faint, menacing smile. "I will give you what you ask, but you alone will have to deal with the consequences." The elegantly dressed man nodded to his servant then: "Leave us—and don't return until I call you."

"Yes, master," the ex-convict said as he turned and began to leave.

"Master?" the psychiatrist said. He laughed in a way that was supposed to be sardonic, but which came out as a nervous squeal.

The elegantly dressed man was not smiling anymore. He waited until the ex-convict closed the door behind him, then he gestured to the ground, saying, "Do you see anything there, doctor?"

The psychiatrist looked to the ground, but there was nothing there. The voice of reason within him kept telling him this was a stupid game. As he had done hundreds of times with delusional patients, the psychiatrist told himself he would pander to the delusion/game to see how far the neurosis went. However:

"Look again, doctor. Do you see it?"

The psychiatrist was about to mask a condescending laugh, but when he glanced at the spot on the floor again, he saw the cat appear out of the nothingness. All of a sudden, it was there, staring at him with those large, aquamarine eyes. He gasped and retreated a step—

"What kind of game is this!" he screamed.

"Touch the cat and receive your answers, doctor," the elegantly dressed man said mockingly.

The cat was approaching the psychiatrist; the man retreated another step. He wanted to scream—to run away and spend the rest of his life forgetting these moments of terror—but when the cat brushed its flank against his leg, it was too late to run....

In those few seconds of contact with the cat, he experienced a million lifetimes. He suffered a million tragedies, and experienced a million moments of fleeting joy...and realized everything was pain. Joy and pleasure were pain; existence was pain, and there was no escape....

When he regained consciousness, he was on the floor. His first act was a frantic search for the cat—for the thing that had brutalized him—but it was gone. Soon, he was shaking and crying like a baby. The individual images of his countless lifetimes had not stayed with him, but the terror and pain remained.

The elegantly dressed man chuckled from the couch, while the psychiatrist groveled on the ground. "I have shown you everything, doctor, and yet your mind is even further away from being able to understand the truth," he said, shaking his head in pity. "Leave this house now, doctor," the elegantly dressed man commanded, and the psychiatrist clambered to his feet, and tried futilely to wipe away tears that would not cease. When he was standing, he swayed before the elegantly dressed man, like a drunkard.

The elegantly dressed man chuckled again, and waved his hand dismissively.

"If your soldier is missing," he began, "then allow him to be lost. You have no business chasing after things you have no hope of understanding. Don't presume to follow the paths walked by gods, doctor. Don't begin a journey beyond the confines of your limited existence. Go home," he said at last, and the psychiatrist slunk away, still sniffling.

When the woman entered the park, it was a little after six in the morning. Joggers were just beginning to come out. She walked to the lake and stood on the bank. As the ducks had come to expect people standing on the bank to feed them, about twenty of them swam over to her. She remembered the food she had in her huge bag, and began to rip pieces of bread and fling them at the ducks. This, she did with a far-off expression. When she looked up, she saw the morning sky was beautiful. In the face of everything, she did not know if it mattered. She only knew she wanted to stand there and let her mind empty itself of thoughts.

A few minutes had passed by the time she heard footsteps behind her. When she turned, she saw a man walking up with a peculiar smile on his face. It was peculiar because it reflected a level of peace and joy she did not think possible anymore.

"I'm here," he said as he stepped up. She looked up at him as if in a daze; after a few moments, she realized it was the guy in her vision/dream—the war hero from television. That realization filled her with wonder and unease. Before she had time to react, he reached out and held her arm with his right hand. She reflexively wanted to protest; looking down, she noticed his left hand was covered in a bloody bandage, and that the sack he was carrying in that hand was also stained with blood. At the same time, his hand felt good against her skin: it was warm and strong. There was something about his entire aura that left her disarmed. His eyes were clear and frank, and beautiful. He laughed then—in the same peaceful, understanding way. Indeed, from the way he looked at her, she had the strange feeling he knew more about her than she did. It instinctively unnerved her, and yet there was something about him that made discomfort unnecessary. Discomfort was a kind of dishonesty, and everything about him seemed straightforward.

"…You know me?" she said at last, still struggling to keep up. The ducks, which she had neglected all that time, had become impatient with her dawdling, and now began to swim down the bank, to where an old woman with a bag of stale bread had stationed herself.

The war hero smiled at her again: "You'll remember everything eventually. You already feel a connection to me, don't you?"

She stared at him helplessly: there was nothing else to be done. His words made no sense to her, and yet she knew, somehow, that there was truth there. "…What's happening to me?" she asked.

The only thing he could think to say was, "We're connected—joined by something."

Glancing down, she again became aware he was holding her arm—and that she liked his touch.

"Everything's fine now," he went on. Then, seeing the lingering confusion in her eyes, he told her about that day in his childhood, when a girl who looked like her emerged from the muddy pit. He told her about the dimension of light and the countless lives they had lived together. He described his time in the war zone, telling her how the cat had miraculously saved him. He told her how he had met her the second time—how she had marched down the street during the protest. When he told her about holding her in the swirling sandstorm, she nodded her head, because she remembered the scene from her vision. …And he went on, telling her about the things that had happened in the hovel, and the events that had made him a war hero. At last, when he sensed her mind was on the verge of collapse, he told her about coming back to the city and seeing her picture in the elegantly dressed man's home.

She was looking up at him wide-eyed when he was done. Objectively, she knew his story was insane, but she knew it was all true.

"…I had a vision," she began, about to tell him about the scene in the sandstorm. However, in that same stream of thought, she remembered her corpse floating in the bathtub. Now that the war hero had opened the door to impossibilities, she felt compelled to tell him about the thing that had happened to her. In fact, she needed to tell him. "...I died last night," she said at last.

"What?"

She told him about how the cat had followed her home—how she had taken a bath and found herself jumping from scene to scene. She told him about having to take the subway home; she pointed out the Catholic school uniform she was still wearing. During her story, her hand instinctively went to his chest; she gripped his windbreaker with her hand, but it felt natural.

She told him how the building superintendent had had let her in—since she did not have her keys. She told him how the superintendent had not recognized her—how she had sensed herself being erased.

The war hero nodded his head then—not because he understood, but because he had come to believe anything was possible. She realized she was gripping his windbreaker, but it felt right. They were practically hugging one another now, but his body felt good next to hers. She almost lost herself in these thoughts, but she shook her head to refocus herself. She looked up into his eyes again, where there was still peace and acceptance, then she told him about the last part:

"...When I finally got upstairs, I went to the bathroom, and that's where I saw myself—my corpse—floating in the tub. I drowned last night," she said simply.

The war hero was deep in thought—or maybe he was beyond thought. "The body's still there?" he asked.

"As far as I know. ...I didn't know what to do. I had to get out of the house—to think about things. But there's no way to make sense of it."

"Let's go to your place," he said.

"Okay," she responded, as if taking him home were the most natural thing in the world.

As they turned to leave, the war hero suddenly found the bloody pillow-case, and the supposed weapon within it, cumbersome and unnecessary. For once, he felt invincible—as if the woman's touch would protect him against anything. He tossed the sack into the lake then, startling the ducks, and annoying the old woman who had been feeding them. Wordlessly, he and the woman began their trek back to her place.

For the most part, they walked in comfortable silence. The emerging day was bright and beautiful. Yet, with the woman at his side, the war hero would have been content if the day had been damp and overcast. For the first time in his memory, he was utterly at peace. The woman, on the other hand, was still anxious. Maybe it was even the strange peace that made her anxious.

"Are you cold?" he asked. She was walking with her arms folded over her chest, and her back hunched—as if bracing herself against a biting wind. She looked over at him as if she had forgotten he was there. "Are you all right?" he asked again.

She shook her head: "I don't think so."

"...We'll figure out what to do," he said calmly. He had no idea what to do, but some burgeoning male instinct told him that speaking calmly and decisively was the key to reassuring her.

At the moment, they were perhaps five or six blocks from her home, walking down commercial blocks. People were beginning to leave for work. They were already congregating at bus stops and descending into subway stations. It seemed like any other day; but just then, an ice cream truck began blaring "Pop Goes the Weasel." The truck was at least a couple blocks away—since she could not see it—but the song seemed impossibly loud. She stopped, looking around uneasily.

"What's wrong?" the war hero asked her.

The song was getting louder. The music box chimes seemed like they were inside her head—

"What's wrong?" he asked her again.

As she was about to tell him, something went through her. At first, she thought something had physically happened to her—that perhaps she had been shot. She swayed and gasped; the war hero grabbed her as she was collapsing. She was panting.

"What happened!" he screamed, holding her.

She began to sob.

"Talk to me!" he pleaded, holding her more closely.

She was mumbling something—like a scared child; tears were already streaming down her face.

"What is it?" he demanded. Passersby were beginning to look at them oddly, so he pulled her into the dark, recessed doorway of a business that had not opened yet.

"Something's happened," she whispered, trembling, "—something bad."

"We need to get you home," he tried to reassure her again, but another fit of sobs wracked her body. He tried to reassure her that things would be fine, but even he was beginning to worry now. He dried her tears with the sleeve of his windbreaker, and held her closely, but she was so despondent that she hardly seemed aware he was there.

In time, they continued to walk. They left the commercial blocks and turned onto residential blocks. She walked as someone who had nowhere to go—who was just out wandering aimlessly. He had his arm around her shoulders now, as if to keep off the cold, but she still shivered. They were about two blocks from her home when she stopped again, and pulled back, beginning to cry once more.

"What's wrong?" he asked again.

"I don't want to go any further. Let's get away," she said with a strange combination of fear and hopefulness. "I have some money," she said, tapping her pocket, "—let's get away from this place: from everything. Let's just go."

"...But what about the body? We just can't leave it—"

She began to cry again.

"Okay," he said holding her again.

At that moment, two police cars rushed past, their sirens blaring.

"Something bad has happened," she whispered as the cars zoomed past. He held her to his chest; as he craned his neck and looked down the blocks, he realized there were several emergency vehicles parked in the middle of the street—in front of what he suspected was the woman's building. A crowd had gathered to look...

"Don't you want to know what happened?" he ventured.

She shook her head, which was still buried in his chest.

Presently, two middle aged black women in pastel blue nursing aide scrubs came up the block, talking excitedly.

As the war hero held the woman to his chest, her back was to the two nursing aides.

"Excuse me," the war hero said, getting their attention. "Do you know what happened down the block?"

The nursing aides seemed excited by the prospect of retelling the story. The first one began, "They found a woman's body in her bathtub this morning!"

The woman shuddered; the war hero held her tighter.

The second nursing aide seemed a little exasperated with the lack of details in her friend's telling of the story, so she added, "The landlord found it. The water from the bathtub was leaking on the floor, and then it dribbled to the apartment downstairs—"

"Yeah," the first one took over again, "—the tenant downstairs called the landlord, and he went to investigate. That's when he found the body floating there naked." The nakedness seemed like a spicy detail, even though finding the body clothed in a bathtub would have been the extraordinary thing.

The second nursing aide took over again, while the first one's wide, suggestive eyes transmitted their innuendo about the naked body. "The landlord was outside when we passed, telling everyone how it had happened. The coroner brought down the body while we were standing there. It was in a body bag of course," she said, disappointedly, "but the landlord said she was young and beautiful and educated. Seems like a waste," she said. However, from the strange way the nursing aides looked at one another, it was as if they felt vindicated somehow—as if it had been education, youth and beauty that had killed the woman; and that as middle-aged, unattractive women with basic education, they had been spared. In fact, despite the story they had just told, morbid smiles came to their lips.

The war hero thanked them, but mostly to get them to leave. They looked at him afresh, as if just noticing he was handsome; they called him "sugar" and made strange eyes at him, as if the woman in his arms were invisible. He thanked them brusquely—almost rudely—since they would not take the hint to leave. At last, he pulled the woman along with him, and fled across the street. Then, they began to walk back the way they had come. The woman now seemed dead in his arms.

"I knew something had happened," she whispered. "...Everything's fading away."

"Stop being silly," he said with a smile that belied his own panic, "—you're here, aren't you? I can feel you and you can feel me. That's all that matters."

"People think I'm dead," she pointed out. "They've found my corpse."

"Let's just walk for a while," he said to put off the topic for now. She nodded faintly, and they walked down the block, holding one another around the waist, like old lovers. Neither tried to account for it: they merely fell into it. She stared down at the ground. She noticed his Army dress shoes: how dusty they were. She realized she disapproved, and that that was ridiculous, considering everything that was happening around them. She held the war hero closer. She liked the smell of him, and the way his muscles felt against her body.

They were about to cross the street, but as his left foot was about to step from the curb, something came over her, and she wrenched him back. She was panting; he looked at her with the mixture of patience and concern he had had since the onset: "What's wrong?"

She looked at the curb, trying to reason it out, but it made no sense: they had the light; no traffic was coming...the strange terror ebbed from her system, and she looked at him apologetically. He smiled at her and she was relieved. He put his arm around her again, and they continued to walk across the street. ...She remembered the money in her pocket. They could buy a ticket somewhere and get away. The fantasy of a fresh start buoyed her for a moment, but that was when a luxury sedan pulled up to the curb. As they stood there in shock, the driver side window went down, revealing the smiling face of the elegantly dressed man. The woman jumped—

"I wasn't expecting to find you both in the same place," the elegantly dressed man began. "It will save me the trouble."

"...What do you want?" the war hero demanded. The elegantly dressed man's presence unnerved him as well, but he was still trying to maintain the outward appearance of strength and confidence.

"I'm here to offer my services. Both of you have made a mess of things," he scolded them, but with a reassuring smile. "As always, I'm here to fix things."

"Who are you?" the war hero said, suddenly aware he had a lump in his throat.

"I am the man offering you a way out of the mess you've made. Get in the car and we'll talk."

The woman had been looking on, mesmerized by the elegantly dressed man's words; but all at once, a feeling of abject fear gripped her, and screamed, "Don't listen to him!" She turned to the war hero now, gripping his arm. "Let's go away quickly."

"Don't you even want to know what I'm offering?" the elegantly dressed man suggested from the car window.

"No!" the woman screamed. And then, returning to the war hero, "Let's go…please. Don't listen to him. Don't allow yourself to hear."

The elegantly dressed man had a calm, confident smile on his face when the war hero looked over; and remembering his own apprehensions during his dinner with the man, the war hero continued to walk along with the woman—to flee.

"You know where to reach me if you change your mind," the elegantly dressed man called from the car window. The glass went up then, and the car drove off.

The war hero could feel the woman's frantic heartbeat.

"You know who he is?" he said, gesturing to the disappearing car.

"No, but…he's horrible. I know it. I met him yesterday."

"Yeah, he told me."

"You've talked to him!" she said, looking up at him with trembling eyes.

"Remember, I told you I went to a man's house and saw your picture?"

"Oh God!" she whispered, trembling more noticeably now. "It's all some kind of trap—don't you sense that?" She went to her pocket and pulled out some of the elegantly dressed man's money. "He slipped this into my bag yesterday. He's been stalking us—*trapping* us."

As she said those words, the war hero remembered all the things the pleasant voice had told him in the hovel. His mouth felt dry—

"We can't allow ourselves to listen to him," the woman went on more urgently. "I'm sure I've met him before yesterday—just as I'm sure I know you. He's *horrible*."

The war hero felt queasy and drained. "Okay, okay," he said, trying to calm them both. He held her closer, and they walked along in silence. Still, they did not feel at peace anymore—regardless of how closely they held one another.

"...Are you sorry you can't go back to your old life?" he asked eventually.

"...No," she said after giving it some thought. "I don't feel any connection with it anymore. Maybe I haven't for months now. I miss some of the people from that life, but...I don't feel as though any of it was real."

The war hero nodded his head at those words. The woman went on:

"I called my mother this morning. ...She wasn't there anymore," she said, her voice taking on a bewildered edge.

"We're together now," he said again, as if that explained and assuaged everything.

She looked up at him, then shook her head, sighing in frustration: "Why don't I remember all the things you said? ...And what about my corpse," she said with a shudder. "If I'm dead, and everyone thinks I'm dead, then why am I still here?"

"...Maybe you're still here because of me?"

"You?"

"All the other times, everyone forgot about you, and you disappeared... but this time, I was there to remember you. I wanted you here. ...You said you were drowning, but then you had a vision where you were with me in the desert. That image has been playing in my mind non-stop for weeks now. I've been dreaming of going back and changing that moment—of bringing you back to life..."

She looked at him uneasily. There was something unnerving about the calmness of his voice—the boundless clarity that was there, despite their enigmatic predicament. "How did all this happen?" she asked again, shaking her head.

"I don't know," he said, "but we were together in the beginning—I know it. We were happy together—everything was perfect—but then something happened, and we lost each other—"

"Just like Adam and Eve?" she teased him.

He smiled: "Maybe." He laughed then, like someone awakening to see the face of a loved one. "What's your favorite thing in the world?" he asked in a suddenly playful voice, "—feeding the ducks, right?"

"…Yeah, I guess," she said, as if surprised by her admission—by the simplicity of it.

"Let's go to the park and feed the ducks. Let's enjoy our time together."

"And then what?"

"And then we decide what we're going to decide." That unnerving clarity was there once more, and she held his arm tighter.

They took a few steps down the block before three dark SUVs pulled up to the curb. An irate general emerged from the middle vehicle, followed by some minions. "Has everyone gone crazy!" he screamed.

The war hero stood stunned for a while (as did the woman); but suddenly remembering he was in the Army, he stood at attention and saluted the general. The woman still held his other arm—

"First that blasted shrink has a nervous breakdown," the general screamed as he stormed up to the war hero, "and now you're wandering around with your girlfriend when you were supposed to be on television an hour ago!" He had pointed accusingly at the woman, as if she were the cause of his lapse in duty and honor: some kind of scheming Jezebel.

"Sorry, sir," the war hero ventured in the uneasy silence.

"Sorry?" he said in exasperation. "Get in that fucking car, soldier!" he screamed, causing huge purple veins to bulge on the side of his neck.

"Yes, s-sir," the war hero stammered. He instinctively pulled the woman along with him—

"Where the hell do you think you're going!" the general demanded of the woman.

The war hero turned around pleadingly; the prospect of further talk frustrated the general, so that he waved his arms in bewilderment and screamed: "Goddamn it, just get in the car!"

As he approached the SUV, the two junior officers ambushed the war hero, or so it seemed to him. He was practically shoved into the vehicle, and then the officers were handing him a dress uniform, telling him to get dressed. In the tussle, he lost hold of the woman. Within the spacious SUV, the two back seats faced one another. The war hero and his two clothiers sat on one side, while the woman sat next to the screaming general. The general began to wax poetic on duty and honor, while he supervised the war hero's disrobing.

The woman felt isolated and vulnerable next to the screaming general. The war hero's shirt was off now. The junior officers helped him to haul down his pants. There was a blank expression on his face. The woman tried to avert her eyes, yet, despite all that had happened to her in the past few hours, she could not deny the longing that was in her as she saw the war hero's body. The strength of the longing left her bewildered, staring helplessly. And then, an image flashed in her mind—either a recollection of something that had happened, a premonition of things to come, or just wishful thinking. She saw a moment of intimacy in a cramped apartment. It was early in the morning; she was lying in bed, smiling as she watched the sweaty elasticity of his muscles. He was getting dressed after their lovemaking. She was content, ready to doze after he left...and then he was gone. It was a simple enough scene, but when the man in the scene left, there was a grim finality about it—something that hollowed her out and made her knees shake—

Even when the scene in her head ended, an unsettled expression remained on her face. The war hero looked up at her as he buttoned his shirt. He frowned and asked her if she was all right. She smiled to reassure him, but he was not convinced. He was going to say something to her, but one of the junior officers started up an electric shaver then, and began to rub it across his jaw. The war hero grabbed the shaver and continued shaving himself.

When the war hero was dressed, and the unsettling buzz of the shaver was turned off, the junior officers changed the bandage on his hand. They had a full first aid kit, as if they had planned for all contingencies. During this time, the screaming general reprimanded him on allowing himself to get injured, and jeopardizing his supposed place in America. Then, after all that, an uncomfortable silence pervaded the vehicle. Everyone seemed drained. The general had exhausted all his aphorisms on duty and love of America, and now basked in a kind of rhetorical afterglow. The war hero looked handsome in the uniform. The woman wanted to touch him, but he seemed so very far away from her now. Something about that realization was debilitating. She felt herself drifting away; without the war hero, she felt she would disappear entirely, like wafting smoke. As if sensing something within her, the war hero stared at her anxiously; she looked back at him from time to time, and tried to smile…

They were nearing the outdoor set of the morning show. It was a city block cordoned off to traffic, where hundreds and sometimes thousands of pedestrians-cum-audience members loitered behind a barricade and clapped like trained seals when given their cue. At the sight of the cheering crowd, the war hero felt a chill. This was the moment of truth. He wanted to run away with the woman and turn his back on whatever horrors were to come—but he was trapped.

The SUV stopped on the periphery of the outdoor set. The hosts' chipper voices could be heard over the speakers. The audience laughed at a punch line.

They all exited the SUV. A sudden sense of desperation or love overcame the war hero, and he pulled the woman to his trembling body. Soon, he was kissing her with wild abandon. She melted into it. His trembling became her trembling. She was breathless when he pulled away—they both were. She blushed when she saw all the eyes on her, but she felt giddy with love—

"Soldier!" the general screamed, losing patience. The man had been watching the scene with the bile rising in his throat. The war hero ignored him, and gripped the woman again.

The general nodded to the junior officers then, and they pulled the war hero away from the woman. They left her standing there alone. The war hero had to twist his body to get a final look at her. "I'll never forget!" he said at the last moment.

Something about his words was icy, and she stood frozen. The Army driver, who had been holding the door open, coaxed her inside, and she went absentmindedly—like an old woman with dementia, who had forgotten where she was supposed to be.

The war hero was being led through the crowd now. People were already clapping; some patted his back. And then, magically, he was on the other side of the barricade. He looked back in amazement, and saw the general and the two junior officers clapping; he looked ahead and saw the two hosts, who were coming up with wide grins on their faces. As the war hero looked around, he became aware American flags were being waved in the air. They must have been distributed to the crowd beforehand. On the giant screen television, a huge American flag was undulating in the wind. The hosts were before him now. The male one shook his hand and patted him on the back, while the female one kissed him on the cheek. The moment dragged on like a horrible torture. The war hero felt a headache coming on—either from the loud cheers, or the pressure that was building up within him. He wished everyone would shut the hell up. Their cheers were ripping the world apart. Then, when he sensed he could not take it anymore, the male host grinned wider and screamed:

"We all love America here!" In response, the crowd screamed louder, so that the war hero grimaced and staggered back. Now, the male host turned to the war hero, saying, "What would you say to someone who didn't love America?"

The crowd quieted to hear his words. At first, the war hero merely stared at the host. His mind tried to churn out something patriotic—something that would keep the crowd clapping—but his soul rebelled against it all. The question was meaningless. Its premises were not facts that could be fleshed out, but religious tenets—articles of faith, national superstitions….The crowd was silent and anxious. The war hero opened his mouth to say something—anything—but now, as he looked around, he remembered the pleasant voice's warnings. This was the time for betrayals and coronations; and just then, he saw a man emerging from what seemed to be the crowd—but which was actually a backstage area. The producers had thought the war hero would have answered the question by now. The question had only been a set-up piece for the next segment. The man stepping from the staging area was the focus of that segment. The hosts, who had been waiting anxiously for the war hero to answer, were sent scrambling when the man was sent out prematurely. The only thing to do was announce him, so they screamed:

"Here is the President of the United States!" The crowd cheered uproariously again, and the war hero nodded his head mechanically, knowing this was the end of everything.

…Time began to slow down. The war hero was able to look up and see something flying through the air—something fist-sized and metallic. It had been heaved from the crowd. It sparkled in the sunlight, then it bounced against the ground once, before rolling to the president's feet. The man stopped, unsure; the clapping waned for a moment—or at least, those in the front, who could see, stopped clapping, while those further back continued to applaud. And then, in that relative stillness, there was an explosion. The president disappeared in a flowing cloud of flames and death. Seeing everything coming to an end, the war hero willed himself into the past—back to the moment of perfect pleasure he had shared with the woman. Even then, the flowing cloud of fire devoured him hungrily. He barely managed to gasp before he was swallowed whole. In the SUV, the woman was instantly rocked by the brutal awareness that the war hero was gone. Even before she could scream, she found herself in that nowhere place beyond time and history…

Then, the very next moment, she opened her eyes to find herself lying in bed: in the same cramped apartment she had seen in the previous vision. Straight ahead of her was the door though which her husband had left. It was perhaps six in the morning—the sun was bright outside her window. She suddenly remembered everything—the countless lives she had lived: countless dead ends; countless moments of pain and suffering… As she looked about the room, she realized she was back at the beginning!

She jumped up from bed and ran to the door. She was about to open it and scream for the war hero—for her husband—to come back. But she saw that she was naked. She grabbed a robe that was draped over the chair of her vanity, then she opened the door—even before the robe was fully around her. She screamed his name then—his real name—but the hallway was empty. She was in a four-story walk-up; she looked down the staircase, but he had already left the building. She ran down the stairs. She was barefoot, but there was no time to waste. Downstairs, she leaped through the front door. It was the middle of summer, and the pavement was warm, even in the early morning. ...And "Pop Goes the Weasel" was playing—blaring like some kind of cosmic alarm.

That was when she looked up and saw her husband at the end of the block. Just as she opened her mouth to say the words of his name, he stepped off the curb and was ploughed down by the speeding ice cream truck. His body was sent flying. She suddenly remembered the premonition she had had when he stepped off the curb, but it was too late now. The ice cream truck swerved after hitting him, and then crashed into some cars; the crash damaged the speakers, so that "Pop Goes the Weasel" was now an out-of-tune dirge. She could not move for at least five seconds. She was back at the beginning, so she knew the thing she had gone through time to stop had already come to pass. Still, after the initial shock passed from her system, she ran to the corner on stiff, unresponsive legs. The war hero was a bloody mess, shuddering from shock and pain, holding himself tensely, as if relaxing would cause his viscera to spill out of his butchered body. She had relived this moment countless times, and each time was a fresh torture to her. She burst into tears then; she went to him, holding him to her, so that her cotton robe was soon soaked with his blood. She screamed then, but he was already dead, so she sat there rocking his lifeless body.

The ice cream truck driver came out of the vehicle with his head bleeding; the woman looked up at him and nodded her head slightly, as if greeting a casual acquaintance on the street. At first, the man was dazed from the accident; but then, seeming to grasp everything all at once, his body slumped—

"We missed it again!" he mumbled. It was the man with the bloodshot eyes. He stood on the periphery, while the woman sobbed and held her husband.

When she heard another set of footsteps behind her, neither she nor the man with the bloodshot eyes needed to look up to know who it was. The elegantly dressed man walked around to her front, and stood watching her with an expression of helpless amusement: amusement that could not be helped, considering the circumstances.

"You two almost made it that time," the elegantly dressed man said, twirling his cane. "You almost remembered."

She looked at him. For a moment, there was boundless rage there. Yet, in the end, she shook her head, knowing it was pointless. "...How many times have we done this?" she asked then, looking down at her husband.

"I've lost count. Shall we try again?" he ventured, looking from the woman to the man with the bloodshot eyes. When the woman looked up again, she noticed the cat sitting contentedly in the elegantly dressed man's left arm. Over the elegantly dressed man's shoulder, people were beginning to gather—people from the neighborhood. She recognized many of them. They milled about out of curiosity—morbid and otherwise. Children held their mother's skirts; men shook their heads at the sight at the "raw deal" that had been meted out by fate.

The woman blocked them out and looked down at her husband. Despite the passage of time, she cried once more—for her husband's death and suffering, and for her own. She thought back to the proposal the elegantly dressed man had whispered into her ears all those lifetimes ago. She had heard the accident from her bedroom and gone out to investigate, pushing past the milling crowd to get to her mangled husband. "Would you like a chance to make things right?" the elegantly dressed man had proposed to both herself and the man with the bloodshot eyes that day. She had been insane with grief and shock; the man with the bloodshot eyes had been blubbering, trying to explain that the brakes and steering column had suddenly stopped responding.

Thus, maybe, in their shock, neither of them had really heard the elegantly dressed man's proposal. The man's shining eyes had held the possibility of hope, and that had been more than enough for them. When the man produced that cat out of the nothingness, and held it out for them, it had probably been curiosity that made them touch the cat. Either way, after they touched the immaculate fur, it had been too late. They had found themselves tumbling through history, trying to remember who they were as time frittered by.

How many times had they gone through it? Dozens of times? Hundreds...? The woman bent down and kissed her husband's bloody forehead, then she cried some more. She had sentenced them both to hell; her desire to cheat fate had damned them. She looked at the man with the bloodshot eyes now, as he stood on the periphery with his head bowed. They had damned themselves—had multiplied their sufferings by trying to cheat fate. Maybe, the woman found herself thinking, she should give up at last—let her husband stay dead, and allow herself to move on with this life. She recalled she had other relatives and loved ones in this life. Maybe it was time to move on—

But the cat was purring; she looked at it and its master warily. The elegantly dressed man was smiling at her—as if he had read all her thoughts and knew them better than she did. "Shall we try again?" he coaxed her.

At first, she looked at him as if he were a monster; and yet, once one had gone down the path of stupidity, and passed a threshold of time, distance and pain, there was no point in turning back. The only choice was to continue down the path in the hope that it would eventually come to an end—or lead somewhere.

"Shall we try again?" the elegantly dressed man asked once more. She looked up at him helplessly; she opened her mouth, but the words eluded her. She looked back at the man with the bloodshot eyes then, to see his thoughts; but as always, his cowed expression told her he would defer to whatever she wanted—

"All I am doing is offering you possibilities, madam," the elegantly dressed man pointed out then. "The choices and consequences are yours to bear."

"...Yes," she mused, as if seeing an essential truth after many years of blindness.

"Good," he said. "Shall we try again?"

"...Yes," she said, looking down at her husband again, and holding him close, "—but let me remember who I was for a little while, before I start all over again."

"No rush," the elegantly dressed man said with a smile, "—we have all the time in the universe at our disposal." And then, "What's the point of living in the past if you can't correct your mistakes?"

While the man with the bloodshot eyes sulked on the periphery, the woman kissed her husband's forehead and continued sobbing. She again saw how her hopes for an impossible future had damned her. Like the generals of a war that had gone horribly wrong, she was beginning to see she would never win; but after so much suffering, the only thing keeping her going was the fantasy that this would all be worthwhile someday. The more she suffered, the more the fantasy became everything to her—and the more she felt she had to continue down this path, in order to justify all the pain and wasted time. It was a self-fulfilling hell. Yet, unlike the generals and presidents and other hopeful warmongers, at least she had a way to forget her stupidity. Considering all she had endured, maybe forgetfulness was the only thing she had left. She nodded to the elegantly dressed man then, and he extended the cat to her. As she stretched out her hand to touch the cat, she reminded herself her love was stronger than the horrors she would face; but as soon as she touched the soft fur, and found herself toppling though oblivion, her love disappeared into the nothingness. In fact, after a while, all that was left was a dull ache.

Author Bio

D.V. Bernard emigrated from the Caribbean island of Grenada when he was nine, and settled in New York City. *Intimate Relations with Strangers* is his fourth novel. He can be contacted through his website: http://www.dvbernard.com

Author's Note

There may or may not be a prequel to this novel, centering on the ex-convict and revealing how all this started in the first place.